THE REGENCY LORDS & LADIES COLLECTION

**Glittering Regency Love Affairs
from your favourite historical authors.**

THE REGENCY LORDS & LADIES COLLECTION

Available from the
Regency Lords & Ladies Large Print Collection

A SCANDALOUS LADY

Francesca Shaw

First published in Great Britain 2002
Large Print Edition 2009
Harlequin Mills & Boon Limited,
Eton House, 18-24 Paradise Road, Richmond, Surrey TW9 1SR

© Francesca Shaw 2002

ISBN: 978 0 263 21032 3

Set in Times Roman 16½ on 18¼ pt.
083-0209-72415

Printed and bound in Great Britain
by CPI Antony Rowe, Chippenham, Wiltshire

01292948

Chapter One

Nicholas Lovell, Earl of Ashby, swung his quizzing glass at the end of its ribbon and listened to the rising hum of anticipation from the well of the theatre below him. From his vantage-point in the box he could see virtually the entire sweep of the Theatre Royal, the swirl of colours from the ladies' silks and satins, the subdued gleam on the gentlemen's formal evening wear. As usual the Bath audience had paid hardly any heed to the curtain-raiser, chattering, gossiping and waving to acquaintances throughout it. But now the mood had changed to one of heightened expectation.

Perhaps, he mused, his friends had not exaggerated the charms and talents of the Royal's chief attraction, Mademoiselle Lysette Davide, the sublime interpreter of Shakespeare. And tonight there was the added piquancy of knowing that those privileged enough to procure a ticket would be witness to her last performance of the season. But, no, despite everything, he could not summon up the enthusiasm to join in his friends' excitement. He closed his eyes and leaned back in the gilded chair.

'For pity's sake, Lovell, do wake up and show a bit of interest. The performance is about to start.' George Marlow leaned over and poked him unceremoniously in the ribs with his quizzing glass.

Nicholas raised one dark brow laconically, and resumed his bored scrutiny of Bath society, chattering in the stalls below.

George, persisting in the face of his friend's uncharacteristic ennui, added, 'I tell you, La Belle Davide is well worth the wait.'

'He's right, you know,' Lord Corsham contributed. 'Worth sitting through that tedious ballet for. Have another glass of champagne, old chap. You haven't had enough to drink, that's your trouble.'

The last of the quartet, Sir William Hendricks, whose box it was, peered anxiously at the programme. 'It isn't Shakespeare, is it? Can never understand a word the fellow's on about.'

Nicholas laughed, roused from his indolent mood by the look on his old schoolfriend's face. He well remembered Hendricks's struggle to concentrate on any literary endeavour at Eton, being more enam-oured of the sports field and cockpit than his books. 'Don't worry—it's not Shakespeare. Why do you bother with a box, old chap? It can't be worth the expense.'

'Well, one does, you know. After all, one never knows when one might want to come along—and I can tell you, ever since we discovered Mademoiselle Davide we've been here virtually every night she's performed.' He sighed gustily. 'If I could just kiss her hand.'

'And the rest of her,' George Marlow remarked, with a meaningful grin.

Nicholas was surprised by his companions' calf-struck demeanours. After all, George had kept a string of actresses for the past few years, yet all the men were behaving like schoolboys whenever this particular woman's name was mentioned.

'So what's stopping you?' he enquired, irritated. 'She's only an actress, and we all know what that means. Enough money and you can kiss her from head to toe, never mind her hand.' It had taken a lot to persuade him to come out this evening. He had only arrived in Bath that afternoon—reluctantly obeying a summons from his elder sister Georgiana—and had had no intention of doing anything but having a good dinner and several glasses of brandy with his brother-in-law Henry.

'Only an actress!' Indignation mottled Sir William's cheeks. 'She is pure, unsullied, a goddess—the Unobtainable!' His companions, equally earnest, nodded solemnly.

They had all of Nicholas's attention now. He swung round away from the stage and regarded the three young men with amused disbelief on his lean features. 'There is no such thing as an unobtainable actress. You three are either getting old or you have all lost your touch!'

'Damn it, Nick,' Lord Corsham growled indignantly. 'No one succeeds with her. It isn't just us. Not even you could storm those unsullied ramparts—I bet you!'

'I can't be bothered to storm anything,' Nicholas rejoined with a quirk of his firm lips. 'Look, the curtain's going up.'

He turned away as Frederick Corsham grabbed his sleeve. 'Not even if I wager Thunderer?'

He had all the Earl's attention now. 'Are you

serious, Freddie? I thought you'd never sell that animal, never mind wager him.'

'It's a safe bet,' his friend replied breezily, sitting back as the limelights were turned up and the curtain rose on the first scene of *The Castle Spectre*. 'Even you couldn't do it.' The other two nodded solemnly. They all knew few women could resist Nick's dark charms if he chose to exert them, but they also knew of Miss Davide's formidable reputation for virtue.

'Done—and I haven't even set eyes on the lady.'

At that moment Lysette Davide was standing in the wings having a furious, whispered argument with Mr Porter, the manager of the Theatre Royal. 'I never thought you meant it!' he said. 'I'll raise your fees to…to…12 pounds a week,' he added wildly. 'Damn it! That's as much as Mrs Jordan was getting in her heyday.'

'Not now, Mr Porter! I am retiring after this performance and that is final. Now, *please* leave me!'

Lysette checked her dark wig again, smoothed down her white diaphanous skirts and took a deep, not entirely steady breath. In the three years she had been on the professional stage she had never lost her pre-performance nerves, and tonight, the very night that she was going to declare her retirement, she felt as nervous as a kitten. And the hissed interchange with Mr Porter had only served to make things worse.

Her cue came and she swept on to the centre of the stage, tall, almost regal. The theatre erupted into a storm of applause from all levels and footstamping from the common folk up in the topmost tier.

From the vantage-point of Sir William's box, overhanging the stage, Nicholas had a perfect view of the Unobtainable Miss Davide. And for the first time that evening he was paying attention. It was not just that she was a very beautiful young woman, tall, shapely, elegant, but that she had great presence. While she was on the stage, even when she was not speaking, she held the eyes of all the theatregoers, and when she did speak for the first time there was a collective intake of breath from the stalls. Her voice was strong, carrying, yet mellifluous, with a slight hint of a French accent.

The play was a farrago of nonsense, of course, a typical fashionable Gothic melodrama, yet she made it sound like Shakespearean verse. For the first time in weeks Nicholas felt his boredom disappear. He had begun to worry about his lack of interest in all his old pursuits. Gambling had lost its excitement, the pursuit of the fair sex had lost its lure, and he had taken to leaving parties early, and more or less sober.

His circle had begun to comment, and the only person pleased with this apparent reform of a notorious rake was his land agent, who found all his correspondence answered promptly and with interest.

The truth was that, at the age of twenty seven, the Earl of Ashby was growing restless with the pursuit of pleasure for pleasure's sake. His sister, the redoubtable Georgiana, had told him he needed to marry and settle down, to ensure the future of the earldom by producing an heir. But, unsettled and restless as he was, Nicholas was damned if he was going to marry one of the eligible ninnies that his sister found for him on a regular basis. And, much as his ancestral estates in Buckinghamshire were beginning to tug at his conscience, the thought of sobriety and conformity with a 'suitable' wife who had neither wit nor conversation filled him with dismay.

His eyes did not leave the tall dark figure as the play progressed. The drama involved ludicrous plots, abandoned orphans and a wicked villain who emerged, cloaked and masked, to seize the heroine, but Nicholas took in none of that. One part of his mind enjoyed the spectacle of Miss Davide's beauty, the other reflected that, if he had to spend a week in Bath at his sister's beck and call, then the pursuit and conquest of such a woman would be more than compensation.

The curtain fell for the first interval and a waiter came in with a tray of champagne and canapés. After the man had departed, all three of his friends turned to Nicholas and demanded with one voice, 'Well?'

Nicholas grinned, stretched out his long legs and raised his glass in a toast. 'To the Divine Miss Davide, and to the three of you for giving me something to do for the next week.'

'You are very confident,' Lord Corsham remarked.

'He's got cause,' George Marlow replied ungrudgingly. 'When has he ever failed with a lady? I don't know how you do it, Nick, but you've got the devil's own luck.'

'Probably signed his soul away to Old Nick.'

'No such thing,' Nicholas protested. 'All one needs is a certain charm, flair…all the things you three are so sadly lacking.'

'I shall ignore that slur,' Sir William said amiably. 'And at least you've cheered up. You'd become so damnably sober we were thinking of sending for your physician. We had better set a time limit on this wager—shall we say the end of next month?'

The interval ended and the play resumed. Miss Davide, not on stage again until the next scene, sat in her dressing-room as her dresser powdered her shoulders and arranged her fichu. She leaned forward, carefully checking her hairline to make sure no betraying blonde curl was escaping, and touched a cloth to her darkened brows.

'First half went well, ma'am,' her dresser, Florence, remarked. She looked at her mistress's reflection in the mirror, automatically checking the heavy stage make-up which covered the naturally pale skin. She always thought it a pity that Miss Davide covered that lovely mass of blonde hair: soft, it was, like spun gold. And the dark eyebrows made her green eyes look hazel. But the perfection of her features was all hers and owed nothing to the artistry of the stage.

'Thank you, Florence. It did go well, did it not? Still, I will confess I am very nervous about my announcement—and Mr Porter is deeply unhappy with my decision. Now, you are sure that you will be content to work for Mrs Scott next season?'

'Oh, it's an honour, ma'am, with her being so well known. But I shall miss you; you've been so kind to me.' Her mistress's slender hand with its long tapering fingers came up and briefly touched her own.

'You will have me crying, Florence. Do not say anything else.' At that very moment there was a knock on the door. 'I must be on stage now. Please bring my hand-glass and powder.'

Despite it being the middle of a scene, there was another storm of applause when Miss Davide resumed the stage. The second half went by as if in a dream: the villain was vanquished, the orphan reunited with his sister and all ended well.

Lysette took four curtain calls, but then held out her hands to still the applause. 'Dear friends, I have an announcement to make. What I have to say is difficult, for I have valued your loyal support these past three years, but the time has come for me to leave the stage.'

There was a gasp, then a cry of 'No! Shame!' but she held up her hand again.

'I know that what I have said will disappoint you, but my mind is made up. Goodnight, thank you and goodbye to you all.'

She swept a final deep curtsey and left the stage, her cheeks hot, tears pricking the back of her eyes, leaving uproar behind her. For many reasons she did not regret her decision, but that was not to say it was not hard to leave behind the thrill of a life so different from that she had been brought up to. Mr Porter rushed up, red-faced, his arms waving in agitation.

'I never thought you would go through with it—now hear what you have done! They are rioting out there!' He had to raise his voice above the sound of rhythmically stamping feet.

'Get a grip, Mr Porter,' the young lady who until a few moments ago had been Lysette Davide commanded briskly. 'They will have another favourite by next season. Your profits will be assured,' she added wryly. Three years' acquaintance with the theatre manager had taught her precisely where his priorities lay.

Her hand was on her dressing-room door when the stage doorman Stebbings came panting round the corner. 'Are you coming along to the Green Room, miss? There's a dozen or so nobs all wanting to see you, and I won't answer for the consequences if you don't make an appearance,' he said anxiously.

Lysette sighed, very tempted to plead a headache, to get the doorman to give her apologies, but then a sense of duty got the better of her. After all, it was for the last time. 'Very well, Stebbings. But only the most faithful gentlemen who always call—you know the ones.'

She hastily checked her appearance in the mirror, whisked a trace of powder over her high cheek-bones and rubbed a smudge of lamp-black from under her lower lashes, then hurried along the dingy corridors, parsimoniously lit by the occasional oil-lamp. Mr Porter was not going to spend money on frills and furbelows behind the scenes, but he had invested in the Green Room, where his actors met favoured members of the audience.

The scene which greeted Miss Davide's eyes as she pushed open the door was a familiar one. A dozen gentlemen clad in evening dress, glasses in hand, were discussing the evening's performance and her astounding announcement, while one or two of the more callow youths glowered at each other in jealous silence from the corners of the room.

As she walked in the room fell silent, then she was surrounded, bouquets and ribboned boxes pressed upon her, and from every side expressions of dismay at her decision and pleas to reconsider rained down. Smiling, nodding, responding with the grace that so marked her, Lysette gave no indication that this was yet another performance.

'Red roses, my lord, they are enchanting!' she was saying encouragingly to the tongue-tied seventeen-year-old heir to one of the nation's greatest families, when the door half opened again and she heard Stebbings expostulating on the other side.

'I'm sorry, gentlemen, but Miss Davide isn't seeing anyone else now.'

'She will see me,' a lazy voice declared coolly, and a tall, dark man strolled in, closing the door firmly behind him.

'Lovell!' Lord Franklin exclaimed. 'Didn't know you were in Bath, old man. Now look here, this won't do, you know—this is in the nature of a private farewell by Miss Davide's most faithful admirers. And quite frankly,' he added, low-voiced as he stepped forward to shake hands with the newcomer, 'we could do without any competition from you!'

Nicholas clapped his old acquaintance from White's Club on the back and grinned unrepentantly. 'I have been a silent admirer of Miss Davide for some time, and I am sure you are going to introduce us.'

Lord Franklin made the best of it, 'Miss Davide, may I make known to you Nicholas Lovell, Earl of Ashby? Lovell, Miss Davide.'

Nicholas bowed low over her proffered hand. 'Madam, your most devoted servant.'

Lysette inclined her head in response. 'My lord,' she responded calmly, not inclined to like this sardonic, self-assured man in his immaculate evening clothes. He was attractive enough, she admitted grudgingly, elegant certainly, without being in any way a dandy, but his self-possession made her want to oppose him on principle.

Despite her long practice in managing attentive gentlemen she found herself swiftly isolated from the rest of the group. His lordship's broad shoulders effectively blocked the others and the way he filled her champagne glass felt almost possessive.

Lysette's irritation grew, but she let none of it show on her face.

* * *

Nicholas, however, was close enough to see the sudden flare of annoyance that turned her hazel eyes green, and the infinitesimal tightening of her perfectly painted lips. He was intrigued. In his not inconsiderable experience actresses were piqued when eligible gentlemen ignored them, not when a new admirer came their way. This was going to prove one of the most satisfying wagers he had ever accepted; suddenly the prospect of winning Thunderer at the end of it was insignificant compared to the delight of conquering Miss Davide.

His facial control was as good as hers, but something of the hunter in his thoughts reached her and she felt herself strangely excited and unsettled by this man. Why this should be when she handled every other importunate gentleman with grace and firmness was a mystery.

Startled by this discovery, she looked up sharply to meet his dark blue eyes. Nicholas looked down and locked his gaze with hers, quite deliberately holding the moment like a caress, his mouth curving in an unspoken invitation. He was not surprised to see the flush that touched the creamy skin over the high cheekbones, but he was taken aback as she haughtily raised her dark brows and remarked coldly, 'I am neglecting my other guests, Lord Lovell. You must excuse me.'

So, she did not like to seem too obvious, Nicholas mused. Well, it would make the chase all the more piquant, and he had, after all, the entire week before he had planned to leave Bath. He was carrying in his breast pocket a small gift he had bought for his sister: an antique cameo he had found in an obscure little jeweller's in the City. It was not particularly valuable, but it was unusual and, even to a masculine eye, pretty. Georgiana, irritating though she might be, was still his favourite sister, and he had purchased it on a whim for her. However, the Bath jewellers would furnish another gift for his sister.

Lysette took a step forward, expecting him to move aside and allow her to rejoin the main group. To her annoyance he did no such thing, remaining still while she now found herself in dangerous proximity to him. She opened her mouth to ask him to move when he forestalled her by producing a small, flat jeweller's case.

'Miss Davide, will you honour me by accepting this small token of my admiration?'

Lysette took the box in her long fingers and regarded him levelly. 'Why, thank you, my lord. Perhaps I should make it clear that acceptance confers no promise of anything else whatsoever. I only ever accept gifts in appreciation of my per-formance *on the stage*.' There could be no mis-taking the implication of her words, and normally such a very frank hint meant that she had no further trouble with the gentleman concerned.

But this gentleman...this one was different, and obviously prepared to be quite as frank as she. 'That is making the situation very clear, ma'am.' His lips quirked in amusement as he moved aside slightly. 'Are you always as blunt?'

Despite the fact that he had given her the space to pass by, Lysette surprised herself by not moving. 'I rarely find it necessary, my lord, to be any more explicit, but I have discovered that many gentlemen have...how shall I put it?...a misconception that all actresses also follow another profession.' Again she felt the flush mounting her cheek. What was it about this man? Why could she not simply ignore him, sweep past him and join the other...safer... gentlemen?

She felt as though she was fixed to the spot, but then he moved again, bowing as he said, 'But I am monopolising you, Miss Davide, especially as this is your last appearance. Perhaps I could call upon you tomorrow. May I have your direction?'

'I never receive at home, sir,' she said repressively as she passed him, but he noted with interest that her previously still hands touched nervously at the dark curls that fringed her neck, and her manner as she began to speak to the other gentlemen was slightly less assured.

Florence appeared in the doorway and began the familiar task of gathering up bouquets and posies. Nicholas watched from his vantage-point, sipping his champagne, as Lysette worked her way round the room, making her farewells and allowing her hand to be kissed by those she knew best.

At last she paused in the doorway, her head held high on the slender column of her neck. He admired the almost classical elegance of her form, the fine gauze shawl draped over her bare arms highlighting the translucence of her skin. The diaphanous stage gown moulded her slender form, emphasising the narrowness of her waist and the grace of her carriage.

What was her background? he wondered. She was a very fine actress—her protestations of virtue just now had been almost convincing—

but surely she had to be simulating that air of good breeding, of being one of the Quality? And then she was gone.

Back in her dressing-room Lysette allowed Florence to help her out of her gown and into the simple walking-dress she had arrived in. She was fastening the bonnet strings as Stebbings tapped on the door.

'I'm a bit worried, miss. There is such a crush out front—and at the stage door too. I'm not sure how long it's going to take me to get you a carriage, or even a chair, miss. I think you had better wait a while: they'll go home after an hour or two—I can fetch you some supper in.'

Suddenly Lysette wanted to be out of the theatre and home more than anything. It was over, all the pretence, all the fairytale glitter and unreality, and she had her real life to return to. The thought of being trapped here for even another hour was insupportable.

'No, Nathaniel, I shall go home on foot.'

'But you'll be recognised, miss,' Florence protested, her face screwed up in worry.

'Give me the cloak I used in Act One, Florence, the one with the big hood. If I take off my bonnet and pull up the hood I should pass unrecognised. Is that basket you brought in last week still here? I can put my reticule in it and I will seem to be one of the dressers going home.'

'Yes, miss, here it is. Look, your bonnet will go in too, and if I tuck this cloth over no one will know.' The dresser pulled up the cloak, twitching the ends together in front to cover the modestly dark walking-dress. 'Oh, do take care, ma'am, I shall miss you!' She gave Lysette a convulsive hug, the tears running down her cheeks, then burst into real sobs as Lysette pressed a package into her hands, dropped a kiss on her cheek and slipped out.

Stebbings had been right; the crowd was thick around the stage door. Lysette drew up the hood close around her face, hunched her shoulders under the heavy folds of the cloak to disguise her height, and slipped, almost unheeded, through the throng.

But one pair of eyes marked her progress, one pair of eyes saw through the disguise. The Earl of Ashby, seated comfortably in the vantage-point of his carriage, watched the huddled figure reach the corner of Beaufort Square, glance back and straighten up to her full height before melting away into the darkness.

Little fool! What the devil was she doing, walking alone at this time of night? He had intended following her carriage or chair in his own conveyance, but now he opened the door and jumped down. 'Go home, William, I will walk.'

Lysette, too, was beginning to regret her decision to walk. Despite the lanterns and flambeaux outside each house, the streets were haunted by pools of shadow and frequent alleyways loomed like black pits. More than once she shrank back as groups of men, some of them the worse for drink, passed her noisily, but most worrying was the feeling that she was being followed. Once or twice she stopped and drew into the side of the path, but she could see no one behind her.

She told herself not to be such a ninny, but it was with relief that she reached Walcot Street. She still had to negotiate the area in front of the penitentiary for fallen women, which often attracted attention from undesirables, but once clear of that the street became increasingly respectable in a modest way.

Again she stopped, the hairs on the back of her

neck prickling, but this time there was no mistaking the fact that she was being followed, and very closely. Two hulking figures in frieze coats quickened their pace and before she could cry out or run she found herself bundled roughly into a side alley.

Frightened though she was, Lysette was not going to give in easily. One man had a callused hand over her mouth and she bit down hard, causing him to yelp and cuff her over the ear. Half stunned, she staggered, but still swung the heavy basket at the other man, catching him on the corner of the head and knocking off his hat. The smell of sweat and drink was nauseating and Lysette's stomach heaved as she struggled with the second man, trying to catch her breath enough to scream.

Increasingly terrified, she reacted instinctively to his groping hands, raising her knee sharply into the man's groin and being rewarded by his croak of pain. He staggered back, swearing viciously and clutching himself. 'Get the bitch, Clem,' he snarled.

'I think not,' a cultured voice said with soft menace, and the entrance to the alleyway was suddenly blocked by a tall figure silhouetted against the lamplight. Seconds later, after a brisk flurry of blows from a cane, both men were reeling off down Walcot Street.

A wave of nausea hit Lysette and her knees buckled. Before she could sink on to the muddy cobbles, strong arms encircled her and she was lifted and held against a broad chest. A familiar voice said firmly, 'Now, you are not going to faint until you tell me where you live.'

'My lord…' she gasped out, relief flooding through her weak limbs. 'Oh, thank you.'

'Do not thank me,' he replied almost roughly. 'You were a damn fool to be out here alone at this time of night. Now, tell me where to take you.'

'Para…I mean, number eight. Just up the road, here on the left.'

Nicholas Lovell did not appear to notice her hesitation, but put her on her feet, took her arm, picked up the basket, and set off slowly in the direction she indicated.

Lysette clutched gratefully at his strong arm, then staggered as the shock of what had so nearly happened hit her. Nausea hit her and she doubled up, drily retching. The Earl shifted his grip, lifted her firmly in his arms and carried her up the street.

'Here we are, safe and sound,' he said soothingly, his breath grazing her forehead. 'Number eight…but there is no light. Surely your maid is waiting up for you?'

Her thoughts were almost too hazy to deal with this situation, but after a moment's panic she found that at least part of the truth would serve. 'My companion had to go to her sister's bedside; her husband is very ill.'

'But where is your maid?' He set her carefully on her feet while keeping a firm arm on her elbow. His eyes were shadowed under the brim of his hat, but Lysette was very conscious of his sharp regard.

'I…er I sent her with Margaret, to carry things…er, calvesfoot jelly…and so on,' she added rather wildly.

'Hmm. Give me your key.' Nicholas unlocked the panelled door, holding it open as she slipped past him into a front room which was dimly lit by a well-banked fire.

Lysette stooped to light a taper from the coals and touched it to a branch of candles on the mantelpiece where it reflected in the mirror, filling the little parlour with muted light. She turned, schooling her face into polite gratitude. 'Thank you my lord—' she broke off as she realised that he was not only in the room, but that the front door was firmly closed.

Before she could protest he had walked past her, through into the kitchen behind, and was trying the back door, satisfying himself that it was secure. He rejoined her and, seeing her pale face, sat her firmly in the fireside chair and stated, 'Tea, I think.'

Weak-kneed as she still was, Lysette struggled out of the chair, only to find herself pressed back into it again. 'My lord, I am grateful to you, but this is entirely unnecessary—and you should not be here!' In her alarm it came out sounding ungracious.

'If you had slightly more regular domestic arrangements, ma'am, I would not need to be!' he rejoined tartly, and without as much as a by-your-leave he disappeared into the kitchen.

Lysette could hear the fire being riddled and the clang of the kettle being held under the pump, and suppressed a half-hysterical giggle at the thought of his elegant lordship involved in domestic chores. She supposed he must know how to make a cup of tea, although it seemed unlikely that he ever penetrated to the kitchen regions in his own elegant home. Goodness knows what he was making of the cottage, which was doubtless far from what he expected of a leading actress's abode.

He emerged from the back room carrying two bone china cups and placed one of them on the table beside her. Lysette took a grateful sip from hers, watching the Earl cautiously over the rim. He stood by the fireside, one foot on the fender, looking as incongruous in the cottage as a big cat in a dog kennel. He drank his tea with a grimace and she pulled herself together with an effort and a passable imitation of her Green Room manner.

'I thank you, my lord, for saving me this evening and for your kind attention. But I must not keep you—I am sure you would far rather be drinking brandy with your friends than sipping Bohea with me!'

'Not at all, ma'am—a refreshing change. And my sister would doubtless tell me it is better for me. Now, how many bedrooms have you?'

'Two…I mean, how dare you, my lord! That is a most unseemly question!'

'Is it?' he asked maddeningly. 'It seems entirely practical to me. I can hardly leave you alone, and I am sure your companion would not wish me to invade her bedchamber. However, doubtless I can make myself comfortable on that couch.'

Lysette jumped to her feet, deeply discommoded. 'Sir, what you suggest is outrageous! My reputation will be in tatters!'

One dark brow rose mockingly. 'My dear Miss Davide, forgive me for stating what may be a truism, but you are—or were—an actress.'

'Oh!' Lysette stamped her foot in sheer frustrated fury. Nothing seemed to dent his assurance and he said the most outrageous things, in such a way as to make them sound common sense. 'I have already told you this evening, I am not *that* sort of actress!'

Nicholas sketched her a bow. 'Oh, yes, you did hint at that earlier. Well, in that case I will be quite safe on the couch, will I not?'

'You…you…you are totally impossible!'

'So I have been told. By the way, Miss Davide, did you realise that when you are angry that slight French nuance in your speech quite disappears?' The dark head bent over the teacup and he appeared quite impervious to her simmering fury.

Lysette glowered at the rangy figure, so very

much at home on the hearthrug, the elegant cut of the dark blue superfine cloth moulding athletic shoulders, the long legs more than capable of standing the fashion for a tight cut. 'As I am not French, it is not surprising that the accent is not permanent,' she snapped. 'Now, my lord, grateful as I am—will you please go?' Although what exactly she was going to do if he chose not to was hard to say.

'My dear Miss Davide—or whatever your real name is—has it not occurred to you that those ruffians may well be hanging around out there, waiting for me to leave? It is highly likely they followed us here:
that type tends to be fairly persistent, in my experience, and I have no intention of leaving you to their tender mercies.'

The irony was that this was not her home, and if only Lord Lovell would leave she could make her escape with safety. But she was in a total dilemma: she could not tell him that this cottage belonged to Margaret, her old nurse, who was indeed away with her sister, but if she did not, he would stay. But at least, thank goodness, Mama would not be fretting. Over the last three years she had grown used to her elder daughter's unpredictably late hours and would have long since retired to bed.

Nicholas Lovell watched the play of emotions suddenly transform the previously well-controlled face of the beautiful young woman before him. He was puzzled, not a state he often found himself in.

She was not French, that much had quickly been established. Nor was Lysette Davide her name, but again, that was normal practice for the stage. Nor, he very strongly suspected, seeing her complexion close up, was she a brunette. But she was a genuine actress of talent, and something more… He stroked his chin, contemplating the enigma as she took an impatient few steps around the room. She genuinely wanted him gone, despite her fear of the footpads—and that was a real mystery if she was what she purported to be. And Nicholas Lovell did not like a mystery he could not solve.

Lysette stopped pacing and stood before him, looking up at him with greenish hazel eyes that were becoming shadowed with tiredness and reaction. 'My lord, please…' It was irresistible, even if it was not what he had intended—yet. Her face was tipped up to his, her lips soft and full, her eyes imploring. The subtle scent she wore, like honeysuckle on a warm summer night, had fretted at his senses since he had first come close to her in the Green Room. Now, so near, it filled his nostrils.

Before he could stop himself Nicholas reached out and stroked one finger gently along the fine line of her jaw. She started, her lips parting unconsciously in an invitation he could not resist. He bent and kissed her, catching her in his arms and drawing her into his warmth, his strength. For a moment the slender, supple figure was pliant in his arms, the lips returned the pressure of his, hesitatingly, with a naïveté that was the last thing he expected. Then she jerked back, abruptly freeing herself, anger turning her eyes a pure, hard green. Instinctively her hand came up to strike him and Nicholas parried the blow with the palm of his hand. The sound of the slap rang through the small room, then she was gone, in a flurry of skirts.

Nicholas listened to her footsteps as she ran upstairs, the slam of a door, the unmistakable click of a key turning in a lock. He stood absently rubbing his tingling palm, a look of rueful surprise on his face. Of all the things he had expected to discover this evening it was not that Miss Davide was not only Untouchable, but, quite literally, untouched.

Chapter Two

Camilla Knight who, until a few moments ago, had called herself Mademoiselle Lysette Davide, leant against the panels of the bedroom door until her convulsive breathing stilled slightly. The sentimental wool-work picture hanging over the narrow bed swam in and out of focus in the firelight and she wondered if she was going to faint. Gradually the image of a child clutching two kittens became clear again and the possibility receded.

'How could he…?' she whispered into the silence of the shadowed room. Then, 'No, I will *not* think about it!' The touch of Nicholas Lovell's mouth still seemed to burn on her lips, but she forced herself to ignore it. It was far more important to think about how she was going to escape and get home with Lord Lovell occupying the front room. Three years of living a double life had left Miss Knight with a skill for ingenuity and subterfuge unknown amongst other unmarried ladies of her class, and one amorous and over-gallant peer was not going to trip her up now, just when she had renounced it all and was about to return to safe respectability. But any amount of ingenuity was not going to make this very real man disappear.

Camilla bent and touched a taper to the smouldering coals in the grate then lit the two candles on the mantelshelf. The simple room that she used nightly to transform a society lady into an actress and back again now seemed unreal in the flickering light. It was stark: there was little in there except a bed, a dressing-table with ewer and jug, soap and clean towels. No clothes, no personal belongings, nothing to hint at the real person who inhabited it for a short while. In contrast the rest of the little house was redolent with the personality of Miss Margaret March, the family's old nurse, retired since Camilla's younger sister left the nursery, but still very much a personality in the household. Once Miss March had been drawn into the subterfuge she had kept her mistress's secret faithfully night after night, despite her somewhat confused disapproval of these 'goings-on'.

But tonight Miss March was at her desperately sick brother-in-law's bedside and this absence threatened to break the secret wide open. Camilla opened the curtains and looked out. The cottages on Walcot Street all had small yards and gardens sloping steeply up to meet the far larger ones of the elegant houses of the Paragon, which arched along the crest of the hill above. The lights in the salon of her mother's house shone out directly above, so much higher that in the darkness it seemed to be on a clifftop. Safety was so near and yet so far away. It could be on the other side of Bath for all the help it was as a refuge to her now.

Normally she would have long since taken off her wig and maquillage, having a short conversation with her old nursemaid as she did so. Then she would have slipped up through the concealed gate in the wall between the gardens, climbing the steep steps through the shrubbery to the back door, left on the latch for her. Now Camilla gazed longingly at her escape route, resting her hot forehead against the glass. It was going to be a long night.

The old clock on the landing produced one wheezy chime, but Camilla could still hear Nicholas moving about downstairs. There was the rattle of the poker in the grate, the sound of the pump in the kitchen, his footsteps on the boards. It seemed he was having trouble settling down to sleep.

Camilla shivered, despite the fire in the grate. She wrapped the quilted counterpane around her shoulders and settled back on the bed, tucking her feet up under her. She was aching for sleep, but determined not to drop off. She had to escape before morning: if his lordship were to see her in daylight her careful disguise would be swiftly penetrated. Stage make-up was never designed to be seen in the harsh light of day.

Now her double life was all over she could hardly believe she had got away with it undiscovered for so long. Three years! But then most people saw only what they expected to see, and that was not Miss Knight, the elder daughter of one of Bath's respectable widows, disporting herself on the professional stage!

Just over three years ago the newly bereaved Mrs Knight had arrived to take up residence in the city with her daughters. Camilla had been eighteen, Ophelia fourteen, and Mrs Knight had been planning her elder daughter's come-out when her unfortunate husband had succumbed to the seizure that carried him off. It had been no surprise to the family that the estate in Cambridgeshire was entailed on a distant cousin, but Mr Knight's sudden demise, and the subsequent discovery that their means were reduced from very comfortable to merely modest, had been a shock.

Mrs Knight had heard that one could live genteely in Bath on the income they had at their disposal and they soon found a respectable house in the Paragon. But the widow had no head for finance, and Camilla had rapidly found herself assuming the responsibility for the family funds. They were fortunate indeed that the elder son of the family solicitor from Cambridge had set up his own practice in Bath, and Mr Arthur Brooke had soon been established in their confidence as both friend and trusted adviser.

The true state of affairs revealed by Camilla and Mr Brooke's study of the account book had been depressing in the extreme. The Knights had been faced with the prospect of moving to dowdy apartments, discharging all but one of the servants and devoting all of their income to day-to-day living. There would be no money for either daughter's come-out, nor funds for dowries.

It was pure chance that had led Camilla to the shocking solution to their problems. After a particularly gloomy session discussing investments, Mr Brooke had offered to take her to the theatre and Camilla had readily accepted, desperate for a little diversion. Besides, private theatricals had long been a passion of hers, and their circle in Cambridgeshire had been unusually rich in other enthusiasts. Visits and house parties in the neighbourhood had invariably included charades, playlets and poetry readings, at which she excelled, and she had missed it very much since their move to Bath.

In the carriage driving back from the play she had been silent, the germ of an idea growing deep within her.

'A penny for your thoughts,' Arthur Brooke had prompted gently in his rather dry manner. Although only thirty, he was already adopting many of the mannerisms of his elderly father. 'Are you thinking about tonight's performance? I thought it very good.'

'I could do that,' Camilla blurted out impulsively.

'I beg your pardon, my dear Miss Knight, do what?'

'Act, go on the stage!'

'But why would you want to do anything so... so improper?' The shock in his voice hardly gave her pause, for the outrageous scheme was growing in her mind even as she answered him.

'Why, to make money, of course! Have we not agreed only this morning that my family's circumstances are straitened indeed? And what other talents have I?'

'But, Miss Knight, only consider what you are suggesting! A respectable match is surely not out of the question? You are educated, well-bred and very, er...' she could almost feel him blushing in the dark '...er, personable, if I may make so bold.'

'And with no dowry and no influential friends to promote my come-out, no amount of education, or even looks, are going to assist me, Mr Brooke. I cannot delude myself. Who,' she finished rhetorically, 'is going to offer for me now?'

There was a short silence, then he said, with shy diffidence, 'I will! Miss Knight, may I have the honour...?'

Camilla rushed in before he said the words.

'No. I thank you, sir, but I cannot accept an offer made out of kindness.'

He managed to keep the relief out of his voice very well, she thought, as they had continued back to the Paragon amicably enough. It had never been mentioned again.

But the idea of making an income from the stage was fixed in Camilla's mind. The very next morning, dressed modestly and heavily veiled, she ventured down to the Theatre Royal and sought an interview with Mr Gordon Porter, its actor-manager. One rendition of a scene from *As You Like It* and Mr Porter was more than interested in this prospect—especially when the anonymous young lady lifted her veil to reveal a lovely, expressive face to match the grace and elegance of a well-turned figure.

The manager was less enthusiastic about the hard-bargained terms she exacted from him, along with a promise never to enquire about the true identity of 'Lysette Davide'. But Mr Porter was no fool, and he soon realised his investment had been a good risk. Miss Davide rapidly became wildly popular, particularly with the gentlemen in the audience, and her salary rose accordingly, season by season.

A heavily disapproving but intrigued Mr Brooke threw himself into the investment of this scandalous income, and by diligence and some strokes of great good fortune they saw the nest-egg grow far beyond Camilla's original modest dream. Now the Knights' comfortable home was secured, Ophelia's future well funded, and Mrs and Miss Knight could look forward to a respectable future.

These comfortable recollections ceased abruptly as Camilla thought about Nicholas Lovell ensconced downstairs, blocking her escape and threatening her with exposure. The clock struck two. Camilla climbed carefully off the bed, knelt down and applied one ear to the floorboards. All was silent—she would have to risk it now.

She crept down the steep stairs, hugging the inside of the treads to minimise the creaking of the old wooden boards, and peeped through the half-open door into the parlour. He was not on the couch! Her hand flew to her mouth as she scanned the room, then her eyes fell on the long shape stretched before the guttering fire.

Nicholas was lying full-length on the hearth-rug, a sofa cushion behind his head. He had taken off his jacket and loosened his neckcloth and his body was totally relaxed in sleep. Camilla stood transfixed on the threshold. He looked younger, gentler, his lean features softened by the depth of his slumber. His lashes lay black on the high cheekbones, and in the flickering firelight his mouth seemed to flex into a smile.

Camilla fought down a totally irrational impulse to cross to him and brush back the lock of dark hair that had fallen on to his forehead. She should be out of the back door and away, not standing here remembering that outrageous kiss and wishing he would wake up and do it again!

With a shiver Camilla pulled her pelisse closer across her shoulders, lifted her skirts and tiptoed into the kitchen. The big back-door key was in its usual place behind the flour-bin. She pulled it out with infinite care, stopping every few moments to listen, the sound of her heart thudding loudly in her ears. She slipped the key into the lock, then with painful slowness turned it.

The lock gave a harsh click which rang out like a pistol shot in the silent cottage and from the room beyond she heard Nicholas Lovell sigh and turn over, but he did not wake. Seconds later she was out in the chill April air, securing the door behind her and running up the steep path to the shrubbery which masked the door in the wall. With trembling fingers she lifted the latch and was through, pausing only to arrange the screen of falling ivy again before she closed it and climbed up between the clipped box hedges to the kitchen door.

Four hours later Nicholas Lovell woke stiff and cold before a fire reduced to a pile of smoking ash. For a moment he lay, eyes closed, trying to remember where he was and how he came to be there. The memory came back with a jolt of pleasurable anticipation and his mouth twisted in sensual recollection. He sat up, stretched, got to his feet and padded through to the kitchen, wincing as his stockinged feet met the chill of the flagstoned floor.

A few seconds with his head under the pump was enough to bring him fully awake and he stood for a moment listening. All was still in the little cottage. It would be fascinating to see what Miss Davide was like in the daylight and discover how she would react to him when they met again… Nicholas hefted the heavy kettle off the range and filled it. He riddled the fire, threw on some more coal, making no effort to do it quietly, and listened again. Surely that would have woken her?

He made the tea absently, his mind on his strategy for the morning. The capture of the intriguing Miss Lysette Davide—or whatever she was really called—was going to be too piquant to be rushed. Besides, he had five days to fill before going back to Town, and the thought of filling them with the chase was pleasurable.

There was still no movement from the room above. Nicholas climbed the stairs, glanced into the front room, the door of which stood open, found it empty and went to tap on the second chamber door. There was no response, so he tried again, calling out, 'Miss Davide? Good morning! I have made some tea…'

Still silence. Could she really be so heavily asleep? Then he remembered the fatigue in those hazel-green eyes the night before. He should really leave her to sleep, but he could not leave without speaking to her, and he must leave soon or risk being seen by the neighbours. She might be an actress, but she would guard her reputation, and he doubted she flaunted her gentlemen callers in such a way.

Nicholas knocked again, then gently eased down the handle and looked round the door. Not only was the chamber empty but the curtains were drawn and the bed obviously unslept in. He stepped inside and for a moment of disbelief blinked at the empty room, not trusting his own eyes. There was no wardrobe, no cupboard or trunk to hide in. The floor under the bed was visible and empty. He strode to the window, but the casement was stiff and had obviously not been opened for some time. He scanned the little yard below, sloping upwards to the high wall of the Paragon gardens above. But even if she had opened the window there was no way to climb down.

The front bedroom was equally unsatisfactory: it was exactly what it appeared—an elderly spinster's chamber, devoid of hiding places. Nicholas went back to the landing, closing the doors behind him. For a long moment he stared down into the little hallway below, his hands on his hips, his brow furrowed in thought. Unconsciously he pushed back the lock of hair Camilla had been so drawn to the night before.

Well, she must have gone out through the back

door; there was no other explanation. But the door was locked and there was no key to be found. The front door was also locked, but the key was on the inside, exactly as it had been left when they had entered the night before. Nicholas went back into the kitchen and peered through the window, but all he could see was the high stone wall all around the yard, and the tangle of ivy and bushes screening the even higher wall at the foot of the gardens of the Paragon buildings.

'How the hell did you get out of here, Miss Davide?' he asked into the silence. 'And why?' It was her house, he was the interloper. But then the memory of that curiously innocent kiss came back to him. Either she was the most accomplished actress he had ever come across or she was indeed as pure as she had wanted him to believe. And if that were the case, then finding herself alone with a man might well have prompted her to take flight. But to where?

Ten minutes later he was locking the front door and slipping the key back under it. He would go home, have a wash and shave and a good breakfast—and send one of the grooms to keep a discreet eye on the little cottage in Walcot Street.

* * *

Mrs Knight was already pouring her second cup of chocolate when her elder daughter wandered, heavy-eyed, into the sunny breakfast parlour.

'Good morning, Mama, good morning, Ophelia.'

'Ah, there you are, my dear!' Mrs Knight raised her rather short-sighted blue gaze from the pages of the *Bath Intelligencer* and regarded Camilla anxiously. 'So unlike you to sleep in on such a lovely sunny morning. I was about to send Blisset up to see whether you were awake yet.'

'Oh, Mama!' Ophelia broke in, 'No wonder poor Camilla is so fatigued. How could you forget? It was her final performance last night!' At almost eighteen, Ophelia had much of the blonde prettiness that had made her mother so admired in her time, but she had too something of her father's sharp intelligence and spirit.

Mrs Knight blinked vaguely at her daughters. 'Oh, yes, I had quite forgot. Do forgive me, my dear. Did it go well?' The widow had managed to cope with her daughter's outrageous career by dint of largely ignoring it, persuading herself that Camilla's performances at the Theatre Royal were no different from those enacted at a private house party. Her understanding of financial matters was not strong, and she had been so sheltered by her late husband that the restoration of their fortunes appeared more as a happy accident than due to the actions of her daughter.

And besides, Camilla acknowledged, it was easier all round if Mama did not think too much about her scandalous behaviour. It was enough to give any respectable matron a fit of the vapours. Well, from this morning onwards the entire Knight family would be precisely what they appeared—respectable, modestly well-off ladies: ornaments of Bath society.

This comforting train of thought was punctuated by a shriek from Ophelia, who had purloined the inside pages of the newspaper from her mama and was conning them whilst demolishing her third slice of bread and butter with healthy appetite. 'Camilla! Look—do look! You are all over the paper!'

Her sister nearly dropped her cup before she realised that Ophelia was reading the theatre reviews. For one wild, mad moment she had imagined that the encounter between herself and Nicholas Lovell had somehow reached the gossip columns. She pressed one hand to her breast as if to still her wildly beating heart, before saying, as calmly as she could manage, 'Do read it Ophelia.'

'*"Finest performance of a dazzling three-year career...Mr Bradley also giving a strong reading..."* oh, never mind him! *"...crowned it all with a shocking announcement to theatre-goers...riot in the pit..."* Were they really rioting? How exciting!' Ophelia's eyes sparkled with excitement. 'Oh, how I would have loved to be there! *"...resolute in the face of the pleas of her loyal audience...a sad loss to the Dramatic Art...noisy scenes outside the Theatre lasting into the small hours..."'*

'A complete exaggeration,' Camilla remarked calmly as she buttered a slice of bread with an almost steady hand. 'There was some disappointment at my announcement, which I confess was very gratifying, but it is a storm in a teacup and will all be forgotten in a week.'

Ophelia was scarcely listening. She was wrestling to fold up the broadsheet pages to show an engraving which purported to be that of Mademoiselle Lysette Davide. 'What a terrible likeness,' she declared, wrinkling her nose.

'So I should hope. Just think what would befall us all if anyone recognised your sister,' retorted her mama faintly, then rallied as a happy thought struck her. 'My dears, I have just thought. We can all go to the theatre again now!'

'Not for a week or so, please, Mama,' Camilla protested. The way she was feeling this morning, she did not care if she never saw the inside of a theatre again!

For his part Lord Lovell spent a restless day, largely engaged in avoiding his sister Georgiana. The Countess of Forres was eager to question her brother as to why he had not returned home until the morning, fearing that he was, once more, reverting to his old rakish ways, instead of conserving his energies for the pursuit of a wife. This had been her intention in inviting him to stay with her, and she expected—nay, demanded—that he dance attendance on her through an elaborate series of social events.

Aided and abetted by his brother-in-law Henry, Nicholas had managed on his arrival to elude her hints, invitations and downright orders to accompany her to dances, soirées and afternoon tea parties, at which he knew full well a succession of

eligible young ladies would be paraded before him.

His valet was just smoothing the set of his
evening-coat across his broad shoulders when
the under-footman appeared at his bedroom
door. 'Martins is returned, my lord, and said you
had asked to see him at once.'

'Send him to Lord Forres's study. I will be down
shortly.' Released finally by his valet, his appearance having passed muster to the standards of
that demanding critic, Nicholas ran lightly down
the staircase of Georgiana's house in the Crescent.
Martins had spent all day watching the little house
in Walcot Street, and surely by now he would
have gleaned enough intelligence for Nicholas to
track down the elusive Lysette Davide. She could
hardly stay away from home all day.

The groom was waiting in the panelled masculine sobriety of Lord Forres's retreat. A
taciturn, self-confident man, he touched his
forelock as his master entered.

'Well, Martins, what news do you have for me?'

'None, my lord, I'm afraid.'

'None?' Nicholas's dark brows rose. 'You have
been there since eight this morning, man,
somebody or something must have occurred.'

'No, my lord. The place has been deserted. No one in, no one out. I took young Ben with me—he's a reliable lad, my lord—and I set him off to find a back way in—but there is none. I left him on watch and tried both the alehouses in the street. Thought someone there would know something.'

Nicholas stood frowning into the darkened garden. 'Good man. And what did you discover?'

'Not a lot, my lord. The house is occupied by an elderly lady—governess type by the sound of it. No one else lives there, no one else visits. She goes out a lot, but keeps herself to herself. Name of Miss March. Shops locally, pays her bills on time, very quiet. Not so much as a pet parrot.'

Nicholas grinned at this unusual touch of whimsy from the groom. 'You are sure about the parrot?'

'Dead sure, my lord. Do you want me to go back and watch the house again overnight?'

'No, you have done enough for one day. Send Wilkins; we will give it one more shot. Now go and get yourself a good dinner.' He tossed Martins a coin.

As the door closed behind the man Nicholas

dropped into one of Henry's wing-chairs and stretched out his feet towards the fire. He steepled his fingers and looked through them at the dancing flames, his mind pondering on the enigma that was Miss Davide. To all intents and purposes she had walked into that cottage as though she owned it; she'd moved about the little rooms with an ease that spoke of long familiarity.

She knew that house well; he was sure of it. Then a thought came to him. Could she be disguising herself as the old lady? After all, she was an actress, and a fine one at that. But then he remembered the bedroom, so obviously and typically that of an elderly lady. Whatever Miss Davide might disguise herself as outside, there would be no need to continue the pretence in the privacy of her own home. And why should she disguise herself in any case?

Nicholas was still pondering pleasurably on aspects of the previous evening when the door flew open and a voice declared triumphantly, 'There you are, Nicholas! Really, what are you about, skulking in here? Benson announced dinner quite fifteen minutes ago!'

'Good evening, Georgiana.' Nicholas got reluctantly to his feet. 'I am afraid I quite lost track of the time. That is a particularly handsome turban. Is it new?'

The Countess inclined her head graciously at the compliment. Never beautiful, she was none the less a striking woman who dressed to advantage to show off her Junoesque figure and height. Strongly coloured silks and taffetas showed off the family jewels and the new pieces which an indulgent husband showered upon her every time she produced for him another child. As the family now consisted of four boys and a girl, her lord had every reason for thus rewarding her.

'Do not seek to divert me, Nicholas; what is going on? Why are you having surreptitious meetings with your grooms in the study?' Her deep blue eyes, so like his, fixed on his face.

'I do not believe Henry objects to me using his study,' Nicholas remarked mildly. 'I can hardly stand around in the mews at this time of night giving my men their orders. May I take you into dinner?' He offered his sister his arm and she gave him a frosty stare as she laid her fingers upon the dark blue superfine of his sleeve and turned with him towards the hall.

'Mmm. Do not think to bamboozle me,

Nicholas! You know perfectly well I have no objection to you using the house as you wish, but you are up to something. Something disgraceful in the way of a wager, I will be bound!'

'How well you know me. I can hide nothing from you, sister dear. It revolves around a particularly fine horse and a wager I have entered into with George Marlow and his friends.'

Lady Forres snorted. 'I should have known it. Now, what are you doing tomorrow afternoon?'

'Er…nothing in particular.' Thinking of Mademoiselle Davide, he realised too late that he had fallen straight into his sister's trap.

'Good. Then you are coming with me to Lady Richardson's. She has just had a sculpture gallery added to her house and has invited a select party to view it. The cultural environment will do you good and I need an escort.' She ignored her brother's upcast eyes and persisted. 'Horses and wagers indeed! Besides, there is someone I am particularly anxious for you to meet.'

'Oh, good,' replied Nicholas in a voice of deep gloom as they entered the dining-room.

Lord Forres was already seated, but he got to his feet as his wife and brother-in-law entered and grinned at the expression on Nicholas's face. 'For goodness' sake, Georgiana, leave the man alone,' he admonished lovingly. 'And let us get on with our dinner.'

Despite the fact that there were only the three of them dining that evening, Lady Forres maintained the standard of food and presentation for which she was justly famed. Course followed course, each accompanied by a fine wine from Lord Forres's extensive cellar.

Georgiana showed every sign of wishing to probe further the question of his bet with George Marlow, and at the mention of a horse Henry's ears pricked and he too joined in the interrogation. Nicholas had no desire to discuss the terms of the bet and seized on the only other subject he knew Georgiana could reliably be diverted upon.

'So who is this person you are so desirous of my meeting tomorrow?' he asked innocently. 'A sculptor? Lady Richardson's architect? A visiting Italian artist, perhaps?'

Henry immediately lost interest and reverted to studying the cheeses before him. Georgiana, however, took the bait and dropped the subject of the wager. 'Do not be disingenuous, Nicholas, it does not suit you—you are too old to act the *naïf*. Mind you,' she added darkly, 'you always were!'

Nicholas tried, and failed, to look hurt. His elder sister had always done her best to order his life, but despite their constant sparring there was a deep affection between them. And, provided Georgiana was not nagging him, he always enjoyed coming to the household with its boisterous children, Henry's affable hospitality and Georgiana's lavish table.

His sister set down her empty glass with decision and looked hard at her handsome brother. Really, the boy was far too good-looking for his own good; and those looks combined with his intelligence, wit, social standing and undeniable wealth made him such a catch she could not believe he had wriggled free for so long. Well, not for much longer, if she had anything to do with it! He was twenty-seven years old; high time he was married and setting up his nursery. If Lady Forres had anything to do with it, Nicholas Lovell would not be leaving Bath unengaged to a highly eligible *partie*.

Recalling herself swiftly, she announced, 'The young person I wish you to meet is Lady

Richardson's niece, Miss Emilia Laxton. Such a well-bred, well-connected young woman.'

'And how old is this paragon?' Nicholas asked warily. This was all too familiar. Georgiana appeared to think that the younger the débutante the more suitable she would be for reforming her rake of a brother.

'Er…I believe she is, er…seventeen.'

'A schoolroom chit, in other words! Save me, dear sister, from yet another vapid giggling miss without an idea in her head—or indeed anything else.'

'No, indeed, you are being most unfair, Nicholas, to dismiss Miss Laxton out of hand. She is extremely well-connected. The grand-daughter of the Earl of Olney and, I understand, the heiress of her uncle, Sir George Laxton. I only want to see you settled and happy, my dear, and she would make you a very conformable bride.'

Nicholas grimaced. He too felt an increasing desire to be settled and happy—but not with some child selected by his sister on the basis of her place in *Debrett's* or the size of her fortune. He wanted a companion, someone with character and intelligence—and looks and spirit, of course.

Someone like…He remembered the touch of Lysette Davide's lips on his last night, the flash of anger and intelligence in her eyes, the piquant mystery of her. Of course an actress, of whatever quality, was totally ineligible, but if he could find a respectable young lady with some of those qualities he would be only too happy to marry her.

Yes, he would go to Lady Richardson's and endure it with every appearance of pleasure, and no expectation of meeting anyone of any interest. Meanwhile there was still a wager to win and the delectable Miss Davide to find and conquer.

Chapter Three

No one observing Lord Lovell's urbane expression as he bowed gracefully over his hostess's hand the next day would have guessed that he was at the reception under duress. Certainly Lady Richardson, intensely gratified by the presence of one of the most good-looking and eligible bachelors of the Ton, read nothing but polite interest in his handsome features as he enquired about her new sculpture gallery.

'Well, my lord, we did feel it was time we found more fitting accommodation for the treasures Lord Richardson brought back from the Grand Tour. For so long they have been in very cramped surroundings in our London residence—they could not be properly appreciated there. But here we have not only space for our own sculptures, but also those my late father-in-law had installed in the Berkshire house.'

Nicholas smiled warmly at his hostess, who responded by turning a hue almost as rosy as her afternoon gown. 'A most striking arrangement, ma'am, and, if I may be so bold to venture an opinion, so very indicative of your own taste.'

Lady Forres shot her brother a warning look over the shoulder of their hostess. Lady Richardson might be fooled into thinking she had just received a compliment, but Georgiana, herself inwardly shuddering at the over-ornate, gilded décor, knew better.

'Well, for myself I cannot wait to look around; it looks quite fascinating,' she interjected hastily. 'Give me your arm, Lovell, and let Lady Richardson attend to her other guests. We must not monopolise her.'

The ladies bowed to each other and Nicholas guided Georgiana off towards the far end of the new sculpture gallery. A footman approached with a tray of glasses and Nicholas secured a glass of Madeira for them both. 'Nicholas,' Lady Forres warned, *sotto voce*, while smiling and nodding to an acquaintance. 'None of your tricks now. Do behave, please!'

One dark brow rose quizzically. 'Sister, dear, what can you mean? I am being perfectly polite about this ghastly room.'

'I know you are, you wretch, so why do I feel as though I am sitting on a keg of gunpowder every time you open your mouth?' Her blue eyes regarded him shrewdly; she was not displeased by what she saw. Even a sister's critical eye could detect no flaw in the cut of his coat or the perfection of his neckcloth or gleaming Hessian boots. And the fashion for tight trousers, while fatal to those of short limbs or a portly disposition, enhanced the rangy elegance of Lord Lovell's frame. As for his looks—well, he took after his father, said by many to have been the best-looking man of his generation.

As brother and sister strolled slowly down the length of gallery, it seemed that an inordinate number of ladies turned to regard them. But Lady Forres, who did not delude herself into thinking it was her new gown that was causing the interest, could see no sign of Miss Laxton, her quarry for the afternoon.

Ah, there she was! Lady Forres spied the young lady sitting demurely on a chaise-longue, partly hidden by an orange tree in a pot. The girl rose politely to her feet when she saw the older woman bearing down on her, but her eyes dropped when she saw Nicholas. 'Miss Laxton, how do you do? You are not acquainted with my brother, the Earl of Ashby, I believe? Lovell, Miss Laxton.'

Miss Laxton dropped a curtsey without raising her gaze to Nicholas. 'Miss Laxton,' he murmured, wishing she would look up. His sister had been right; she really was the most beautiful child: dark brown curls clustered round a small, perfectly shaped head and cascaded on to her slender white neck. Her features were regular, her face heart-shaped and her complexion one of true roses and cream. After a long moment she shyly met his gaze, revealing a pair of pansy-brown eyes and an expression of apprehension.

Lady Forres saw her friend Lady Richardson advancing on them and permitted a small smile to play around her lips, answered by an almost imperceptible nod from the betoqued head of the older woman. The two of them had put their heads together over this meeting, and both had agreed that the match was highly desirable, for many reasons.

'emilia, my dear,' Lady Richardson cooed, 'why

do you not show his lordship the fountain at the far end of the gallery? I am sure he will enjoy the view afforded of the orangery from there.'

'That sounds delightful,' Nicholas responded, offering Miss Laxton his arm. Her fingers, as they settled lightly on his sleeve, trembled slightly. As they moved away from the two matrons he said lightly, 'Come, Miss Laxton, I am not so much of an ogre as to make you tremble, am I?'

'Oh, no, my lord!' she protested, her startled eyes flying to meet his amused gaze. 'It is just that my aunt said that you were such a connoisseur, and I know nothing about classical art. In fact,' she added, all in a rush, 'I think these statues rather ghastly.' She looked so conscience-stricken at this admission that Nicholas laughed out loud.

'In what way?' he asked encouragingly.

'So cold and white. And there are bits missing— see, that one has no arms! Why could they not be mended before being placed in the gallery? And then there are all those huge men wrestling with sea monsters—it really is not the sort of restful thing one would like to live with, is it?'

Nicholas obligingly viewed the fountain to

which she was referring. It had been set into the end wall of the gallery and indeed, over-muscled marine gods appeared to be locked in mortal combat with improbable sea creatures. 'I have to agree with you, Miss Laxton, not restful at all. I suspect the architect has seen the Prince Regent's latest additions to Carlton House and has been inspired by them.'

This interchange appeared to have exhausted Miss Laxton's source of conversation for the moment and they stood side by side in silence in front of the tumbling water, Nicholas wondering just how soon he could politely make his escape. Miss Laxton was undoubtedly a delightfully pretty débutante, but five minutes in her company was more than sufficient.

Outside in Laura Place a hired chaise drew up and three ladies descended on to the flagged pavement before Lady Richardson's house. Mrs Knight ran a critical eye over her daughters' gowns and, more than satisfied, ushered them into the hallway. 'One good thing, my dear,' she remarked to Camilla as they climbed the stairs to the reception room. 'Now you are no longer going to the th...I mean, going out in the evenings, you will be able to accept so many more invitations for parties and dances.'

'Indeed, Mama,' Camilla responded, as a maid conducted them into a side room to remove their pelisses and tidy their hair. 'But I shall have to account for the sudden improvement in my health which now, after three years, allows me to go about in the evenings.'

'Oh, that is easily done: the Bath air, the waters, a new physician—there are any number of reasons one can give.' Mrs Knight flapped her hands vaguely and led her small party out to meet their hostess.

Camilla stepped confidently into the salon behind her mother. She knew she was looking her best, in a new afternoon gown of pale moss-green with a simple flounce. Her tall, slender figure needed no distracting frills or ornamentation to detract from any faults, and in keeping with her unmarried status she wore only a simple pearl necklace and matching earstuds. Although her clandestine life had forced her to make excuses for rarely attending evening events, Camilla had nonetheless a wide social circle, many of whom would be present at this reception.

Passing through the salon, she was soon

caught up in conversation with a cheerful group of young ladies of her acquaintance. She accepted a glass of orgeat and eyed the over-ornate gallery warily. Lady Richardson was an excellent hostess, but unfortunately her money and connections did not confer good taste in interior design. Camilla maintained a lively debate on the quite dreadfully unflattering hat brims which had just come into fashion, while mentally stripping the room of its ornament and substituting a few well-placed statues and potted palms.

Ophelia, wandering wide-eyed at her mother's heels amidst the crowd of classical sculptures, was inclined to giggle at her elders' flowery enthusiasm for the display. After a few moments she glimpsed Miss Laxton at the far end, made her excuses and hurried towards her best friend.

On reaching her side she was pulled up short by the sight of Miss Laxton's companion, a dev-astatingly handsome man. Emilia was directing an anxious, silent signal for help to her, and Ophelia was only too happy to oblige. What was Emilia doing with this man when Ophelia knew she had contracted an attachment to Edward

Ormond, the younger son of Sir James Ormond, the City banker?

Well, if her dear friend needed help with this particular gentleman, Ophelia was only too ready to oblige! 'Miss Laxton, good afternoon. What a charming party!'

'Good afternoon! My lord, may I introduce Miss Ophelia Knight? Miss Knight and I attended Miss Atherton's seminary together. Miss Knight, may I make known to you the Earl of Ashby?'

Ophelia dropped a curtsey, and raised bright eyes to his lordship. 'My lord, are you resident in Bath?'

'Visiting my sister Lady Forres, Miss Knight. I am rarely in Bath, but I realise now what I have been missing, and will visit more frequently in future.' This child was enchanting, and with none of Miss Laxton's shyness.

Ophelia twinkled back responsively. Unlike her friend, she had not the slightest objection to flirting with a handsome man such as his lordship. 'Oh, so you are attracted by classical sculpture then, my lord? Is there none to be seen in London? Surely the British Museum is full of that sort of thing.'

'I was referring rather to the charming

company one encounters in this city, Miss Knight,' Nicholas responded gallantly. Miss Knight intrigued him: she was very young, as young as the gauche and silent Miss Laxton, but there was something about her…

'Have we met before, Miss Knight?' he enquired as the three of them turned and began to stroll back up the gallery.

'I think not, my lord. I have not been to London since I was quite a child, and I do not come out until this Season.'

'Forgive me my error,' Nicholas responded lightly. But that strong sense of having met either Miss Knight or someone very like her persisted.

'There is your sister, dear Ophelia,' Miss Laxton cried, still anxious to widen the circle and remove herself from the uncomfortable presence of Lord Lovell.

Nicholas turned at her words and saw Camilla framed against an empty niche. She was laughing at a story one of her group was telling, her head tilted back slightly, her blonde curls falling from a high knot. Her profile was almost Grecian in its purity and cool perfection of line, and Nicholas thought he had never seen a more beautiful woman.

He glanced automatically at her left hand, but she wore no wedding band. He guessed her age to be perhaps twenty or twenty-one, slightly older than the other débutantes. Perhaps that accounted for her poise and air of quiet self-assurance. And if her younger sister's features had stirred something within his memory, then that feeling was much stronger now.

'Will you not introduce us, Miss Ophelia?' He had met her before—but where? Surely he could not have forgotten such looks and presence?

Ophelia, with an inward sigh, for she was well aware that in the presence of her sister no attractive rake was going to be sparing any attention for her, led the way over.

Camilla had perhaps two heartbeats' notice of the arrival of the man she had spent half the previous night with. For a moment she thought she was going to faint, the shock of seeing him was so great. Then, with an almost superhuman effort, she called up every vestige of acting skill she had ever possessed and stood with nothing but an expression of polite interest on her face.

'Camilla, may I introduce the Earl of Ashby, who is anxious to be made known to you? My lord, my sister Miss Knight.' Ophelia wondered why her sister had gone so pale and why she was suddenly so still, so rigid. Why, Ophelia thought with a sudden flight of fancy, one might almost think she had stepped out of the empty niche behind her, a statue come to life.

'Miss Knight, good afternoon. You will forgive me, but have we not met before? In London perhaps?'

'Good afternoon, my lord.' Camilla murmured. 'I am afraid I do not recall our having been introduced. Perhaps you are mistaken.' It was not the truth, of course, but it was not quite a lie either: after all, he had been introduced to Lysette Davide, not to Miss Knight. He had not recognised her, she was sure of that, but something about her had piqued his interest, that was certain. There was a look in those quizzical blue eyes that worried her. It was obvious that her cool words had not satisfied him and he would not give up until he had placed her in his memory. The impression of him as a hunter that had come to her in the Green Room was back.

She caught a glimpse of her own reflection in one of the long glasses which lined the room between the niches and was reassured. No, surely he would not recognise in this blonde, pale, composed and calm English débutante the brunette actress with her husky French accent and bold stage make-up. And the chaste simplicity of her gown spoke of nothing but the débutante.

'Are you in Bath long, my lord?' she enquired politely. 'Will you be subscribing to the Assembly Rooms and concerts?' With any luck he would say he was just passing through, hated Bath and would never set foot in the place again!

'I am staying with my sister, Lady Forres, and I had intended a short visit only on this occasion. Normally I do not find much to keep me in Bath. However, I feel I have greatly misjudged the city and I may well extend my stay.' How he managed, without any change of expression or tone, to imply that this was entirely due to her presence, Camilla was at a loss to know. The man was an accomplished and dangerous flirt, if not an out-and-out rake.

In one part of her mind she was amused to have the unique opportunity to observe his technique with women from—as he thought—two very different worlds. But, intriguing as that might be, she could not but be aware that she was in very grave danger, and a tension far greater than any stage fright she had ever suffered was gripping her nerves. One word from Lord Lovell and she would be ruined, irretrievably and for ever. And Ophelia would be tarred with the same brush.

His lordship was signalling for a waiter, and when the man arrived he took two glasses from the tray and offered one to Camilla. As she accepted it her hand shook slightly, and observing it Lord Lovell was taken aback. Why was this cool, poised creature trembling? He was used to displays of nerves from very young débutantes, but in this woman it seemed at odds with her outward assurance.

Camilla glanced round for her sister, anxious to turn this dialogue into a three-way conversation, but, thoroughly bored and somewhat resigned to his lordship's lack of interest in anyone but her older sister, Ophelia had rejoined her schoolfriend at the end of the gallery. Now they sat, heads close together, giggling behind their hands at the carefully placed figleaf on a statue of a very minor Greek god.

'I am sure Lady Forres must be delighted that you are extending your stay, especially if you do not normally find Bath congenial,' Camilla observed, wondering if she sounded as banal as she thought she did.

Nicholas grimaced. 'I had intended staying five days. But now I have made a wager with some of my friends. To win it I must stay in Bath for a while. So…' he smiled at her, transforming his lean and somewhat saturnine features, '…my plans for next week are overset and I think I will have to console myself by experiencing all of Bath's attractions.'

He was rewarded by a slight blush on Miss Knight's pale cheeks. She might look as though flirtation was beneath her, but she could respond to it like the next woman.

Camilla had indeed been in no doubt as to which attractions he had been referring to. Try as she might, the memory of his mouth, warm, experienced and demanding, came flooding into her mind and the blush deepened. Her fingers crept to the curls clustering against her throat, and she smoothed them unconsciously. Nicholas frowned, his memory piqued again by that gesture.

Collecting herself with a huge effort, she smiled back at him. 'Somehow, my lord, I do not think you will find taking the waters to be an attraction, but if you have not spent much time here before you may not be aware of how delightful the countryside is around the city.'

'That does indeed sound more attractive than sipping sulphurous waters—not that I had intended to try, I must admit! Do you know of any rides in particular that you could recommend?'

Camilla, not seeing the trap, fell right into it. 'Yes, indeed, my lord. My sister and I often ride out: there are many routes through the woods or across the hills which I can recommend.'

'Capital!' Nicholas smiled warmly into her green eyes. 'Then might I hope you will act as my guide? Perhaps, if this fine weather persists, you and Miss Ophelia might like to ride with me tomorrow afternoon?'

'Why, thank you my lord. What a kind thought. However, we have a previous…'

'Riding!' Ophelia appeared beside them as if by magic, her arm linked through that of Arthur Brooke, whom she had obviously just waylaid. 'How lovely! With spring so much in the air, I am longing to gallop along the downs. Thank you, my lord.'

'Unfortunately Miss Knight was just telling me you had a prior engagement,' Nicholas said with a wicked glint in his eye, looking from one sister's eager face to the other's warning frown.

Ophelia turned a puzzled face to her sister. 'No, no, Camilla. What can you be thinking of? Why, it was only this morning we were agreeing how dull this week was set to be!'

'Yes, well, we can discuss that later, Ophelia. Mr Brooke must think our manners have gone wandering! Good afternoon, Mr Brooke, how pleasant to find you here admiring the new gallery.' In her relief at seeing him, Camilla was rather warmer in her manner than normal in greeting her old friend and man of law, a fact reflected in the smile that appeared on his normally serious face.

'Indeed, yes, I am. And a most pleasant surprise to find you all here, Miss Knight. An interesting interpretation of the Graeco-Roman style, but I think the architect has succeeded in carrying it off.'

'I must confess to finding it somewhat chilly,' Camilla replied with a smile. 'But I am forgetting my manners. Lord Lovell, may I make known to you Mr Brooke? Mr Brooke, the Earl of Ashby, who is staying in Bath with his sister Lady Forres. Mr Brooke has a legal practice in the City, my lord, and is an old and good friend of ours.' She laid a hand on Arthur's sleeve as she spoke, acting on an instinctive desire for support, and saw his lordship's brows draw together slightly at the intimacy.

'My lord.' Mr Brooke bowed somewhat stiffly, disliking the sight of a man of fashion standing quite so close to Miss Knight. He had never met his lordship, but he knew of the other man's reputation as a rake and was well aware that he was attracting many feminine glances as he stood there in his London clothes.

Ophelia had been waiting with poorly concealed impatience for the introductions to be over. 'Camilla, you must be mistaken about our engagements tomorrow, for I am certain we have none. Surely you recall discussing it?'

With a rather stiff smile Camilla capitulated, knowing from long experience that Ophelia would be blind and deaf to looks and hints. 'How foolish of me to have confused the days! It seems, my lord, that we are able to take up your kind invitation after all. I wonder if we would be able to make up a small party...Mr Brooke, would you be able to accompany us?'

Arthur, aware of an almost infinitesimal

pressure on his arm, replied with deep regret, 'I am very sorry indeed to have to refuse such a treat, but tomorrow I am engaged with one of my clients—a very elderly lady who is in the very frailest health—and I cannot see my way to changing the appointment.'

Nicholas, aware that there was an undercurrent present, glanced from Arthur Brooke's face to Camilla's and wondered if, despite the solicitor's sombre appearance, he would find himself with a rival to cut out. 'What a pity you cannot join us. However, may I call at two o'clock tomorrow? And if I might enquire of your direction?'

'We live in the Paragon, my lord.' She opened her reticule and handed him a card. As she looked up she saw a reminiscent smile playing around his lips.

'Lord Lovell? I have said something to amuse you?'

'I beg your pardon, Miss Knight. I know little of Bath and yet it seems that on this visit I am drawn to that particular district. Why, only last night I had a most singular encounter in Walcot Street.'

'Indeed, my lord?' Camilla said repressively. 'I understand that parts of that street have an unfortunate reputation. It is not an area my sister or I would frequent.'

'Well, my experience did begin with a rather unpleasant encounter with footpads, but ended rather more…pleasurably.' A reminiscent smile curved his firm lips, earning him a severe look from Arthur Brooke, who suspected that expression had something to do with the location of the house for fallen women in Walcot Street.

Camilla's heart was beating in her chest like thunder. He knew! He must know! He had recognised her. Then as her shock subsided she realised he was not teasing her, nor looking to entrap her. No, what she had glimpsed had been a genuinely private recollection of pleasure. The thought that he recalled her like that set her heart fluttering, and once again her own memory of that kiss returned to heat her blood.

'I see my mother is waiting for us. Goodbye, Mr Brooke, I do hope you find your client in better health. Until tomorrow then, my lord, but please do not trouble if the weather turns bad; we will not look for you in that case. Goodbye.' Camilla extended her gloved hand and Nicholas took it, returning the pressure slightly in a formal handshake. But the movement brought her close to him, the hem of her skirts fluttering against his legs as she turned from him towards the door and a slight waft of the warm honeysuckle scent she wore touched his nostrils.

He swung round to watch her as she walked through the door into the salon, her mother and sister at her side. That nagging memory was back again. Where on earth…?

'Lovell!' Georgiana was at his side, looking disapproving and most effectively breaking across his train of thought. 'What have you been about, monopolising Miss Knight for so long? People will talk. And you have neglected Miss Laxton disgracefully, I quite despair of your manners!' Seeing his eyes following the departing Knights, she added, 'Very good family, but no money—that matters not to you, of course— but I tell you frankly, Nicholas, she would not have you. No young lady who has been in society as Miss Knight has will tolerate your wayward behaviour and raking about. You need a nice little innocent who will adore you for what she thinks you are,' she added tartly.

His sister's complaints rolled off Nicholas's broad shoulders, preoccupied as he was with the mystery of Miss Camilla Knight. Frowning, he turned to his sister. 'I beg your pardon, Georgiana. Were you saying something?'

'Oh, you are quite impossible, Nicholas!'

The Knights' carriage was making its way with painful slowness over Pulteney Bridge, which was choked with carrying chairs, pedestrians and several riders making their way towards Sydney Place. 'Oh dear,' Mrs Knight lamented vaguely as she looked out of the carriage window. 'I had meant to walk up from Laura Place and call in at Miss Little's for that bonnet she was trimming for me. Oh, well, never mind. We can walk down tomorrow...'

'We cannot accompany you, Mama, unless you choose to go before luncheon,' Ophelia said with excitement, patting her curls. 'Camilla and I have been engaged to ride out with Lord Lovell.'

'Lovell,' her mama echoed, as if searching her mind to place the name. 'Oh yes, indeed, Lady Forres's brother the Earl of Ashby.' She looked sharply at her daughters. 'He should have presented himself to me before engaging to take you anywhere. And where did you meet him, my dears?' Her mind, although normally vague, was sharp enough when it came to the subject of eligible men and her lovely daughters.

'Why, in the sculpture gallery, Mama,' Ophelia prattled happily, not noticing how unusually silent her elder sister was. 'You did not venture in, I believe.'

Mrs Knight gave a delicate shudder. 'No, indeed. I stayed in the salon. All that chilly white marble, and those unclothed figures… Hardly the place I would have thought suitable to entertain young ladies. But you were saying about Lord Lovell?'

'He is rather old, of course,' Ophelia opined solemnly. 'Why, he must be all of thirty.'

'More like seven and twenty,' Camilla interjected suddenly, then returned to gazing out of the window.

'Well, that is old anyway. And everyone says he is a terrible rake, but he does not look like one to me…'

'I sincerely hope you have no idea of such things!' Mrs Knight protested. 'When I was your age I would not have heard the word, let alone thought to use it in the presence of my mama! And if he is,' she added firmly, 'then you are certainly not riding out with him tomorrow or indeed any day.'

Up to that moment Camilla would have been delighted to hear her mother deny Lord Lovell the house. Now, perversely, she felt a stab of alarm and a strong inclination to soothe her parent's fears. 'No, indeed, Mama, I believe Lord Lovell has suffered the fate of many eligible bachelors. Because he has—doubtless unintentionally—raised the expectations of many a matchmaking mama, he has been labelled a rake. He seemed most truly a gentleman, and of course, we will take Higgins.'

The image of their dour and deeply respectable groom rose in Mrs Knight's mind in a truly reassuring manner. No, there would be no inappropriate behaviour with Higgins to hand! 'Very well, my dear. Indeed, if one can be assured he is not, er…what Ophelia said…it has to be admitted he is a most eligible man.'

Aware she was being regarded beadily by her mama Camilla flushed, but said steadily, 'Now, Mama, you know we have agreed that the circumstances of my…' she hesitated '…former occupation dictate that I may never marry. I am now, as we have agreed, quite ineligible.'

'Oh dear, I know you say so, Camilla, but surely, after perhaps a year, there will be not the slightest danger that anyone will ever find out? You cannot condemn yourself to spinsterhood, though I appreciate your offer to remain at my side as a support and companion in my old age.'

'Mama, you know it would be quite dishonourable of me to marry a man knowing there is a risk this might come out—imagine the scandal if it did! And no man would marry me if he knew. But it is not something we should be discussing now. And as to Ophelia, she is far too young for Lord Lovell.'

'*Well,*' Ophelia declared, 'you may say so, but I know that Emilia's aunt Lady Richardson, and Lord Lovell's sister Lady Forres, are plotting to marry Emilia off to the Earl! And she is the same age as I am! So there!' She leaned back with a triumphant smile upon her pretty young face.

'That would be an excellent match indeed!' Mrs Knight exclaimed. 'I must congratulate Lady Richardson, for if this is true she is a most notable matchmaker. Little Emilia Laxton and an earl—why, it gives me hope for your prospects, Ophelia dear!'

'Well, I cannot dispute that I would like to be a countess,' Ophelia agreed. 'And Lord Lovell is very handsome,' she added, with a sideways look

at her elder sister. 'But he is also very old...
What exactly does a rake do?'

'Did I not hear that Miss Laxton had formed
an attachment?' Camilla enquired hastily, hoping
to turn the conversation somewhat from the
subject of his lordship. She was inclined to agree
with Ophelia's first statement, and heartily
disagree with the second. It was not Lord
Lovell's age that troubled her...

'Oh...er...no, not really,' Ophelia said hastily,
with a glance at her mother. But she only
managed to look the picture of guilt and Mrs
Knight caught her up immediately.

'If you are helping Miss Laxton conceal a clandestine flirtation, Ophelia...' she began warningly, her pale brows furrowed.

'No indeed, Mama,' her youngest daughter
hastened to assure her. 'It is no secret. She makes
no secret of her attachment to Mr Ormond, but
despite his papa's great wealth, her mama will
not countenance the match.'

'A City banker! Well, I am not surprised. And
he is a younger son, is he not?'

'Yes...but he is going to have a wonderful
career as a university professor and make his
name, you know. He is ever so learned and

already something frightfully important at Oxford…or is it Cambridge?' She broke off, her nose wrinkled with the effort of remembering.

'emilia Laxton married to a scholar?' Camilla exclaimed. 'What an inappropriate match! She is a sweet girl but she does not—and I suspect never will—have a serious thought in her head!'

'She knows she is not bookish, but she says that is not what Edmund needs. She says he needs a good wife, someone who will look after him when he becomes too immersed in his studies to eat, and she will be that. Emilia says she will nurture his genius!'

'Goodness!' said Mrs Knight weakly. 'How forward young people are these days. Well, the sooner she is married off to the Earl of Ashby the better, is all I can say.'

'Indeed,' her elder daughter agreed with somewhat less conviction. Why should the thought of Miss Laxton's marrying Nicholas cause her heart to jolt so? She scarcely knew him, and she had acknowledged that she would—could—never marry. But almost unbidden her gloved fingers came up to caress her lips, as if re-tasting the sensation of being kissed by him. Suddenly very anxious that the subject should be closed, Camilla turned her gaze once more to the honey-stone terraces of Bath, and the thronged streets through which the coachman was making his careful way back to the Paragon.

The Earl in question was also seated in a carriage and gazing out of the window, doing his best to ignore his sister's steady flow of observation, criticism and general commentary on his character, prospects and lack of stability. 'Settle down and raise a family,' she was saying firmly. 'It is about time you had an heir. You are not getting any younger…'

'Doubtless you are right, Georgiana.'

'I am always right! Do you not wish to be settled? Can you not imagine the benefits of marriage to Miss Laxton?'

'I am not averse to marrying and settling down, my dear, but, beyond the undoubted charms of Miss Laxton's countenance and youth, I can think of few worse things than to be leg-shackled to a pretty little chit with nothing between her ears than the latest Paris fashions or the newest novel!'

'Nonsense, Nicholas! I agree she is young, and by no means a bluestocking, but then you are not noted for intellectual or cultural pursuits,' Georgiana added, tartly, before continuing, 'but she is malleable. You can mould her to suit you...'

'I do not wish to marry a lump of clay. I want to marry a woman of character and intelligence,' Nicholas protested, then turned a wicked look on his indignant sister. 'Not, of course, that I am averse to a pretty face, a well-rounded figure, a pair of warm lips...' As he expected, she shot him a furious glare and subsided into silence. The conversation was becoming scandalously inappropriate.

A pair of warm lips...soft and inviting...now that did stir memories. He resumed his unseeing scrutiny of the street and turned his mind back to that moment when Miss Davide had quivered responsively in his arms, her face upturned to his, her full lips trusting yet eager against his own, the scent of her filling his nostrils, warm and seductive.

The scent of her! Why, of course, that was it—that subtle, lingering sweetness of honey-suckle, warm against a summer wall, but here warmed by her skin, *that* was what had been in the back of his mind, and that was what he had smelt again that afternoon as Miss Knight had turned to leave!

It couldn't be…the idea was too preposterous to entertain…Camilla Knight was so fair, so un-adorned with paint or patches, so undoubtedly respectable. But he knew that women could transform themselves with the application of maquillage, and to cover that pale glory with a wig, a brown hairpiece, would be simplicity itself, especially to one who had all the skills of the theatre at her disposal. He remembered again how the younger sister had piqued his memory when he had first seen her.

But if it were true why should someone like Miss Knight, undoubtedly of the Quality if not of the very first ranks of the Ton, take to the stage? The whole world was aware of how society regarded any young lady who had an as-sociation with the boards. After all, the term 'actress' was often no more than a euphemism for a whore, the fiction of being on the stage a cover for being kept by a gentleman as a com-plaisant friend, always willing, always avail-able…

'Lovell!' Georgiana repeated sharply, her previous words lost on her oblivious brother. 'I begin to wonder if you are quite well. Perhaps you need to take a physick!'

'Sorry, my dear, I was admiring Mr Nash's artistry. You were saying?'

'I will ask you again. Are you dining in this evening?'

Nicholas pulled himself together. 'I think not. I agreed to meet George Marlow and Sir William Hendricks this evening. I shall be out till late, so please do not concern yourself on my part.'

And over dinner and a hand of cards he would make a few discreet enquiries of his theatre-loving friends about the history of the mysterious Mademoiselle Lysette Davide. Before the evening was out he intended to discover if she and the graceful Miss Camilla Knight were one and the same woman.

Chapter Four

'Lovell! Are you going to bid or sit there gazing at the wallpaper all evening?' George Marlow asked plaintively. He had an excellent hand which was getting no support from a partner who appeared to have his mind on something else entirely.

'Um? Oh, yes, right…three hearts.'

George sighed inwardly and cast his eyes up to the ceiling moulding, a careless gesture which did not go unnoticed by the other pair, who hastily changed their tactics.

'Not got your mind on this, have you, Lovell, old man?' Lord Corsham enquired slyly. 'Now, what can you be thinking of, I wonder?'

The three friends were agog to discover what had transpired between the Earl and Miss Davide the previous night. In the scrimmage outside the Theatre Royal they had entirely lost sight of him and were now waiting to hear how the bet was going. On the other hand, none of them was going to broach the subject directly, and Nicholas Lovell was being quite infuriatingly discreet.

Sir William Hendricks played a card and winked across the table at his partner. 'Been out on Thunderer today, Freddie? Making the most of him while you've still got him?'

'Judging by our comrade's silence, I believe I have little to fear,' Lord Corsham replied languidly, taking a sip of his brandy. 'I haven't noticed any message asking me to hand him over…'

Nicholas lowered the fan of cards in his hand and grinned with a sudden flash of white teeth at his friends. 'There is no need to fish, gentlemen. The answer to the question you are all studiously avoiding asking is "not yet". Now, can we finish this hand?'

'Not if you aren't going to concentrate,' George said bitterly, poking a plump finger at the diminishing pile of coins in front of him. 'I can't afford to play *against* you at any time, but I'm damned if I'm going to play *with* you if you can't keep your mind on the cards!'

The ice having been broken, the other two were not going to give up. Freddie Corsham raked in his winnings and picked up the scattered cards. 'Turned you down flat, then, did she?' He shuffled the cards and began to deal. 'An unusual experience for you, Nick.'

'I wouldn't call escorting a lady home being turned down, exactly,' Lovell replied calmly, picking up his cards and eyeing them impassively.

'She let you take her home!' Hendricks choked on his brandy. 'You lucky dog! Where does she live?'

It was the opening Nicholas was looking for. 'Oh, don't any of you know?' They all shook their heads mutely. Damn! He let none of the disappointment show on his face and kept his eyes on his hand. 'Two diamonds.' The bidding went round twice before he continued. 'I would have thought you faithful admirers would know everything there is to know about the Divine Miss Davide. Surely you are on her doorstep daily with bouquets of flowers?'

George looked particularly downcast. 'Her love of privacy is notorious, old man. Even that old rogue of a theatre manager doesn't know where she lives: we've all tried to bribe the information out of him.'

'And Mr Gordon Porter would sell his own mother for ten guineas,' Hendricks added darkly. 'So if he won't sell the information it means he doesn't have it.'

Nicholas won a trick and scooped the cards towards him, thought for a moment and led with trumps. So, Miss Davide was secretive to a quite extraordinary degree. That tended to support his theory that she and Miss Knight could be one and the same woman. But even as he thought it he wondered again: it was such an incredible suspicion to have. It was possible to believe that a rather fast young widow might hazard her reputation on the stage, but a well-bred, single girl of great beauty…why she would be risking everything! Any hope of a marriage of even the most modest respectability would be lost if the knowledge of such a double existence came out.

Nicholas and George won the next two hands, which cheered up the impecunious Mr Marlow to such an extent that he pulled the bell and, when his butler arrived, ordered the best brandy to be brought up. Nicholas ignored the light badinage between the three men that filled the interval, his thoughts again turned to Camilla Knight.

If they were one and the same, then it seemed inconceivable that the débutante he had encountered today would permit any behaviour of the sort that would win him the wager—and in any case, there was no circumstance in which he was going to start seducing virgins!

Unless of course Miss Knight was such a good actress that playing the innocent was just another role and she truly was leading a double life, with or without the knowledge of her mother and sister. And that would be such an incredibly dangerous thing to do—why, if it came out the entire family would be ruined, including young Ophelia. But could even the most accomplished actress have feigned the innocence in that kiss last night? He could have sworn she had never been kissed by a man in her life before.

On the other hand he could be completely mistaken, taken in by a look, a gesture, the scent of honeysuckle. It was hardly conclusive. The other three were still watching him, obviously hoping for further revelations about their goddess. He had no intention of telling them any more about his evening—and even less about the night. On the other hand he had his pride, and leaving them with the impression that he was on the verge of success when it seemed highly likely that however this turned out he was not going to win the wager, was not a good move.

'However, despite my limited success last night, I have to tell you, gentlemen, that I am not making room in my stables for Thunderer yet.' He won his trick and took his time over his next card, letting the other three hang on his words. 'Miss Davide appears to have left town.'

'Ah, standard female tactics!' Freddie advised wisely. 'Playing hard to get: you remember that little filly I was keeping in that apartment off Drury Lane last year? Took me weeks to win her over, but it was worth it...'

There were howls of outrage from Marlow and Hendricks. 'Come off it, Freddie! Hardly the same class of girl at all! She was just hanging out for more money. How can you compare Miss Davide to an opera dancer!' George spluttered.

'What are you going to do?' William asked, intrigued.

Nicholas pushed his chair out from the card table and stretched his long legs out. 'Go home and go to bed, I think.' He ducked as George lobbed a guinea at his head and grinned. 'I've left a groom keeping watch on the house—and no, Freddie, I am not going to give you her direction. I have no intention of being cut out by you, you rake! But it's a long chance of finding her, I suspect.'

'So, giving up and running back to Town, are you, old boy?' Hendricks asked.

'No such luck! Georgiana has me pinned down for a full week of endless soirées and parties. Have you seen Lady Richardson's new sculpture gallery yet? No? Well, take my advice and steer well clear of any invitation to do so. I was dragged along there today for an interminable afternoon in the company of cold marble and silly débutantes. Mind you,' he added casually as he got to his feet, 'I did meet a Miss Knight who seemed something out of the commonplace. Haven't come across the family before—anyone know anything about them?'

He kept his face indifferent, but was surprised at the frisson of excitement that he felt at mentioning her name. Obviously the excitement of the chase, he told himself.

George and Freddie shook their heads, but William Hendricks replied, 'Oh, yes, quite a good Cambridgeshire family, I think. My mother knows Mrs Knight, and there's a younger sister too, who's quite a lively girl, but the older sister doesn't go about much. A bit of an invalid, I think—Mama used to invite them all to evening parties, but only the mother used to come. Young Miss Ophelia isn't out yet.'

So, Miss Knight did not go abroad in the evenings because she was delicate! He had rarely seen a healthier-looking young woman— so unless she had made a recent miraculous recovery she had other things keeping her busy in the evenings.

Bidding farewell to his friends and refusing the butler's offer to call a chair, Nicholas strolled along Charles Street from George's lodgings, around Queens Square and turned uphill into Gay Street.

The clock of St Mary's Chapel was striking two as he passed it and the town was quiet, although candlelight in many windows and the scurry of the occasional sedan chair bearing its occupants home showed that not everyone was abed.

Nicholas stopped in the Circus and looked up. The sky was clear, which explained the nip in the air, and the stars twinkled icily. Despite the brandy his head was as clear as the sky above and his blood raced in his veins. If he had been at home on his country estates he would have taken a horse out and galloped away this restless excitement; as it was, he carried on walking, striding up Brook Street briskly despite the slope.

Tomorrow he would see Miss Knight again, and then, with the knowledge he had gained this evening, he should be able to solve this puzzle. But it would be a pity if they proved to be one and the same woman...he was not quite sure why, but, yes, it would be a pity.

While the Earl was losing sleep puzzling over her identity, Miss Knight was experiencing just as much trouble sleeping herself. When she woke from a fitful doze, the sunlight was slanting across the polished boards of her bedroom floor from the window looking eastwards over Walcot Street and the river.

For a moment, as she rubbed the slumber from her eyes, she wondered why the sight should make her heart beat faster, then she remembered she was engaged to ride out with Lord Lovell that afternoon. If the unpredictable spring weather turned showery then the excursion would be cancelled, which was, of course, the best possible outcome under the circumstances.

She pulled the bellrope for her morning chocolate and wriggled to sit up against the pillows. Smoothing down the counterpane, she studied her long fingers, unadorned by rings and likely to remain so. The realities of her new life as Miss Camilla Knight, respectable spinster of Bath, were beginning to dawn on her. It had been all very well not having much of a social life when she could go to the theatre every night, experience the thrill of danger as she stepped out onto the stage, the fizzing of excitement through her veins as night after night she overcame stagefright, honed her skills in a particular part, curtseyed again and again to tumultuous applause.

And who would miss the insipid company of débutantes and chaperons when one could have the adoration of gentlemen admirers, safe in the confines of the Green Room? Shy young men at parties proffering compliments and nosegays were as nothing compared to outrageous adoration, the offer of diamonds and pearls, sumptuous bouquets of heavy-scented hothouse blooms…

She had spoken with genuine conviction of the impossibility of her ever marrying and of her intention to support her mama and see her sister well married. But the emptiness of it all suddenly yawned before her on this beautiful spring morning. Even spinsters past their first flush of youth—as she soon would be, she told herself bitterly—could hope for late happiness and a suitor. But the risk of discovery of her scandalous past would never leave her. If she was discovered they would all be ruined, and in any case, she could never enter into marriage dishonestly deceiving her husband.

It meant she couldn't even flirt, Camilla thought dismally as she sipped her cooling chocolate. And Lord Lovell was most certainly a man with whom it would be a pleasure to flirt! Camilla could not recall ever feeling this way about any man she had met before: attracted, excited, and not a little afraid, both of herself and of his reputation as a man who was never short of female company, a man who would never have to try too hard.

Her fingers strayed to her lips as if to retrace

the impression of his mouth on hers. It must be because he had kissed her, that was all. She recalled with a shiver the sensation of his lips, then pulled together her unruly thoughts. After all, one would remember one's first kiss; it did not mean that one was seriously attracted simply because the memory was so vivid, so real...

Her thoughts were rudely interrupted by the eruption of Ophelia into her chamber. The younger Miss Knight was wearing her new riding-habit, a garment of deep sky-blue and of a rather more fashionable cut than her mama really approved of.

'There you are! Why are you still in bed? Look what a gorgeous morning it is!'

Ophelia tugged back the curtains to their fullest extent and gazed out over the city.

'I am thinking,' her sister responded coolly. 'And why on earth have you changed so soon? We are not going out until two, and not at all if it rains.'

Ophelia pouted prettily and Camilla felt a little frisson of alarm at the sight of her little sister aping a grown-up so charmingly. The thought of Ophelia catching Lord Lovell's eye was curiously unsettling, despite the fact that she had just convinced herself that he, along with every other eligible man, was not for her.

'It is quite the nicest thing I have,' Ophelia was explaining, fidgeting around with the things on her sister's dressing-table. 'Maria Frogmorton is coming around this morning and it is *miles* nicer than the riding-habit she has just had tailored. Hers is positively *dowdy*.'

'So it is not for Lord Lovell's benefit, then?' Camilla teased, feeling somewhat reassured. The response was even more consoling, and very typical of Ophelia.

'Oh, no! After all, he is *so* old... But on the other hand, it would be wonderful if my friends were to see me with him; he has *such* a reputation. And I think he is handsome, do you not?' She did not wait for Camilla's answer, but twirled round from the dressing-table, a string of rose quartz beads in her fingers. 'You never wear these, Camilla. May I borrow them to go with my new afternoon dress? You know, the deep pink one.' Ophelia lifted them to her throat without waiting for a reply.

Camilla knew perfectly well what 'borrow' meant in Ophelia's vocabulary. 'Yes, you may have them.' After all, rose quartz beads were not the sort of thing that dutiful spinsters wore with their sensible twill dresses in anything but deep pink... Yes, it really would be best if the weather were to change and it poured with rain this afternoon.

As she thought it a black cloud moved in front of the sun and she jumped out of bed with an exclamation of alarm. 'Oh, no! Look at that cloud!'

'It is all right,' Ophelia reassured her, 'it is just the one—look, it is passing over now. I am starving. I will see you in a minute in the breakfast parlour.' She bounced out, leaving a sudden silence behind her. Camilla sighed, pushed back the coverlet, and padded barefoot to the washstand.

The morning passed with agonising slowness. More than once Camilla crossed the morning-room to the mantelshelf and tapped the clock, as if in doing so she could hasten the minutes. Fortunately her mama and Ophelia were occupied about domestic concerns, and were not witness to her restlessness.

After a cold collation, Camilla went to her chamber to change from her simple morning-gown into her riding-habit. Unlike Ophelia's, it was not newly tailored, and not quite in the highest kick of fashion, but the soft green suited her colouring and moulded itself to her slender,

high-bosomed figure. Her maid was just posi-
tioning the light veiling on her hat when Camilla
heard the front door open, and the sound of
voices in the hall below as the footman admitted
their visitor.

Her heart turned a giddy somersault in her
chest, and she spread her fingers across the front
of her jacket, as if to calm its hectic beating. She
counted slowly to one hundred, an old trick to
counter stagefright, and pushed in her hatpins
with a firm hand. Breathing deeply to quell the
sudden spark of panic at the thought of confront-
ing Nicholas again, she descended the staircase,
then, summoning all her ability to act the part of
the proper young woman engaged in a pleasant
afternoon's activity, Camilla pushed open the
door and entered the drawing-room.

Nicholas Lovell got to his feet with an easy
grace that belied his height. He was dressed for
riding in a coat of deep blue that echoed the
colour of the warm gaze he now turned upon her.
In two strides of his gleaming boots he was
across the Turkey rug, bowing over her hand, but
not before she had glimpsed the gleam of sensual
appreciation in his eyes. Her cheeks felt warm
and she felt her fingers curl into his.

'Miss Knight, good afternoon. As you can see, the weather has favoured us: it is quite clement for our excursion this afternoon.'

Camilla released her hand and replied coolly, 'Indeed sir, although it seemed less than favourable earlier on.'

She crossed and seated herself primly on the sofa next to her mama, who looked pink-cheeked, animated and almost pretty. Lord Lovell had obviously charmed her in a very short time, and Camilla doubted that her mother's strictures against rakes, uttered only yesterday evening, prevailed this afternoon!

Ophelia had not yet made her entrance, and for a brief moment Camilla wondered if she had deliberately delayed her entrance so as to make a bigger impact. This unworthy thought, and the twist of jealousy accompanying it, she swiftly suppressed.

'I must apologise for Ophelia's time-keeping, my lord,' Mrs Knight gushed. 'It is a failing quite frequently found in the young, I regret to say. I am happy to add that my elder daughter is always punctilious in such matters, are you not, my love?'

Camilla knew her mother was complimenting her for Lord Lovell's benefit. Mama was always so transparent in such things, and appeared to have acquired no more skill or subtlety as she grew older. She would be praising her harp-playing, which was non-existent, or her embroidery—which was indifferent—before long.

Nicholas's smile was almost a grin. 'Indeed, ma'am. I am sure Miss Knight aims to act to the highest standards in whatever she undertakes.'

Camilla was half-way to raising a glass of ratafia to her lips, and only the keenest eye could have detected the momentary pause this comment gave her. Had she imagined the emphasis his lordship had placed upon the word 'act'? She swiftly chided herself against over-reaction to such a slight comment, and sipped her refreshment.

Any further chit-chat was forestalled by Ophelia finally making her entrance. She looked young, fresh and absurdly pretty in the blue habit, but to her relief Camilla noticed that his lordship scarcely reacted, bowing over the débutante's hand with polite correctness, before resuming his seat and picking up his glass of Canary once more.

A short silence ensued, then the three ladies verbally collided as each spoke at once.

'Well, I hope the outing is enjoyable…' Mrs Knight began.

'If Maria Frogmorton calls, tell her I am out riding with his lordship, will you, Mama?' Ophelia supplied eagerly.

'Perhaps we should go, while the weather holds…' Camilla suggested.

Lord Lovell got to his feet, bowing to Mrs Knight. 'Do not concern yourself, ma'am. I shall ensure that the ladies are returned secure to you by four o'clock.'

Mrs Knight's hand crept up to her lace cap as if to correct its angle, and she smiled at the Earl. Really, the gossip surrounding him must be sadly amiss if this encounter were anything to go by. Lord Lovell was not only dashing and handsome in his superbly cut riding clothes, but his manners were of the highest order of correctness and charm, a combination one seldom encountered, the widow reflected wistfully.

Could she dare to hope for an alliance of one of her daughters with such an eligible man? Of the two, Camilla was closer to his lordship in age and interests, and unless she was very much mistaken the true source of his lordship's attentiveness. But Camilla had declared that her sac-

rifice was absolute: she could never marry, for
fear of scandal. And yet… For the remainder of
the early afternoon Mrs Knight fell to pleasant
musings on how such an outcome might be
achieved. Her daughter a countess…

Camilla noticed with an inward touch of satisfaction the way Lord Lovell's eyebrows rose at
the sight of the two mounts which Higgins led
round to the front door. Miss Knight, who
normally kept a prudent eye on the family expen-
diture despite their now comfortable circumstances, had no trouble at all in opening her
purse strings for either carriage horses or her
own and Ophelia's hacks.

It gave Mrs Knight, as she confessed to her
daughters, a 'warm glow' to drive around Bath
behind a pair of outstanding dapple greys which
quite outshone those of her less fortunate friends
in both manners and appearance, but it was the
Knights' riding horses which were the envy of
every other young lady with aspirations to cut a
dash in local society.

The late Mr Knight had been a keen rider to
hounds and had enjoyed nothing more than to
spend the day in the saddle, whether going about
his business on the estate or indulging in some

sporting exercise or another. In consequence he had had a knowledgeable eye for a horse and had been happy to see both his daughters well mounted—provided they'd met his exacting standards of horsemanship.

Camilla had inherited his excellent seat, and had also learned well from his example when it came to choosing her horses. Ophelia, equally confident on horseback, made up in somewhat reckless enthusiasm for her less elegant style and was more than happy with the rather showy, although sweet-tempered black mare her sister had found for her.

However, it was not Blackbird, whiffling hopefully into her young mistress's gloved hand for a piece of apple, who caught his lordship's eye, but the chestnut gelding who was attempting to drag the leading rein from the groom's hand as he took violent exception to a piece of paper blowing past.

'Stand still, drat you, you stupid bru…animal,' Higgins growled, turning his own mount to keep from getting entangled in both sets of leading reins. 'Now then, Miss Ophelia, don't you stand there like a ninny, girl! You take Blackbird's reins while I sort out this… Stand, will you!'

Ophelia ran to the head of her mare, not at all put out by the groom's plain speaking. Having freed one hand, Higgins took a firmer grip on the chestnut, but found the Earl already at its head, one hand on the bridle just above the bit.

'Yes, yes, I know…it could have been a wild panther in disguise. You were quite right to be alarmed,' he was saying soothingly. The gelding rolled one eye at him, obviously unconvinced, but prepared to stand there all day if his ears were scratched in the precise way Nick was doing.

'That there animal doesn't have the brains it were born with,' Higgins said forthrightly, his Norfolk accent strong. 'And I don't care how much you say about his looks and his gait and his staying power, Miss Camilla!' He swung down out of the saddle and, looping his rein over his arm, went to toss Ophelia up on to Blackbird.

'Well, I agree he is hardly the most intelligent horse in the world,' Camilla agreed, smiling her thanks to Nicholas as he offered his clasped hands to give her a leg up. 'But he is a wonderful ride if one just does the thinking for him.' She settled in the saddle and arranged the folds of her riding-habit one-handed, holding the reins firmly in the other. 'Thank you, my lord, Kestrel is quite calm now. He really is quite provoking, because he will stand like a rock in the face of real danger, like a fierce dog or a bull, but he imagines all sorts of monsters in shadows or paper.'

Nicholas took the reins of his own horse from his groom and mounted, saying, 'That will be all, Little, thank you. I will not be needing you for the rest of the day.' He swung round to ride alongside Camilla, his eyes on Ophelia, who was riding ahead of them, engaged in an earnest argument with Higgins about whether her new riding-boots were suitable.

'Frippery things,' he was grumbling. 'You take a toss and have to walk home five miles in those and you'll be sorry.'

'Nonsense,' Ophelia retorted. 'I would ride Robin and you would walk in your nice sensible boots!'

'An unconventional groom,' Nicholas observed drily to Camilla.

'He is indeed,' she laughed. 'He taught us to ride, you know, and found us a terrible trial. And, what was worse, our old nurse Margaret used to tell him off for using strong language! There he would be, poor man, with one or other of us at the end of the leading rein, shouting, "Keep those bl…heels down Miss!" and going red for want of all the words he would like to be using. But he was a good teacher, and the most reliable and sensible man you could hope to find. Papa placed the greatest confidence in him, and Mama does the same. She even listens to him when he says she cannot take the carriage to visit some friend or other who lives up a particularly steep hill, in case it is too much for the horses, so she takes a chair instead, although she says it makes her seasick.'

'I can see he was a good teacher,' Nicholas commented.

'Yes, she does ride well, does she not?' Camilla watched her young sister confidently handling the black mare as they negotiated the busy junction of Broad Street, the Paragon and Lansdown Road.

He did not answer until they too had turned into Lansdown Road, for Camilla was waving at the occupants of a passing carriage and was then occupied in convincing Kestrel that Bath chairs—which he saw every day of his life—did not conceal tigers, and that he could quite safely trot on up the hill.

'Miss Ophelia has a very confident manner on

a horse,' he said at length, 'but it is not on her riding that I formed my opinion of Higgins's expertise as a teacher.'

To his surprise Camilla neither blushed at the compliment, nor disclaimed modestly. 'You think I ride well?' she enquired, smiling at him. When he nodded she added disarmingly, 'Well, I can take no credit for it: after all, Papa had us well taught, gave us good horses and every encouragement, and I expect I inherited his talent for it, so I can hardly congratulate myself.'

'Despite what you say, you are a better horsewoman than your sister, who one supposes has had the same advantages, so I think you may claim it as an accomplishment.'

Camilla laughed. Out in the fresh air with the natural roses blooming in her cheeks, not a trace of artifice about her and with her well-bred and charming frankness, Nicholas once again found himself convinced that he was mistaken in thinking that in Miss Knight he had found the elusive Mademoiselle Davide.

The riders slowed to a walk as the long hill stretched in front of them. Camilla told herself firmly that the Earl doubtless made agreeable conversation, well sprinkled with compliments, to any young lady he found himself in company with. Further, she thought, with even more resolution, allowing herself to be charmed was a thoroughly dangerous weakness with any man, but especially this one.

It was very pleasant to be made to feel that you were the centre of his world and that he found you endlessly fascinating and highly attractive. But the sensible thing to do would be to turn the conversation away from personal matters and to put him firmly in his place by discussing the weather, the view and the latest programme of concerts at the Lower Assembly Rooms.

She was therefore somewhat surprised to find herself, as though under some inner compulsion, smiling at Nicholas and saying lightly, 'I must thank you for telling me I have an accomplishment. I have very few, you see—only two, as I thought—so it is a great relief to be told I have a third!'

'And what are the other two?' he asked quizzically. An unusual young woman indeed! He was going to be disappointed if she admitted to excellence in playing the harp and doing water-colour sketches.

'They are a secret, my lord.' Her eyes twinkled

at him and he smiled back wickedly, making her heart miss a beat. Hastily she added, 'At last we are nearly at the top! It is one of the disadvantages of Bath that everywhere one goes there are hills. The views, of course, are superb, and one can hardly complain about a lack of exercise.'

The Earl was not to be diverted. 'It is really too bad of you, Miss Knight, to tease me with secrets! Surely you cannot be ashamed of your accomplishments?' Unless, he thought, one of them was a talent for acting...

'Hmm...perhaps I will tell you one then, provided you promise not to tell anyone else, for my attorney says it is a most unfeminine talent.'

Ophelia trotted up, interrupting their *tête à tête*. 'Which way shall we go? Straight on towards Lansdown is the best for a gallop.' Blackbird sidled and curvetted, impatient at being kept sedately by the other horses.

'Are you wishful to gallop, my lord,' Camilla enquired, 'or would you prefer to hack around the top of the hill and admire the views?'

'Let us gallop and shake the fidgets out of our horses' feet. We can admire the views later at our leisure.'

That was enough for Ophelia, who touched

her heels to Blackbird's sides and was off at a brisk canter, Higgins swinging in behind her at a distance, but still keeping a sharp eye on the flying figure.

Camilla would have followed her example if Nicholas had not leaned over and put a hand on her rein. 'Not so fast, Miss Knight! You promised to tell me a secret and I really cannot let you go until you do so.'

Chapter Five

There was a heartbeat's silence as Camilla, the previous conversation blown from her mind by the wind on the hill, met Nicholas's steady, unsettling, gaze and felt her conscience give a guilty lurch. Had she mentioned a secret? Then she remembered—her so-called 'accomplishments'. Really, she must keep a tighter guard on her tongue around the Earl. He was far too perceptive!

'Oh, very well.' She laughed across at him. 'Do you promise not to tell? Well, I am an accomplished investor, even Mr Brooke our attorney says so, although he does not approve. I am prudent, of course, for we cannot afford to take risks, but even with allowing many tempting gambles to go by I flatter myself that I do very well.' For a moment she thought a look of disappointment crossed his face at this revelation, but it had to have been a trick of the light. 'Are you shocked by my secret, my lord?'

'By no means! We will have to compare notes, for I too enjoy speculating. But I am sorry to hear that you are not more of a gambler, Miss Knight: do you never take risks?'

The long look Camilla gave him revealed nothing of her thoughts, then she smiled and said frankly, 'I cannot afford to take risks, my lord: neither with my money nor with my reputation. What a man—what the Earl of Ashby—may do with impunity, Miss Knight must approach with great caution. But we are being left behind by Ophelia, do let us gallop!'

Nicholas reined back his horse to enjoy the picture of Camilla, perfectly balanced on the chestnut, her veil whipping back with the speed of its pace. It was tempting to ask the Knight family to stay at Ashby during the hunting season. On second thoughts, perhaps that would be raising expectations in Mrs Knight's breast. Her daughter was an unconventional young woman, he mused. Unconventional enough to lead a double life? But surely not. That speech about not taking risks had rung true. With a slight shrug he touched his own mount with his heels and gave it its head.

Two sets of hooves pounded over the short clipped turf, and Nicholas was just thinking that the nibbled grass was a sure indicator of rabbits, and therefore of holes, when Camilla swung to the left, calling back, 'Mind the warren!' over her shoulder. Yes, she would look magnificent on the hunting field, tireless and fearless.

His more powerful animal came up neck and neck with hers and for a moment they let the horses race before reining back as they approached Ophelia and Higgins. They had come to a halt at the edge of the hill where the gorse grew thickly and the groom had withdrawn to a respectful distance while Ophelia, who appeared to have spotted something in the scrub, urged the reluctant mare forward.

'What on earth is that?' she asked the groom, her voice just reaching the other two as they trotted up.

She was leaning down, prodding something with her riding crop, when Higgins suddenly shouted, 'Leave that alone, Miss Ophelia!' and spurred forwards.

It was too late—with a furious buzzing a cloud of wasps rose in the air around the black mare and her rider. Ophelia was flapping at them with one hand, struggling to control the panicking mare with the other, then there was a shrill whinny from the horse and it bolted clear out of the mass of furious insects and past them.

'Oh, no, Blackbird has been stung! Higgins…' Camilla had no need to finish the sentence, for the groom was already spurring his horse after the retreating mare.

Nicholas stood in the stirrups, watching the two riders as they vanished over the slope. 'He is catching her up.'

'I thought he would,' Camilla said calmly, although she looked a little pale as she stroked a soothing hand down Kestrel's neck. 'There is no cause for concern. Ophelia has a very good seat, and I have rarely known her take a tumble. Blackbird will calm down once she is clear of those wretched insects. Honestly! It is just like Ophelia to stir up a wasps' nest!'

'Shall we follow them, Miss Knight?'

'No, not immediately, if you do not mind, my lord. She will be mortified that you have seen her lose control of her mount, and it will be worse if she has an audience for Higgins telling her off and lecturing her all the way home on the correct way to treat wasp stings in horses! We will ride round the crest for a short way, if you like, and admire the view, then we can return without making too much of a to-do about the entire incident. That would only alarm Mama.'

'Certainly; I would be sorry to cut short our ride, so long as you are sure there is nothing I can do. Will you lead on? I am sure you know the best—' Nicholas broke off as her mount suddenly bucked violently, snatching frantically at the bit and shaking his head wildly.

'Oh, no! Kestrel has been stung too!' Camilla concentrated on keeping her seat and tried to head the frantic horse away from further danger, for the stragglers from the wasps' nest were still buzzing ominously.

Camilla was conscious of Nicholas keeping his mount close to hers, but not crowding her, and she was grateful that he did not make matters worse by rushing to take her reins, for that would only panic Kestrel more. Then she was suddenly stabbed by a burning pain in her right wrist, just as Kestrel gave another wild plunge. She dropped the reins and found herself clinging to the pommel as the chestnut took the bit between his teeth and careered off towards Lansdown.

Faintly behind her she could hear the sound of pursuing hooves, then all her attention was focused on trying to hang on despite the pain as the furious wasp, trapped in the cuff of her glove, stung her again.

She tried to drag her right glove off with her teeth while reaching for the reins with her left hand, but Kestrel, panicked by pain, was plunging through the gorse so erratically that she had to keep grabbing the pommel just to keep her seat. And in front of her the steep scarp edge was coming closer and closer. It was perfectly possible to walk a horse down the slope, but a frightened animal at the gallop would inevitably fall, taking her with him.

Camilla had just reached the conclusion that she must kick her foot free of the stirrup and jump clear when she was aware of Nicholas's bay pulling up on her right side. He turned its head, attempting to force Kestrel away from the edge and on to the flat plateau, but the chestnut, further excited by the other galloping horse, would not be turned. Just when Camilla was convinced they would all go over the edge together Nicholas leaned over, seized Kestrel's bridle and dragged his head round.

Both horses plunged to a halt in a mêlée of hooves and tossing manes, and Camilla fell off with a thump that knocked every vestige of breath from her body.

She was sitting there whooping with the effort of dragging some air back into her lungs when she realised that Nicholas was kneeling beside her tugging urgently at her glove. 'Aargh!' was all she could manage to gasp out as the pain of the kid cutting into her swollen wrist lanced up her arm.

'Keep still,' he commanded roughly, pulling a pocket knife out and slitting the fine kid until he could peel it back over her hand. 'There. How many times did it sting you?' he asked, shaking out a thoroughly squashed wasp and stuffing the glove in his pocket.

Camilla was still gasping and wordless. Her wrist hurt abominably, her whole hand was on fire and her head was spinning. The part of her mind that was treacherously female was also telling her that she looked frightful and undignified and that Nicholas was being quite revoltingly unsympathetic and practical.

'At least twice by the look of it,' Nicholas remarked, his head bent over her wrist as she lay back on a tussock, too shaky to sit up. Why could he not just make it better and stop touching it? she thought irrationally. Then her nose was full of the smell of spirits and something cold splashed on to her skin. For a moment it burned appallingly, then amazingly the pain began to ebb into something that was almost tolerable.

Her breath came back with a rush and she sat up, pushing off her hat and veil which were hanging by two pins from her disordered hair. It brought her breast to breast with Nicholas, who was kneeling beside her, her hand still in his.

The realisation hit her that she was sprawled on the ground, her habit almost to her knees, her hair round her shoulders and so close to Nicholas that she could see that his eyes were not pure blue but had flecks of black in them. Her wrist felt as though it were on fire, but that was suddenly nothing beside the fact that she had fallen off her horse in a most undignified manner in front of this man, after as good as boasting about her skills as a rider.

There seemed to be only two options: she could burst into tears, which was very tempting, or lose her temper, which she proceeded to do. 'Well, help me up!' she demanded sharply. 'I cannot sit here all day while you splash brandy about!'

'You termagant!' he said indignantly, and promptly leant over and kissed her full on the mouth.

With a gasp of surprise Camilla fell back and found herself trapped under Nicholas's body, his mouth still fastened on hers, his hands exploring the weight of her tumbling hair.

It might be only the second time she had ever been kissed, but there had scarcely been a waking hour when Camilla had not thought about that moment in the cottage when he had taken her in his arms. This time, despite being dizzy, half-stunned and thoroughly unprepared, she responded to him instinctively. Her lips opened softly to his demand and Nicholas responded immediately, his tongue entering to seek out her own. Almost of its own volition, her tongue-tip met his, tasting, inciting him to deepen the kiss. She felt his fingers tighten in her hair as he shifted his body weight above her, and her hands came up to cup his head. It was as though another Camilla altogether was in his arms, answering him kiss for kiss, meeting his ardour with her own untutored desire.

Nicholas groaned, deep in his throat, an exciting, primal sound that stirred her very bones. Then his lips left hers, trailing warm kisses across her cheek to her ear, nuzzling until his teeth found and teased the soft lobe and the sweet honeysuckle scent of her hair.

Camilla gasped, her body arching instinctively towards his. For one electrifying moment it felt as though every inch of their bodies were touching, then he pulled away, supporting himself on his elbows as he looked down into her face with an unreadable expression.

The hot blush swept up from her toe-tips to the roots of her hair as the enormity of what she was doing hit Camilla. 'My…lord,' she managed to stammer out. But she could not tear her eyes from his, however much she wanted to close them, blot out the reflection of herself in those dark blue depths.

Suddenly he smiled down at her, then his fingers gently smoothed the tangled curls off her hot forehead. 'We really should not be doing this, you know,' he drawled.

'Of course I know we should not!' she retorted angrily, the hot blush being replaced with a cold realisation of just how outrageous her behaviour was.

Nicholas shifted his weight slightly, sending a

wave of aching desire through her prone body. 'Stop that!' she snapped, pushing at his chest, then breaking off with a cry of pain as her stung wrist rasped against the cloth of his jacket.

Nicholas got to his knees, gently supporting her into a sitting position. 'Your poor wrist. I know I ought to apologise, but you are *such* a temptation, Miss Knight,' he said ruefully, pushing his hair back off his face. The look of mingled indignation and shame on her face prompted him to add, 'I took advantage of you, I know it. Berate me as you will, you cannot reproach me as much as I reproach myself. I must take you home. Your poor mama will be frantic with worry.'

Camilla still found herself unable to speak. With eyes downcast she let herself be lifted gently to her feet. For the second time in three days she was supported shakily in Nicholas's arms, but this time her entire body was crying out at the shaking the fall had given her. As the excitement of his passionate kisses ebbed from her, the pain of her wrist and the protest of her bruised muscles flooded in.

'Ouch!' She winced as she took her weight on both legs, looking around for the horses.

Nicholas bent to retrieve her hat, then used his long fingers to untangle her hair. Transfixed, she stood almost meekly as he pulled the pins from the curls, then gathered the heavy mass in his hands and twisted and pinned it back into a semblance of order.

Camilla put up her hands and was surprised at the competence with which he had restored her coiffure. Shakily she put on her hat, straightening the veil. 'Thank you, my lord,' she said formally. Then, trying to lighten the atmosphere, added, 'You make a very good ladies' maid.'

His eyes crinkled as he grinned wickedly. 'Thank you, ma'am, it is all down to practice.'

Camilla blushed hotly again and began to limp towards Kestrel, who was standing meekly beside Nicholas's bay, cropping the grass and looking as though nothing on earth would disturb his calm manner. She took a trailing rein and began to check him over for stings, taking refuge from the necessity to look at or speak to Nicholas. 'You silly boy, did those nasty wasps hurt you, then?' she crooned to the gelding, stroking the soft muzzle.

Nicholas's voice close behind made her jump. 'Can you ride, or do you want to sit up in front of me?'

The very thought made her gasp. 'No…no…I will be fine, thank you, my lord!' She forced herself to turn and face him. 'Please, if you will just give me a leg up.'

Nicholas bent to do as she asked, looking up with concern at the involuntary murmur of pain she made as her bruised behind made contact with the saddle. 'I am all right, my lord, I will merely be somewhat bruised tomorrow.'

'I do wish you would call me Nicholas,' he said softly as he checked Kestrel's girth. 'After all, I think we know each other well enough by now.'

The blush stained Camilla's cheeks again as she dug her heel into Kestrel's side. 'There is no need, *my lord*, to taunt me with my forward behaviour. I would be very grateful if you could manage to forget everything which has passed between us this afternoon: my wits must have been disarrayed by the fall.'

As Nicholas swung up into the saddle and followed her back towards the Bath road he murmured to himself, 'And you, Miss Knight, have disarrayed rather more than my wits.'

The sheer discomfort of her bruises forced Camilla to rein Kestrel into a walk, although she was in a fever to get home and bid goodbye to the Earl. His behaviour was still causing her deep confusion as she rode, gaze fixed between Kestrel's alertly pricked ears, cheeks still flushed red with embarrassment and mortification.

If he was a rake, then why had he not ravished her as Mama always warned most men would do, given the slightest encouragement? In fact, the whole of polite society appeared to be organised to protect innocent young women from the inevitable ruin that would result from finding themselves alone with a gentleman for more than ten minutes!

Nicholas had certainly taken advantage of her quite dreadfully forward behaviour—but only up to a point. It was he who had drawn back, not she who had resisted him. Even in her innocence she was aware that her response to him would have goaded most men beyond restraint.

Camilla risked a sideways glance at the Earl as he rode level with her, but a full ten feet away. He was looking at the road ahead, sitting relaxed in the saddle, the reins in his right hand, the left one resting on his thigh. As though he felt her eyes on him, he looked across and asked, 'Are you sure you can hold the reins? I will lead Kestrel if your wrist is paining you.'

She managed a mumbled refusal and a shake of her head, then her eyes shot back to him as he remarked, almost conversationally, 'You should not feel ashamed of acting naturally, you know.'

'Naturally!' The word came out as a cross between a gasp and a squeak. Camilla got control of her voice and said, as repressively as she could, 'I am well aware that gentlemen regard that sort of thing in quite a different light, but I can assure you, sir, that kissing gentlemen in any way at all, let alone…' Words failed her.

'Passionately?' he supplied helpfully.

'P…well, yes, passionately…I mean, that is not something which is natural to a lady.'

Nicholas snorted with amusement. 'Not to all ladies, I must admit, but in my experience the vast majority…'

'We are discussing *ladies*, are we not?' Camilla demanded, not at all wishing to hear about his previous experiences.

'Indeed we are, as well as their weaker sisters. Really, Camilla, what *do* you think happens once people are married?'

She looked so scandalised that he laughed out

loud. 'No, I do not mean the er…practical details, I mean in people's heads. Do you imagine that all young ladies, once married, go through life shrinking from their husbands or calmly putting up with the incomprehensible desires of men?'

Camilla's brow wrinkled as she thought about it. Mama, in her few guarded references to the subject, had intimated that the marriage bed was something that a well-bred lady endured in order to present her lord and master with an heir and that she would achieve her own happiness in the production and upbringing of children. Loose women, Mama implied, either pandered to men's base nature for material gain, or in a few quite frightful instances because their own unnatural passions led them astray. 'Lady Caroline Lamb!' she would whisper in appalled accents as the worst example she could think of. The scandalous wife of the long-suffering William Lamb was a byword for outrageous abandonment to sensuality and excess.

But the sensations Nicholas aroused when he kissed her felt anything but unnatural, and it was very hard, even after the event, to think of them as wicked. Embarrassing, yes, thoroughly shocking, certainly…but oh, so very natural!

He had been watching the play of emotion on her face and said gently, 'You know, you are a very beautiful, very intelligent, very talented young woman, Camilla. It is no good looking suitably modest, because you are not a fool. You know your own worth. You have just discovered that you are also a very warm, very passionate woman and one day a very lucky man is going to discover that too. Then you will discover the pleasure such passion brings between a man and a woman.'

His words filled her with such emotion that her eyes swam with tears and she had to bite hard on her lower lip before replying calmly, 'This is a most improper conversation, my lord, but before we terminate it and while we are being so frank I should tell you that I have no intention of marrying—ever—so the entire subject is quite irrelevant.'

'Not going to marry! Of all the damn fool…I beg your pardon…incomprehensible decisions! Why on earth not?' He made no attempt to conceal his incredulity.

'I intend being a support to Mama in her widowhood,' Camilla said repressively. 'Oh, look! Is that not Higgins coming towards us?'

Nicholas stood in his stirrups and shaded his

eyes with one hand. 'Indeed it is—your knight in shining armour coming to save you from the dragon.'

The thought of the irascible Higgins in the role of St George was so diverting that Camilla was smiling as the groom cantered up. Once he had dealt with Miss Ophelia his thoughts had immediately turned to his other charge, left all alone with A Man, and he had hurried back. He could see little to concern him in her expression but the state of her hair and her habit were another matter.

'Miss Camilla, what have you been doing?' he demanded with his usual lack of respect. 'You look as though you've been pulled through a hedge backwards!'

'Kestrel was stung and so was I and I fell off. But other than bruises and a very painful wrist I am quite all right,' Camilla replied soothingly, ignoring his disapproving sniff, for she understood the depths of his concern for her. 'His lordship has been looking after me,' she added, not able to resist seeing how Nicholas would react.

The Earl shot her a very old-fashioned look before informing Higgins that as far as he could see Kestrel had come to no harm either. 'And how is Miss Ophelia?'

The groom turned his horse's head and fell in beside them. 'Fell off,' he said curtly.

'What! Oh, no! Is she hurt?' Camilla demanded.

'Only her pride and her…er…seat. But your mama has put her to bed and called in Dr Willoughby.'

'Goodness! I hope she does not ask him to see me as well. I hate being physicked. Please do not say anything when we get back, Higgins.'

'She'll take one look at you and see what you've been up to,' Higgins said dourly, fortunately unable to see Camilla's hectic blush from his position alongside Nicholas. 'Falling off! And you call yourself a rider!' He dropped back a few paces, but could be heard muttering to himself as they began to descend towards the city.

Nicholas caught Camilla's eye and raised his left eyebrow quizzically, throwing her into even more confusion. 'Falling off indeed, Miss Knight…'

'I will turn down Guinea Lane. There is less chance of being seen by anyone I know than if we go straight down to the junction with Broad Street. I am very much obliged for your escort, my lord, but there is no need for you to continue further than that point,' she added coolly. To be seen with a man and in such a state of disarray, even accompanied by her groom, would cause eyebrows to be raised and tongues to wag for the rest of the week.

Nicholas fortunately grasped the situation without having to have it spelt out and parted from them with a polite bow. 'Thank you for a most delightful excursion, Miss Knight. I enjoyed it immensely and I feel I have experienced more of the true beauties of Bath than less fortunate visitors may hope to. Please present my compliments to Mrs Knight, and my best wishes to Miss Ophelia for a rapid recovery.'

Camilla was so cross with him that she could do no more than incline her head in response. Beauties of Bath indeed!

Fortunately she and Higgins managed to reach the front door without encountering any acquaintances, and Camilla's luck continued to hold, for her mama was so taken up with her younger daughter that Camilla was able to slip into her room without being seen.

Tugging the bellpull for her dresser, Camilla cast off her hat and veil and began to pull a brush through her hair, wincing at the pain in her wrist.

Mary bustled in, all ready for a good gossip about the afternoon's ride, only to be confronted by the sight of her mistress, hair full of tangles, riding-habit stained with grass and with a swollen and reddened wrist.

'Oh, Miss Camilla, what have you done? Not fallen off as well, have you?'

'Yes, Mary, I have indeed. Now, can you get hot water sent up? Because if I do not sit in a bath straight away I am going to be so stiff tomorrow I shall not be able to walk. And can you get something for my wrist? I have been stung by a wasp.'

Mary immediately set to, organising a footman to bring up the wide saucer bath and set it before the fire she insisted on lighting, bullying the maids into staggering up and down stairs with cans of hot water in double quick time and hurrying in and out herself with towels and soap.

The resulting bustle was sufficiently distracting to keep Camilla's mind off her troubles for a few minutes, but once her dresser had helped her out of her habit and into the bath, arranged the screen modestly around her and left her to soak, there was nothing to keep Nicholas Lovell out of her thoughts. She tried to focus her mind on soaping herself while keeping her right wrist, bandaged with some herbal poultice that Cook swore by for stings, out of the bath, but for some reason the silky warmth of the water, the scented glide of the soap over her skin, only made the re-membered sensations more acute.

She let her thoughts play over those moments in his arms, recalling the warm, demanding pressure of his mouth on hers, the arousing weight of his body, the springing life of his hair under her palms. If he ever kissed her again, she would have learned… He must be right that she was naturally passionate—but could she believe him when he implied it was something to be admired and welcomed? Or was it just the ploy of a seducer?

But if he had wanted to seduce her, why had he not done so there and then? Camilla's sense of the ridiculous gave her the answer: seducing virgins was probably more comfortable and con-venient in a bed than on hard, scratchy ground in plain view of any passing rider, and one was certainly at less risk of being stung by wasps!

Or if he was not intent on seduction, then was he simply amusing himself with an extreme form of flirtation? Unless he was heartlessly setting out to ensnare her feelings there was only one other explanation—he was seriously intending to pay court to her. And that, Camilla told herself firmly as she reached forward to wash between her toes, was ridiculous. The highly eligible Earl of Ashby would not be looking to modestly circumstanced daughters of deceased county gentlemen for a bride! Every scheming mama in society would have the Earl of Ashby at the very top of their list of marriageable men, as he would know very well. He was rich, well-bred, well-connected—and undeniably charming and good-looking.

Her breath caught on a little sob and she lay back against the high back of the bath. Of course he did not have marriage in mind! And if he did…if he did, then it would be even more painful, perhaps the most painful thing she could imagine, for she could never marry him. And what could be worse than having to refuse the man you loved? she thought drearily, trailing her fingers through the cooling water.

Then her rational mind caught up with her wandering thoughts and she froze. She loved Nicholas! No surely not, surely one could not fall in love on the basis of four—no, five—encounters?

Painfully, for her bruises were stiffening,

Camilla climbed out of the bath and reached for a large towel. Swathing herself in the folds of fine linen, she curled up in a chair by the fire and thought back. Nicholas in the Green Room: arrogant, assured, devastatingly handsome, a big cat on the prowl. Nicholas in the alleyway fighting off the footpads: courageous, strong, physical. Nicholas in the cottage: immovable in his insistence on protecting her, disturbing with his kiss, vulnerable as he slept. Nicholas in the gallery: urbane, an aristocrat with his society mask in place, yet with a dangerous current of provocation running deep in everything he said. And finally the Nicholas of that afternoon: a pleasant companion, a fine horseman, a man who was prepared to have a frank conversation with her, an arousing lover…

Oh, yes, Camilla thought miserably, she *was* falling in love with Nicholas Lovell, Earl of Ashby. There was no doubt of that. She loved everything about him, from the way his eyes crinkled when he laughed to his arrogant self-confidence. She would never be free of the yearning for his kisses, for his caresses, for the sound of his voice and the touch of his mind. And he, whatever his intentions, had awoken her with a kiss like the Prince with the Sleeping Beauty—only there would be no happy ending to this particular fairytale.

Chapter Six

Nicholas stifled a yawn behind his napkin, resisting the temptation to consult his pocket watch for the third time in as many minutes. He had returned from his excursion with Camilla to find Georgiana waving a gold-edged invitation and upbraiding him for forgetting that they were engaged—yet again—to go out to dinner. This time his indefatigable sister had manoeuvred a meeting with Lady Cynthia Fitch, the sister of the fifth Earl of Langford. The lady in question was seated beside him, prattling endlessly about whatever crossed her mind. She appeared to be able to do this without engaging her brains in any way, he thought, savagely rehearsing exactly what he was going to say to his sister when they returned to the Crescent that evening.

Lady Cynthia was undoubtedly well-bred, extremely well-dowered and even, if your taste ran to china dolls, pretty. She was blonde, with a mass of natural curls. Her dimples were constantly on display as she simpered and her long black lashes swept down frequently to veil her somewhat protuberant blue eyes every time his lordship addressed her.

God! Nicholas thought, passing her the salt, three hours married to this peahen and he would either have committed murder or have gone insane. What a contrast to his companion of that afternoon! Camilla was another blonde, to be sure, but her eyes reflected her thoughts, the working of a lively intelligent mind. Companion was the right word for her—it was a pleasure to be in her company. But more than that, when he kissed her... Nicholas firmly repressed the thought, which was undoubtedly an arousing one and highly unsuitable for the dining-room.

He looked across the candlelit table and saw Georgiana watching him beadily from the other side of the ornate epergne. As far as he could see, for the intervening heaps of hothouse fruit and flickering candles, she was glaring at him. Obviously he was not making the required effort with Lady Cynthia. Ruefully he raised his eyebrows at her and received in return exactly the look with which she had greeted his return from illicit outings with the gamekeeper when he had been a boy.

'And a more charming pair you could never hope to see,' Lady Cynthia twittered beside him. Nicholas, who had no idea what she was talking about, found himself instinctively glancing at her plump cleavage, then catching the eye of his brother-in-law, who was sitting on her other side. Henry turned a snort of amusement into a polite cough and looked away, dabbing his eyes with the corner of his napkin.

'Pair?' Nicholas asked, firmly swallowing a feeling of incipient hysteria.

'Why, yes, did I not say? My dear brother has bought me a *pair* of lovebirds. One has to keep them together, my lord, or they pine away.' She lifted her eyes coyly to meet his. 'They are so sweet, the way they bill and coo.' Despite what her mama had said, she had been finding the Earl somewhat hard going, but now she had his attention she was not going to let the opportunity slip away. Emboldened, she added, 'You must come and see them my lord. Tomorrow, perhaps?'

Appalled, Nicholas sought for an excuse. 'Why, thank you, Lady Cynthia, that sounds er... enchanting. However, as tomorrow is Sunday I was going to church...'

'You will be attending Matins in the Abbey? Why, so do we. Perhaps you would care to return afterwards for luncheon? Mama would be delighted to meet you.'

Nicholas was conscious that Lord Henry was watching him with scarcely veiled amusement at his predicament. 'Er...actually I was intending to attend the church in Walcot Street. The sermons, I understand, are particularly uplifting. And long,' he added desperately, 'very long. I do find a long sermon particularly satisfying, and this particular clergyman draws heavily on comparisons between the Old Testament and classical scholarship.'

His brother-in-law was now red in the face and choking. Georgiana, unable for reasons of decorum to speak across the table, sent her incorrigible husband a look which promised later retribution.

Nicholas's guess that the threat of a long intellectual sermon would effectively quash Lady Cynthia's enthusiasm for mutual church-going proved correct. She seemed momentarily daunted, then, remembering her Mama's instructions, rallied. 'But you could join us for luncheon afterwards, my lord? And tell us the more interesting portions of the discourse? I am sure that if *you* explained it to me I would be able to understand it.'

'Delightful as that sounds, Lady Cynthia, I regret that I am engaged for the remainder of the day.'

'Oh, dear.' Deflated, Lady Cynthia turned to converse with Lord Forres and Nicholas breathed again.

His sister, having overheard most of his shameful prevarication, was not amused. 'I sincerely trust the sermon at St Swithin's will be every bit as lengthy and scholarly as you say, Lovell,' she said later that evening as they travelled back in the carriage through the night streets of Bath. 'I am delighted, of course, that you have turned to the church, even if it is somewhat belated. But why on earth St Swithin's?'

'Oh…I spotted it when I was riding by this afternoon and thought it looked interesting.'

'The day you take an interest in church architecture, Lovell,' Georgiana remarked grimly, 'I shall eat my bonnet! You are up to something.'

Nicholas, who had had no idea until he said it that he had even noticed the church which stood at the fork of Walcot Street and the Paragon, realised that it was undoubtedly the church attended by the Knights. Camilla must be on his mind even more than he was consciously aware of. Well, he would confound his sister by attending Matins tomorrow.

The next morning dawned sunny and bright and Nicholas strolled along the Paragon in good spirits. Exposure to Lady Cynthia the night before had had quite the opposite effect to that intended by Lady Forres. Far from being captivated, he had come firmly to the decision that all the débutantes he had met in the last year were either vapid, boring or too conventional in their obedience to society's rules for young ladies. The only woman he had met whom he could imagine spending his time with was Miss Knight. One would never be bored with Miss Knight—provoked, stimulated, irritated, perhaps—but never bored.

Startled, he found himself seriously considering her as a wife. It would not be a brilliant match, but not an ineligible one either. As Earl of Ashby he had no need to marry for either money or connections—provided he chose a well-bred woman, he could do as he pleased. And Miss Knight pleased him very much...

But what if his faint suspicion that she was Miss Davide were true? An actress was quite another matter. And yet...and yet Camilla was patently innocent, however passionate she was in his arms. Her responses to him were instinctive, not learned: he had enough experience to recognise artifice when he encountered it. Opera dancers and actresses were skilled in being whatever their protector of the moment wanted them to be, and both of you played the game of make-believe. Yet she seemed to have that damned sobersides of an attorney in her pocket: surely a man like that would not represent such an abandoned creature as an actress. Unless of course he was courting her himself...

Nicholas pulled himself together as he found himself in front of the Knights' door. It was opened by the footman, who expressed himself deeply regretful that the ladies were not at home. 'They have gone to church, my lord.'

'Rather early, surely?' Nicholas queried, wondering if after all they had not walked down to the more fashionable Abbey.

'Services at St Swithin's do commence rather early, my lord. Would you care to come in and wait?' Samuel had heard all about the interesting Lord Lovell from Camilla's maid and, in common with the rest of the servants' hall, thought he sounded just the ticket for Miss Camilla.

'Thank you, no. I will meet the ladies out of church.'

A short walk further along the Paragon brought his lordship to the small forecourt in front of St Swithin's. The verger at the door opened it for him, but one swift glance inside revealed the Vicar in full flow in the pulpit. A soft snore from the elderly gentleman in the back pew was hardly a vote of confidence in the engrossing nature of his discourse, so with a polite nod to the verger Nicholas retreated to the sanctuary of the churchyard. It was a pleasantly sunny morning, it would be no hardship to lean against a tombstone and await the emergence of the congregation.

Inside it was cool and dark. Camilla wrenched her attention back to the Ephesians for the fourth time with a guilty start. She had welcomed the necessity to attend church this morning: not only would the need to concentrate on the service banish all thoughts of Nicholas, but it would also give her the opportunity to reflect in tranquillity on her forward behaviour of the day before.

Her eyes rested on her prayerbook, clasped between her gloved hands. Unfortunately the exercise of penitential thoughts about her behaviour simply raised the most vivid recollection of the nature of her transgression—and her partner in it. Camilla shut her eyes as a little frisson of remembrance shot up her spine. His hands, his lips, the turf yielding beneath their bodies...her near compliance.

'No!' Camilla realised she must have whispered it aloud, for Ophelia turned her head and gave her a puzzled look. Camilla stared back repressively, noting that Mama was dozing, very discreetly, her head hardly nodding. That was a relief; she was unlikely to notice her elder daughter's shocking lack of attention to the service.

She felt as heavy-eyed as though she had not slept, although quite the opposite had been true. She had fallen into a deep, dreamless sleep, almost as though she had been drugged, then woken with a sense of excitement. Camilla had swung her legs out of bed, then winced with the shock of stiff limbs and aching bruises. At once the memory of the fall and all that had followed it had filled her mind and she had not been able to banish it since.

Mrs Knight had been too preoccupied with worrying whether Ophelia was well enough to attend church to notice that her elder daughter was also moving with less than her usual grace and was uncharacteristically silent.

The Vicar droned on, and in an effort to focus her mind Camilla fixed her eyes on the altar rail. This did not answer the purpose at all—quite the contrary, for the image of herself walking slowly towards it rose unbidden in her mind. She saw Nicholas waiting expectantly for her to join him, the pews full of her friends and relatives, the church heavy with the scent of orange blossom and lilies; she heard the swish of silken skirts as she trod the stone flags on her uncle's arm. The scene in her mind was softened by the fine gauze of her wedding veil…

This fantasy was enough to see her through the last hymn and the dismissal, and even their departure from the church, with the organist playing softly in the background, did not dispel it until they reached the door, where the Reverend Mr Wise was paying close attention to the Quality in his flock, shaking hands and effusively replying to his patron's comments on his sermon.

'Indeed, yes, my lord,' he was saying, 'a most interesting interpretation of the text, I always think. Good day, my lord! Ah, Mrs Knight, Miss Knight, Miss Ophelia: I trust I find you all in good health on this beautiful spring morn!'

Leaving her mama to make polite conversation, Camilla wandered a little way away to look at the view. St Swithin's stood at the point where Walcot Street climbed steeply up to meet the end of the Paragon. The church, built of golden stone, jutted out on a raised platform to allow for the difference in level of the two streets which met on the far side of it. There was a fine view across the valley of the River Avon from the west end, but from this side, where the small church-yard sloped in two directions, the view was of the rear of the Paragon buildings, their gardens sloping steeply down, and of the Walcot Street cottages and their own rear yards.

And standing there, both hands resting on the

iron railing surrounding the burial plot, was Nicholas Lovell. Camilla could see nothing of his face, and all his attention seemed riveted on the view. Her heart leapt with joy at the unexpected sight of him before the inevitable apprehension filled her. Camilla felt the colour rise in her cheeks and was thankful for the fact that she had seen him first and could compose herself before facing him again.

What was Nicholas doing here? Camilla walked slowly down the slope towards him, taking in the sight of his broad shoulders in the admirably cut blue superfine jacket, the length of his muscular legs moulded by the tightly strapped trousers, the curl of his hair just visible at the back under his hat. Then she saw he was looking at the back of their house and her heart leapt again: he must be thinking about her!

Nicholas was thinking about Camilla, certainly, but not in a way which would have given her cause for anything but deep anxiety. Twenty minutes spent leaning on the fence in the sunlight, imagining Camilla Knight once more in his arms, had been curtailed abruptly. Some unconscious part of his mind had been regarding the landscape spread before his unseeing eyes, and now his gaze sharpened. Nicholas slowly looked up at the towering buildings of the Paragon stretching along the crest to his right, then he studied the way their gardens tumbled down to the wall of the yards belonging to the cottages facing on to Walcot Street.

Eyes narrowed against the sunlight, Nicholas counted along until he could identify the Knights' residence, then repeated the process for Miss Davide's little house. The garden of one met the yard of the other, wall to wall. So that was how it had been done! Nicholas realised he was gripping the iron railing so hard it hurt, even through the leather of his gloves. 'Mademoiselle Davide' had had a key, had let herself out of the kitchen door as he'd slept and must have slipped through an unseen gate in the dividing wall. Once the other side she had become, once again, the highly respectable Miss Knight.

'Damn!' He said it out loud. 'Hell and damnation!' Just when he thought he had found an eligible bride, a woman he could not only tolerate being tied to but one with whom it would be a positive pleasure to spend the rest of his life, she turned out to be an actress!

Nicholas dropped his head and stared at his clenched hands on the railing. And yet…her reputation as the Unobtainable was no lie, no fabrication for the billboards. Mademoiselle Davide—Camilla Knight—was the virgin that her background and breeding would lead one to expect. An outspoken and passionate virgin, but a virgin none the less. He remembered her behaviour in the Green Room, the skillful way she had handled importunate gentlemen, the way she had made her terms for accepting gifts quite plain.

And yet…she was still quite ineligible. Whatever her reasons for taking this quixotic path—and he assumed they were financial—she had placed herself beyond the boundaries of polite society. If anyone were to discover just who Mademoiselle Davide really was, the Knight family's only recourse would be an immediate retirement to a life of seclusion in the country. Thank goodness he had found out before he had made her a declaration! What would she have said? Her vehement statement that she would never marry made sense now: but the cynical part of his mind, the part that remembered the constant scheming of society mamas, made him wonder if her resolution to do the right thing would have remained firm in the face of a declaration by the Earl of Ashby. It was a good thing he had not gone into the church: he could leave Bath now, not see her again. No harm had been done…

The muffled sound of footsteps on the turf made him turn round slowly. Walking down between the gravestones was Camilla, a graceful figure in a deep amber walking-dress and pelisse, a velvet bonnet in the same shade with a curling brown feather on her head. She smiled at him, a smile of such pleasure and warmth that his breath caught and every sensible resolution flew out of his head.

'Lord Lovell! I did not look to see you here!' She held out her gloved hand and shook his, apparently unaware that Nicholas was uncharacteristically lost for words. 'Will you not join us for luncheon? I know Mama would be delighted.'

Camilla was pleased with the calm air of social poise she had conjured up. Inside her heart was beating frantically and she had a wild urge to throw herself into his arms, but she told herself firmly that this was just another part to play and continued to smile.

'I…I am afraid I am leaving Bath this afternoon, Miss Knight. I called to say goodbye and to enquire about your health and Miss Ophelia's after your falls yesterday. Your footman told me you were here.'

'Oh!' All Camilla's disappointment showed on her face and her lip quivered very slightly before she gained control of herself. 'Oh, your friends will be sorry to lose your company, my lord. Must you go?'

Nicholas knew he should say he had urgent affairs to attend to on his estate, in Town— anywhere but here. He had never before had the slightest trouble ridding himself courteously and generously of any romantic entanglement; now he found himself incapable of simply saying goodbye and walking away.

'Well…I… Perhaps there is no great urgency for a day or two,' he capitulated. God, he was a fool, but the look of sparkling pleasure on her face was reward enough.

'Then you will have lunch with us,' Camilla pressed, trying to achieve a more ladylike control of her emotions, which had been turned upside down by the sight of Nicholas. Her common sense, her sense of what was right and honourable to do, was telling her that she must be true to her resolution never to marry. Her fantasies and hopes were quite different: she wanted to be in his arms again, she wanted his lips on hers, she wanted him to fall in love with her.

They turned and walked up the slope to join Mrs Knight and Ophelia, who were unfurling their parasols and looking round for Camilla. 'My lord! Good morning!' Mrs Knight beamed with approval at the sight of her elder daughter on the Earl's arm. What a handsome couple they made! 'Were you in church too? I did not see you.'

'Good morning, ma'am.' Nicholas doffed his hat and bowed to the ladies. 'I am afraid I arrived too late for the service.' He caught Ophelia's eye: she was giving him the quizzical look of a young lady who knew perfectly well he had had no intention of attending divine service. 'I called at the house to enquire about Miss Ophelia's health after her fall yesterday.' He felt Camilla's hand clench on his arm. So! She had not told her mama that she too had had a fall. He closed his arm up to his side, squeezing Camilla's hand for a fleeting moment.

Reassured by the unspoken message, her heart pounding at the momentary contact with his body, Camilla managed to say brightly, 'I have invited Lord Lovell to luncheon, Mama.'

Mrs Knight's thoughts flew to the menu for luncheon, desperately recalling what she had agreed with Cook for today's meal. She had planned only a light cold collation for luncheon, but there was the lobster for this evening: that would do if Cook prepared a hollandaise sauce and some syllabubs for dessert…gentlemen did so enjoy sweet things. None of this frantic thought showed on her face as she made polite conversation with Nicholas while they walked down the Paragon.

'Such an interesting sermon you missed, my lord,' she said, without a blush for the fact that she had slept through a good part of Mr Wise's discourse. 'Such a stimulating speaker…oh, good morning, Mrs Frobisher!' She broke off to bow to a passing acquaintance. Hah! so much for her snide implications that her Daphne would find an eligible husband long before either of Mrs Knight's two girls. 'That was Mrs Frobisher—the Dorset Frobishers, you know,' she confided. 'She has three daughters, quite charming. They rise above the handicap of the family features by sheer force of personality.' Having thus reassured herself that if Lord Lovell came across the three Misses Frobishers he would be already prejudiced against them, she carried on happily along the Paragon, bowing and nodding to other members of the Quality, who like the Knights, were returning home from church.

Once inside the door she shed her bonnet and pelisse and turned to her daughters. 'Do take his lordship through to the Green Salon, girls, I will join you shortly.' As the door closed behind them she bustled downstairs. 'Mrs Powes! Mrs Powes! Here is Lord Lovell come for luncheon, now what can we do with that lobster?'

'Lord Lovell? Oooh, ma'am! What a good thing Miss Camilla's home. Mary, get that lobster out of the scullery and the pan on the boil. Now, don't you worry, ma'am, we'll get you a luncheon up fit for His Majesty, poor man, let alone Lord Lovell.'

Upstairs in the Green Salon, Camilla sat on the sofa watching her sister flirting outrageously with Nicholas Lovell, who was teasing her back in much the same way as he would a favoured niece. 'Did you really come round to ask about me, Lord Lovell?' she was asking, opening her hazel eyes wide at him.

'But of course, Miss Ophelia. I was hardly able to sleep a wink last night for thinking about yesterday.'

His voice held the slightest hint of wickedness, and although he was not looking towards her Camilla knew perfectly well what he was referring to. She took a large sip from her glass of ratafia and almost choked. She had no fear that Nicholas would tell anyone about what had happened between them yesterday, but equally she had no illusions that he would not refer to it again, however obliquely, to tease her. And if he was telling the truth, the thought that he had lain awake thinking about her made her feel quite hot and confused.

Ophelia, who knew just how well the dark green brocade of the curtains set off her colouring, had perched decoratively in the window-seat and was half turned to look down the garden. Despite her preoccupations Camilla smiled slightly, knowing how long her sister had been practising in front of the mirror to achieve just the right turn of the head to show off her enchanting profile to perfection.

'Do come and look at this view my lord,' Ophelia was saying. 'It is one of the reasons we took this house. See—' she patted the seat beside her encouragingly '—if you sit here you can see right across the Avon.'

Nicholas strolled over, but did not sit. He stood, one hand on the window-frame, looking down. Camilla, suddenly irrationally jealous of her little sister, got to her feet and joined the two of them.

With his eyes fixed outside the room she risked a long look at his averted face. Then she saw that he was not focused on the charming view across to the wooded slopes behind, but was looking down into their garden. Camilla followed his gaze and realised he was staring at the gate in the wall between their garden and the back yard of Miss March's cottage in Walcot Street. Hidden by hanging ivy on the far side, on this face of the wall the gardener kept it trimmed and clear and the route which took her from being Mademoiselle Davide to being Miss Knight was plain to see.

Her eyes flew to his face and saw his eyes narrow speculatively. Camilla gave a little gasp and immediately his attention was all on her. Surely he must have guessed! At any moment the accusation would come and her double life would be exposed. But Nicholas's face revealed nothing but polite interest in the view. 'Yes, it is a fine view, and what a charming garden you have.'

His blandly expressed words concealed his feelings. What he could see from the window confirmed what he had suspected in the churchyard. He had had time to get over that shock, but Camilla's face had betrayed, fleetingly, her guilty secret. She swiftly had her face under control again, but her eyes were still wide with shock and fear, startlingly green. The sensible, the kind thing, to do would be to contrive to send Ophelia out of the room and to reassure Camilla that her secret was safe. And, after lunch, pursue his plans to return to London, putting the whole thing behind him as a pleasant but disappointing interlude.

Camilla wondered vaguely if she was going to faint. It seemed very probable. Her body stood there, apparently calm, while her stomach seemed to have disappeared and her brain whirled. Ophelia's chatter seemed to come from a long way away. What was he going to do? Leave in disgust at her deception? Tell polite society that she was beyond the pale? Expect her to behave as an actress was supposed to behave—the way she had so very nearly behaved yesterday?

He did none of these. Instead he was all

concern, taking her lightly by the elbow and steering her back to her seat on the sofa. 'You are pale, Miss Knight. Are you sure you are fully recovered from your fall yesterday?'

For once Ophelia proved a welcome distraction. 'A fall? Camilla, you did not tell me? Does Mama know you fell off too?'

'No, she does not,' Camilla replied sharply. 'And I beg you, Ophelia, do not tell her. She will only worry—and do you want her to forbid us to ride out?'

Ophelia jumped to her feet. 'Heavens, no! Do you think Mama would?'

At that most awkward moment Mrs Knight swept in, full of confidence that her luncheon table would not shame the most exacting society matron. 'Would do what, my dears?'

Ophelia and Camilla looked blankly at each other, momentarily lost for words. They need not have feared, for Nicholas interjected smoothly, 'I had just asked Miss Knight and Miss Ophelia whether you would all be my guests tomorrow night at the first fireworks and musical evening of the Season in the Sydney Gardens. The weather appears to be holding well, and of course I will reserve a box.'

'Please say yes, Mama,' Ophelia pleaded. She had never been allowed to attend such a grown-up entertainment before. Camilla simply sat back against the sofa cushions and felt a wave of relief sweep over her. He had not guessed! He could not have done and still have invited them all out. She had been mistaken, had panicked unduly. For the first time she truly realised what a very dangerous game she was playing, yet like a gambler in the grip of his addiction she could not stop, could not do what she knew she ought and let Nicholas slip out of her life for ever.

Mrs Knight had not the slightest intention of saying no to such a flattering invitation and one which, she hoped, would bring her girls to the notice of society matrons who might include them in further expeditions. To go to the Sydney Gardens in the company of the Earl of Ashby had a cachet indeed! It was true that Camilla was insistent on her ridiculous refusal to consider marriage, and Ophelia was a little young for him, but Mrs Knight still had hopes of Camilla relenting, and at the very least he could only lend them all consequence.

It was a splendid luncheon, and Ophelia for once demonstrated tact and did not comment on the unusual lavishness of the spread. Mrs Knight was feeling ten years younger with the presence of such a handsome young man in the room, and charmed by his lordship's thoughtfulness and attention to her wishes. 'Is there perhaps another gentleman of your acquaintance who you would like to join us tomorrow evening, Mrs Knight? There is no shortage of space in the box and it would balance the party and—should you permit dancing—would provide another partner accept-able to you.'

'How thoughtful of you, my lord.' Mrs Knight beamed, hiding her racing thoughts. Who could she invite who would not distract Camilla in any way from his lordship? Ah, yes, the very man! 'Shall we invite Mr Brooke, my dears?'

Ophelia, who would not have cared if her mama had invited the Archbishop of Canterbury just so long as she could be seen in Nicholas Lovell's company, agreed instantly. Camilla, saying nothing, recognised the danger to her daydreams in the invitation. Arthur Brooke, emi-nently sensible, aware of every detail of her scandalous other life, and knowing her as well as he did, would immediately tell her to sever a connection which could only lead to exposure.

The fact that he would be perfectly right was no consolation whatsoever!

'Then that is settled,' Mrs Knight said happily. 'I will send Samuel down with a note this afternoon. It was so fortunate that your invitation is for tomorrow night, my lord, for we would have been unable to accept otherwise.'

'Why is that, Mama?' Camilla enquired calmly, trying to pull herself together. The entire meal felt like the sort of nightmare she used to have when she dreamt she was acting in a ten-act play without knowing any of the words.

'I had quite forgot to tell you, my love, today has been so busy, but I have received a letter from Lady Ellwood—our close friends and neighbours from when we lived in Cambridgeshire, my lord—and she has confirmed the invitation to the house party she spoke of in her last letter. We must leave on Wednesday, for I am sure she will want my assistance in preparing for so many guests.'

Ophelia squeaked with pleasure. 'Mama! How wonderful!' She turned to his lordship and began to prattle happily. 'Lady Ellwood always has the most wonderful house parties—so many people, and you would never think they would all get on together, but she is such a wonderful hostess and everyone enjoys themselves. Even the Archdeacon joined in the theatricals last time…'

'Theatricals?' Nicholas asked lazily, passing the sugar to Mrs Knight.

Ophelia caught Camilla's horrified expression and blushed scarlet to the roots of her hair. She might be scatterbrained but she was not stupid and she understood, far more clearly than her Mama, the necessity to keep her elder sister's scandalous secret.

'Oh…merely charades, a little verse-reading, you know. After all, the Archdeacon would hardly participate in anything else…' Her voice trailed away and she looked down into her empty syllabub glass.

'Cambridgeshire?' Nicholas enquired, apparently unaware of Ophelia's confusion and the silence of the other two ladies. 'Is that the Lord Ellwood who has such a fine string of race-horses? I believe my father knew him.'

The relief around the table was almost palpable. So the entire family knew what Miss Camilla had been up to. He supposed, now he thought about it, that it could hardly be otherwise, given the practicalities of running a double life.

Mrs Knight was earnestly remarking on Lord Ellwood's success in the Derby, but Nicholas's mind was elsewhere. The Ellwoods lived on the Cambridge–Suffolk border, handy for Newmarket. Later that week Freddie Corsham was returning home to his country estate not ten miles from Newmarket. And Nicholas had a standing invitation to Freddie's house…

As he walked away back to Georgiana's house Nicholas acknowledged that after tomorrow night the best thing to do would be never to see Camilla Knight again. But some devil was not going to let him do that just yet. He would take up Freddie's invitation—his friend was bound to know the Ellwoods—and then…and then he would just have to see what happened.

Chapter Seven

'Will you not walk a little along the central promenade and view the lights, Miss Knight?' Mr Brooke enquired earnestly and with a meaning look. He had already risen from his seat in Lord Lovell's box and was offering his arm to Camilla.

Good manners suggested that she should immediately accept but Camilla hesitated, puzzled and somewhat nettled by the solicitor's proprietary air. Arthur Brooke was acting as though he were her elder brother, chaperoning her in company of which he did not quite approve. His manner was correct, but to someone who knew him as well as she did, it was clear he was obviously out of countenance.

'Thank you, Mr Brooke, but I am so much enjoying watching the world go by from here—

and drinking this delicious punch—that I would prefer to remain where I am for a while.' She smiled sweetly at him before turning back to watch the throngs that filled the evening's fête in the Sydney Gardens. Rumour had it that two to three thousand people could be accommodated in the pleasure grounds, but this evening, so early in the year, it was quieter, although none the less interesting for that.

At this hour the orchestra was only playing light airs and the dancing had not yet begun on the portable floor which had been laid before the pavilions and boxes. Couples strolled back and forth, admiring the myriad fairy lights and lanterns strung from trees and leading back into the darker grottoes and intriguing labyrinths.

Mr Brooke flicked up the tails of his very correct evening-coat before sitting down again with some emphasis. Camilla wondered why he had positioned himself quite so firmly between Lord Lovell and herself. She would have liked to be able to speak to her host, at least! As it was she could hardly see him, never mind exchange words with him with Mr Brooke's disapproving bulk in the way.

For her part her younger sister, sitting next to

his lordship, was in seventh heaven. He was too old, of course, but undeniably handsome and *so* well dressed in his dark evening clothes which fitted like a glove, impeccable white stockings and exquisitely tied cravat. For once Ophelia had no need to compete with her sister, for she could see that Arthur Brooke was keeping Camilla entertained, leaving Ophelia free to bask in the jealous glances of her friends and acquaintances.

It was wonderful—they all seemed to be here tonight, but *they* were all promenading demurely with their parents, and none were seated in such an exclusive box as she was! Maria Frogmorton almost tripped over her own feet, so agog was she by being greeted by Ophelia, who waved languidly from her seat next to the Earl of Ashby. Her chagrin was not helped by her mama, never a subtle woman, speculating audibly on how those Knight girls had acquired such an eligible escort.

All three Frobisher girls, each cursed with their father's large nose, were Ophelia's next triumph. To their mother's irritation they rushed over to speak to their friend, forcing their reluctant mama to follow them and engage Mrs Knight in conversation from between clenched teeth.

Mrs Knight, keeping her triumph off her face with some difficulty, was ecstatic. She had been patronised once too often by Mrs Frobisher, who was the third cousin to an earl and never let anyone forget it. Now she had seen the Knights in company with the Earl of Ashby twice in two days! She would soon be spreading that around all her friends and the invitations to Ophelia and Camilla would flood in.

Nicholas, very much at his ease, knew exactly what was going on and was, surprisingly, enjoying himself. He found Ophelia's puppy-love amusing and rather endearing: he had no fears that she would break her heart over him. He was a convenient foil for her flirtations and a trophy to parade before her equally young friends, that was all.

No, it was her elder sister he was interested in. Not that his plans for the evening in that regard were going very well, thanks to the disapproving presence of Arthur Brooke. Quite what the lawyer had found so unacceptable in Nicholas he could not imagine, but take against him he most certainly had. There was nothing to criticise in his dry, proper manner, but the man was acting like a dog in the manger—it felt almost as though he would growl at any moment.

Nicholas leaned forward and offered to fill Camilla's glass. She smiled and accepted, allowing him another opportunity to admire her elegant evening gown with its pale yellow net overskirt, showing off the amber satin slip beneath. Camilla's white shoulders and the gentle swell of her breasts rose enticingly from the silvery lace of the low-cut neckline which, to her surprise, her mama had approved. Mama had even lent her the best amber set of drop earrings and necklace which Great-aunt Augusta had left her.

It was the first time Nicholas had seen Camilla in evening dress and the effect was yet another nail in the coffin of his good resolutions to break the connection. Last night he had almost talked himself out of his scheme to stay in Newmarket with Freddie Corsham. Camilla Knight was ineligible, totally ineligible. He was certain now she was Mademoiselle Davide, and the sensible thing to do was to obey his head and walk away. But something else was conflicting with the voice of reason. It could not be love: that was not what he was seeking after all. He needed a suitable wife. Outside marriage all that was required was an intelligent and attractive mistress—one who would keep him satisfied in all respects.

Camilla Knight was too virtuous to become any man's mistress, and her past would not allow her to be any man's wife. So why was he so drawn to her? Camilla stood up to exchange a few words with an acquaintance and he was once more struck by her grace and charm. His eyes lingered on the smooth length of her neck, the soft curls of blonde hair gleaming gold in the bright candlelight of the box. Unbidden, the memory of the sensation of her skin, satin against his lips, of the scent of her in his nostrils, the way she had responded when he kissed her, filled his mind.

His thoughts must have been visible in his eyes, for he realised with a start that Mr Brooke was regarding him with overt disapproval. Damn it! The man must be in love with her himself: if he was not very careful Nicholas would find himself called out!

The two men were still eyeing each other warily when the band struck up a dance tune and the first couples took to the floor to form sets for a quadrille. Nicholas got to his feet and asked, 'Will you do me the honour, Miss Knight?' He scarcely waited for her reply before he took her hand and swept her out of the box and on to the dance floor.

Camilla took her place in the set, her eyes glowing, her gloved hand tingling as though he had touched her naked skin. The measures of the dance separated them, brought them together, separated them again, but their eyes kept meeting. Every time it was she who broke the glance first, feeling as though an electric shock had jolted her heart, frightened that her feelings for him were showing all too plainly.

How she got through the intricate dance without a mistake she never knew, but finally the last chords were struck and she was curtseying to her partner, and joining the other dancers in clapping the band. Automatically she turned to return to the box, but Nicholas was beside her, his hand under her elbow.

'What a crush! I do not think you would wish to be jostled by the crowd, Miss Knight. Let us walk a little.'

Almost before she knew it, Camilla found herself strolling along one of the lantern-lit pathways which edged the bowling green. It was away from the dance floor and the pavilions and on the other side from the famous labyrinth and grottoes, so that even on such a festive night it was relatively quiet.

They walked a short distance in silence, although Camilla was convinced the urgent beating of her heart must sound as loud to him as it did to her. However, when Nicholas spoke his words came as a surprise. 'Is Mr Brooke related to you?'

'Why, no!' Camilla replied, puzzled. 'His father was our family solicitor for years, and now Mr Brooke manages our affairs here in Bath. Why do you ask?'

'He is so very protective of you, that is all. I half expected him to demand to know my intentions. If he is not a relative then I can only assume he is in love with you. He is within an inch of finding cause for a quarrel so he can call me out.' Nicholas sounded quite matter-of-fact.

Camilla stopped in her tracks, completely taken aback by the idea. '*Arthur Brooke* in love with me! Ridiculous!'

Nicholas looked down into her indignant face. 'You are very severe on the poor man. I agree he is not the most brilliant match, but he seems well-bred and is doubtless a good-looking enough fellow if he ever stops scowling.' He added drily, 'And I have never known a poor solicitor yet.'

'You misjudge me, sir, if you think I would look down on Mr Brooke for his profession. He is a good, kind and respectable man, and will make some young lady an admirable husband. But not me—and in any case, he is not in love with me!'

'Are you sure?' Nicholas enquired slyly. 'Why else should he be so antagonistic to me? Miss Knight? I do believe you are blushing.'

'I am not!' Camilla said indignantly, but she was seized by a sudden pang of conscience. She had always taken Arthur's solicitude for granted, never given his friendship a second thought, beyond a strong feeling of gratitude for his help. She had been so sure that Arthur Brooke's declaration that day in the carriage had been purely a kind gesture—but what if he had meant it from his heart? She had treated it so lightly at the time...

'I am certain you are blushing,' Nicholas teased, taking her chin in his hand and turning her face to the light. 'There, I told you so—your cheeks are quite charmingly rosy.' He bent suddenly and brushed cool lips across her burning skin. If Camilla had not been blushing before, she was now. With a gasp she turned on her heel and ran along the gravel path and down a turning towards the sound of tinkling water. She found herself quite alone in the charming little grove, not much larger than an arbor, lit only by a few lanterns and with a cascade of water falling into a pool of artificial rock at the back.

Camilla unbuttoned one glove, pulling it back from the wrist so she could scoop her hand into the falling water. She gasped out loud at its chilly touch, then dabbed it on to her hecticly coloured cheeks. When she straightened she heard Nicholas's footsteps behind her.

He put his hands on her bare shoulders, the fingertips stroking down the satin slopes, gently, insidiously. 'Camilla...' His voice was husky, the note, even to her inexperienced ears, one of sensual longing.

'My lord, this is most improper...' But even as her back stiffened a shudder ran through her frame. She wanted to lean back into the strength of him, to have him encircle her with his arms, his warmth. She wanted to feel his lips on her skin again—and she knew that this was all wrong, that she was behaving like a loose woman, that she must send him away...

A breeze struck the grove and the sharp gust

caught the cascade of water, showering her in cold droplets. Camilla cried out at the shock of it and twisted under Nicholas's hands. The movement brought them breast to breast.

Nicholas needed no further prompting. His arms encircled her, holding her tight against him, and his mouth found hers in a long, unhurried, deeply sensual kiss. Camilla melted against him, her hands reaching up to encircle his neck, her fingers first exploring, then tangling, in the springing curls at the nape. Her fingertips discovered the surprising softness of the skin there and she stroked it, innocently unaware of the effect it was having on Nicholas.

Her lips opened under his, inviting the invasion of his tongue-tip. She had been shocked at her own response when he had kissed her on the Downs, but now she was learning her own power to arouse him. Nicholas groaned deep in his throat and his hand moved down from the slope of her shoulder to the soft swell of her breast. Camilla gasped, both at the intimate touch and at the immediate response of her own flesh under his insidious fingers.

The rising tide of her feelings for him pushed back and then overwhelmed the small voice inside her that said, *No, this is wrong!* But then another voice, almost an instinct, replied, *How can it be wrong when I love him?*

His mouth left hers and she gave a small murmur of protest which turned into a soft gasp of pleasure as he began to nuzzle the exposed curve of her breast above the line of lace. Her fingers closed in his hair and she bent her own head to kiss the dark head, inhale the scent of Russian Leather from his cologne.

Nicholas was aflame, his senses intoxicated by the scent of honeysuckle, by the satiny smooth sensation of Camilla's skin under his questing lips and by the innocent, trusting passion this young woman showed at his very touch. He had known many sensual, practised women, some of the finest practitioners of the arts of love, but none had been as erotic, as arousing as Camilla in her artlessness. And that was why he had to stop this *now…*

He was already lifting his head when two strident female voices broke the silence of the little grove. Feet crunching on the gravel presaged the approach of the speakers. There was only one way out, the way they had come in: the moment he thought it two long shadows fell across the exit. Swiftly Nicholas stepped back behind the only cover, a statue of Venus standing in a large seashell, pulling Camilla with him. She found herself held tight against him, his hand pressed warningly against her lips. She started to protest, then fell silent, shrinking against Nicholas in the shadows as she too heard the voices.

'Shall we rest awhile, Mrs Frobisher? See, there is a bench here.'

'Indeed, Mrs Frogmorton, it looks most pleasant, and I confess I am quite fatigued by the crush of the crowd surrounding the dancing. Chaperonage is so fatiguing.'

The two matrons picked their way across the grove, straight towards the curved bench which stood at the foot of the statue of the goddess of love.

'Oh, good, it is quite dry. I would not wish to stain this new satin overdress,' Mrs Frobisher declared before settling herself.

'A London *modiste*?' her companion enquired sweetly. 'You are so fortunate in being able to wear that difficult shade. On so many people it would make the complexion quite sallow.'

'If one is to speak of shades,' Mrs Frobisher rejoined tartly, 'did you not observe that dress

Ophelia Knight is wearing? Periwinkle-blue, and she is not even out! One would have expected white, or cream, perhaps. Although what Mrs Knight is thinking of to allow such a child to attend an evening event of this nature I cannot imagine.'

Nicholas felt Camilla stiffen in his arms and tightened his grip warningly. The two ladies were so close it seemed impossible they would not hear their breathing or the rustle of Camilla's gown against the encroaching box hedging.

'You speak of Miss Ophelia—I am more concerned with Miss Knight herself!' The two shadows nodded in unison: they had finally reached the issue which had been burning in both bosoms all evening. It was quite impossible to give the matter the full attention it required with the eager ears of their daughters so close, but a private stroll gave ample opportunity to thoroughly air the scandalous affair. 'What can Mrs Knight be about?'

'You need to ask that, my dear?' Mrs Frobisher enquired archly. 'I would have thought it was obvious. She might bring that dull lawyer and that chit of a girl along for propriety, but it is the merest window-dressing. Her motive is obvious:

she intends to ensnare the Earl of Ashby for her eldest daughter!'

It was Nicholas's turn to stiffen, but worse was to follow. '*Intending* to ensnare him? I would have thought she had already succeeded, such a significant degree of interest he is showing in the girl. Hardly a day passes when they are not seen together, I have heard. He is even escorting the family to church.'

Mrs Frobisher laughed patronisingly. 'Oh, no, he is not yet in her toils. When one moves in such circles, one recognises the situation instantly. My cousin the Earl suffered in just such a way. Encroaching mamas, pressing attentions upon him under every conceivable circumstance. And occasionally…' she paused and lowered her voice '…a gentleman can find himself unwittingly in a delicate situation where quite unreasonable expectations have been aroused by the merest politeness on his part. Naturally, those of the Ton, those with a sophisticated understanding, would not expect anything to come of it, but others have their ambitions fuelled by what is the merest politeness and condescension.

'The Earl of Ashby is too refined to make a sudden, humiliating break from the Knights, but mark my words he will be gone within the next few days and that will be the end of Mrs Knight's little plan. A moment of glory for Miss Knight, but fleeting, fleeting, my dear.'

Mrs Frogmorton, smarting at the implication that she was less well-connected and sophisticated than her friend, swallowed her chagrin and lowered her voice in turn. 'That is as maybe, but things may have gone too far for an honourable withdrawal on the Earl's part.'

There was a sharp intake of breath from Mrs Frobisher. Camilla thought they must discover her at any moment, her heart was beating so hard it sounded like a drumbeat in her chest. 'What *can* you mean, my dear Mrs Frogmorton?'

'Mrs Knight—although the family is well-bred enough—can have no real hope of securing such a brilliant match for her daughter, as you so rightly point out. The Knights are obscure, rural—except of course that very odd uncle one hears about. They do say he has been shut up now, with paid attendants, but that is by the by... Is it not possible that in her eagerness to promote the affair Mrs Knight has been, shall we say, lax in her chaperonage?'

To Camilla, standing in Nicholas's arms, her

skin still tingling from his caresses, these words were coals of fire. Her mama had indeed been lax, but how could she ever have imagined her daughter could behave with such shocking impropriety? She wanted to bury her face in his shirtfront, but all she could do was to stand as still as the statue which shielded her, the hot tears of humiliation trickling down her cheeks.

'Surely not!' Mrs Frobisher gasped, half-horrified, half-thrilled at the revelation. 'Surely a man as worldly wise as Ashby would not allow himself to be entrapped by a scheming mama and those rather obvious good looks. Obviously, there is his reputation…'

'Indeed! And one has to admit he has always previously confined his attentions to married ladies with complacent husbands. There has never been a whiff of scandal.'

'You say so, but what about the youngest Turner child? I saw her out with her nursemaid the other week, and I cannot recall any others in that family with such dark hair…'

'My dear! You do not suggest…?' Mrs Frogmorton's voice was full of appalled eagerness.

'I will say no more, but the dates are significant.' There was short silence following this scandalous *on dit*. 'Do you not think a quiet word with Mrs Knight would be a kindness?'

'Oh, no, dear! She would not take it in the kindly spirit in which it was meant. And besides, however much Mrs Knight may scheme, and Miss Camilla throw her cap over the windmill, Ashby is too canny to let himself be trapped by such provincial manoeuvrings.'

Having thoroughly picked over and criticised the manners, morals and motives of both the Earl of Ashby and the entire Knight family, the two ladies fell silent at last. At length Mrs Frobisher rose to her feet. 'I do declare I am feeling quite peckish. Shall we stroll back to our box? I do not like to leave girls too long with only their governess. One cannot be too careful.'

With a self-important rustle of silks the two ladies swept out of the grove, blissfully unaware of the devastation they had left behind them.

For a long moment Camilla stood frozen in Nicholas's arms, then with a jerk she freed herself and stumbled into the middle of the clearing. Her skin burned still, not with his kisses but with scalding humiliation. That her name should be bandied around was bad enough, but that Nicholas should hear it was almost beyond endurance.

'Camilla...those old tabbies...' Nicholas began, taking a step towards her. He was stopped by her upflung hand.

She stood, her face averted from him, calling on every vestige of her hard-learned stage control to help her through the difficult speech which lay in front of her.

'No, my lord, let me speak. I must apologise for the vulgarity of my acquaintances and for the embarrassment that I have exposed you to.' He began to protest, but she stilled him again with a gesture. 'No, please let me finish. My mama, as any careful mother would, wishes Ophelia and me to make good, suitable matches.' She paused, drawing a difficult breath before continuing. 'We are an old family, a good, well-respected family, but we have never aspired above our station. And as I have told you, I have no intention of marrying—*ever*.' Her voice shook betrayingly and she paused for a moment to regain control.

'That said, I cannot deny that I have behaved... indecorously when you have...when we have—' She broke off again, defeated by the impropriety of what she was trying to describe. 'But I have *never* sought to entrap you in *any* way. I have been very weak, but…even if you were to offer for me, which I realise is quite out of the question and never your intention, I would refuse you.' As she said the words they seemed to echo in her head with a dreadful finality, and Camilla realised just how much she had secretly hoped he would make just such a declaration. It had been madness, of course, a complete fantasy, but denying it was the hardest thing she had ever had to do.

Camilla's voice became entirely suspended in tears and she broke off, gesturing with both hands to keep Nicholas away. Somehow she controlled herself and turned to face him, her head high. Suddenly salvaging her pride and her family's honour seemed the most important thing. 'As I say, my lord, I have no intention of marrying, certainly not for considerations of the rank or fortune which I readily agree you would bring me. Nor—' she swallowed painfully '—will I allow my judgement to be swayed by strong physical attraction.'

Nicholas, who had only been waiting for her to stop talking to take her in his arms and kiss away the tears, stopped abruptly. He was well used to the cut-throat gentility of the chaperons' corner, where soft words and appearances of concern were simply a front for ambitious mamas, each aiming to place her own daughter higher in the social tree than her neighbour's child. He had been furious to find himself the subject of such malicious tittle-tattle, having been the subject of it many times before. He knew perfectly well how to value it and would not have thought for a moment to blame Camilla or her mother for the rumours.

But her words struck at the core of pride in the family name and in his lineage, the pride which had nagged him to go away from Bath, not allow himself to become entangled by a young woman who had risked compromise and scandal in such a way. So, Camilla Knight would not allow considerations of his rank and fortune to influence her, would she? He knew perfectly well that he was considered by society—and by the standards of his own family—far above her in rank, fortune and breeding. But it was up to him to decide whom he might favour with an offer of marriage, not for some young woman—however beautiful—to kindly inform him that she valued neither his rank nor his kisses before he had even hinted at an offer!

Nicholas's conscience was pricking in a way which was painfully unfamiliar, but injured pride overrode its promptings. Conveniently forgetting that he had sought out Camilla's company in a very marked manner which would inevitably lead to gossip, he now found himself furious that such gossip had in fact occurred. Dammit, the old biddies were right. Camilla should be extremely grateful to receive a proposal of marriage from him, not coolly telling him that he need not trouble himself to make one!

His face was rigid with suppressed emotion but his voice was cool as he replied, 'Rest assured, Miss Knight, that I perfectly remember your words on the subject and that I had absolutely no intention of putting you to the distress of refusing an unwelcome declaration. It might be felt that I could be forgiven for misinterpreting the warmth of your responses, but let me also assure you that I had no intention of making you any other kind of offer either...'

'Sir! How dare you?' His outrageous words were like a blow: Camilla's eyes blazed and her back stiffened. The fact that he was entirely right and she had behaved outrageously enough to provoke the offer of a *carte blanche* only served to fuel her anger. The only alternative was to blurt out that she loved him, and that was quite, quite impossible.

Now equally furious with both himself and her, Nicholas strode across the short distance which separated them and took her by the wrist. 'Come, come, Miss Knight! Why so proper all of a sudden? You showed none of this delicacy when my lips were on your breast just now. If those two old witches had arrived a little later, would they have found that bench otherwise occupied?'

Camilla brought her left hand up and slapped Nicholas's face so hard the sound rebounded off the rocks of the waterfall. He released her wrist and stepped back sharply, his eyes narrow slits of fury. Camilla swept out of the grove on to the gravel path, intent only on getting back to the box. What must she look like? She dabbed frantically at her eyes with her handkerchief as she went rapidly through the winding dells. Just before she reached the path encircling the dance floor she found Nicholas at her side. He took her arm.

'What do you want? Go away!'

'Be quiet and think,' he snapped. 'Do you really want to give the old biddies something more to talk about? Compose yourself and dry your eyes. We will stroll back to the box as if nothing untoward has happened and you will then doubtless develop a convenient headache and have to return home. And one last thing before we part…'

'*Yes?*' she snapped in her turn.

'I have never had a relationship of any kind with Lady Turner, and the parentage of her youngest daughter is nothing to do with me.'

Camilla turned and looked at him with icy eyes. 'How very sensible of Lady Turner. One can only admire her judgement.' She found herself at the door of their box and opened the door with the air of an actress making a stage entrance. She moved to Arthur's side, 'Oh, Mr Brooke, please would you drive us home? I have *such* a headache. It must have been the punch.'

Chapter Eight

It was the hardest letter Camilla had ever had to write, but after spending Monday night in a state of sleepless, humiliated misery she was determined to put an end to the whole sorry affair with some shreds of her dignity intact.

If she really had been setting out to ensnare the Earl then she would be seeking to retrieve the situation of the night before. The only way to convince him that this was not the case was to end their connection immediately, however painful that was. Camilla screwed up yet another sheet of expensive hot-pressed notepaper and, pushing back her chair, crossed to gaze unseeing out of the window.

'Oh, Nicholas,' she sighed, resting her hot forehead against the cool window pane. 'I love you…' It was the first time she had ever said it out loud, and although it was hopeless it gave her some pleasure to speak the words she would never say to him.

Outside the weather had turned showery and a cold gust sent a spiteful rattle of rain against the window and buffeted the newly emerged blossom on the shrubs in the garden below.

Camilla returned to her writing-desk and dipped her quill in the standish again.

Miss Knight wishes to convey to the Earl of Ashby her deep regret that he should have overheard the unwarranted speculations of some of her acquaintances last evening. Miss Knight begs his lordship to ignore this incident, attributing it to no more than spiteful tittle-tattle.

However, painful though this is, Miss Knight would wish to take this opportunity to assure his lordship that her intentions, and those of her family, have never been other than those of sincere friendship. A gentleman of his lordship's experience will be able, after careful consideration, to place the correct interpretation upon some of Miss Knight's actions which, however foolish, arose only from an inexperienced and passing affection.

Camilla broke off, nibbling the end of her quill. Well, that was the most difficult part over, and she was not displeased with the tone. She had portrayed herself as, at worst, naïve. It was humiliating, but at least it disguised the true depth of her regard for him. Her fingers drifted unconsciously to the edge of her fichu as she recalled the touch of his lips on the skin beneath. He must never know how much she loved him. Resolutely she dipped the nib again.

Under the circumstances of Miss Knight's imminent departure for Cambridgeshire this letter may also serve as a farewell and an expression of Miss Knight's grateful awareness of his lordship's kind attentions to her family.

The letter seemed to end a little abruptly, but Camilla could think of nothing further to add which would not fatally betray her true emotions or the truth which lay behind its painful composition.

She reached out and tugged at the bellpull, dusting the page with sand while she waited for Samuel to appear.

'You rang, Miss Knight?'

'Please fetch me a candle and some wax and then take this letter to the Countess of Forres's residence immediately.'

Camilla pressed her seal firmly into the melted wax and handed the letter to the footman before she could lose her nerve and snatch it back. She heard the front door shut behind Samuel with mixed emotions. What did she want to happen now? The rational part of her wanted to receive back a polite note begging her to give the matter not a second thought and assuring her that the Earl entirely disregarded anything which had passed the night before. She could almost see the page open before her, the letter ending with polite expressions of his best wishes for the future and a clear, and final, farewell.

Yet the irrational side of her wanted him to send back a missive telling her of his regard for her, and of his intentions to call round to see her as soon as possible.

* * *

But even as Camilla was penning his direction on the folded letter Nicholas was bidding farewell to his sister.

'Why are you rushing off like this, Lovell? I thought you were staying at least another week.'

'No, I only said I might.' Nicholas edged towards the door of Georgiana's bedchamber. 'That is a prodigiously fetching nightcap, my dear.'

Lady Forres patted the lace confection complacently. 'Mechlin lace, the finest. But do not seek to divert me, Nicholas. What are you about? Is this anything to do with Miss Knight?' Her clear blue eyes, so like his own, appraised him from amongst the pile of pillows heaped against her immensely fashionable Egyptian headboard. 'A nice girl, as far as I can tell.'

Nicholas gritted his teeth, but produced a convincing air of uninterest. 'Nice enough, I grant you, but the family is hardly what one would call the best match for a Lovell.'

Georgiana put down her chocolate cup upon the nightstand with some emphasis. 'I have never heard such specious nonsense! Since when have you cared for rank? There is breeding there, and sense. You have no need to marry for money or land, let alone connections! Miss Knight is as charming as she is beautiful.' Infuriated by her brother's silent resistance, she warmed to her argument. 'You complain when I introduce you to débutantes, saying that they are shallow and vapid. Just what are you looking for in a woman, Nicholas?'

Nicholas tightened his lips and regarded his sister through narrowed lids. 'I know precisely what I want in a wife, Georgiana, and I will know it when I see her.' As in fact he had already done, not that he had any intention of confiding *that* error of judgement! 'You seem to forget, sister, that I am not twelve years old. I will thank you not to meddle and to leave me to arrange my own affairs.' Lady Forres said nothing, but from the speculative gleam in her eyes Nicholas knew he had done nothing but arouse her interest. 'Now, I must be on my way. I have to call upon Freddie Corsham before I leave Bath. I will write to you from Town.'

Half an hour later Nicholas found Freddie just risen from his bed, sitting at the breakfast table and eyeing the roast beef with a queasy eye. 'Morning Lovell. Sit down—quietly, damn you!—and help yourself to coffee. Evans, a cup for his lordship.'

'Hung over, Freddie?' Nicholas enquired un-sympathetically. He had had a fractured night himself, but at least he had not got over-indulgence in brandy to add to his troubles. He helped himself lavishly to bread and beef and fell to with sudden appetite.

Freddie watched him liverishly. 'What are you doing here anyway? Thought you were going up to Town before coming on to Abbotsford.'

Nicholas waved away the proffered coffee and accepted a tankard of ale from Freddie's man. 'That's why I'm here. I'm not coming to Suffolk, I'm afraid. Pressing business.'

'What?' Freddie exclaimed, then winced. 'But I promised my mama that you'd be there! Can't let me down now, old boy.'

'I have no choice. I have to return to Town.'

Corsham held a hand to his aching head and groaned again. 'My aunt Cecilia is coming with her bevy of daughters. Mama was delighted that you'd be around—helps balance the numbers and spreads the burden of entertaining them. We haven't got enough men, even with you there. Please come. I am a desperate man.'

Nicholas, seeing his old schoolfriend look so green, almost relented, then hardened his heart.

The last thing he needed was to be among more young women; after the last few days he was determined to confine himself to strictly male company for a while.

He noticed a knowing look suddenly cross his friend's face. Despite the hangover, and his never very alert wits, Freddie was putting two and two together. 'Aha! You don't fool me Nick—you've tracked Mademoiselle Davide down, you cunning dog! You devil!' he added admiringly, seeing Nicholas's mouth tighten. 'I thought you'd given up, but I should have known better. Mind, you've only got until the end of the month to, er, conquer her. I still think Thunderer's safe—and if you come to Suffolk you can ride him and see what you've lost.'

Rejuvenated by his unusual perceptiveness, Freddie seized the knife and carved himself a slab of beef.

'Stop fishing, Freddie, and pass the mustard.'

The two men ate in silence for a while. Freddie's hangover was still severe enough to keep him quiet, while Nicholas had his own thoughts to contend with. Why not go to Suffolk? He did not particularly want to be in Town, that had merely been an excuse for

Georgiana, and the thought of going back to his estates in Buckinghamshire did not appeal. It was those very estates which were tugging at him, making him restless for a new life, a wife, a family. He would undoubtedly dwell on what might have been with Camilla Knight, and that was pointless. That incident, that connection, however pleasurable, was at an end.

'You win, I'll come, Freddie. You've worn me down. But I warn you, if your aunt thinks she's going to marry me off to one of your cousins I'll be on my horse and out of there before you know it.'

Freddie paused, a forkful of meat half-way to his lips, a look of appalled sympathy on his face. 'Good God, man! What do you take me for? I wouldn't wish them on any man, let alone a good friend! No need for alarm, though, I'll hold 'em off!' And for the first time that morning he grinned, wondering why his friend looked so serious.

By Thursday afternoon Camilla had come to the conclusion that two days in a closed carriage had given her far too much time to dwell on the events of the last week. Again her mind ran on the footman's return with the same painful effect as probing a sore tooth with the tongue tip.

'Did you find Lady Forres's house easily, Samuel?' she had asked.

'Oh, yes, Miss Knight. His lordship had gone up to Town, ma'am, but the butler said he would forward your letter.'

'Oh…' was all she had said.

Goodness knows when he would receive the note, but that, now, was of secondary importance. Nicholas had left Bath without so much as a word of farewell, not even the chilliest and most formal note.

The words of Mrs Frobisher echoed in her mind. She had remarked that the Earl was too well bred to make a sudden, humiliating break with the Knights. But that was precisely what he had done, driven by circumstances unknown to Mrs Frobisher, the catalyst.

Mrs Knight was snoozing gently in the corner, the occasional mild snore escaping her. Ophelia had taken the opportunity to remove a novel from her reticule, given to her as a surreptitious parting gift by her friend Miss Laxton, but certain to be unacceptable to her mama.

Camilla leaned back against the squabs and

wished she too could sleep. Last night, spent at a friend's in Oxford, had been convivial, but despite her fatigue she had found it hard to sleep in an unfamiliar bed. She just wished that the journey would end and she could submerge her thoughts in the bustle of arrival at Fulbrook Hall and the warm reception she knew they would receive there.

The rolling outline of the Gog Magog hills was increasingly familiar, as was the rest of the quiet Cambridgeshire countryside through which the carriage was passing. Not far away lay their own old home, now occupied by Cousin Stephen Knight, upon whom it had been entailed on the death of their father. Stephen was a second cousin once removed, a pleasant young man, deeply sensible of the distress his arrival at Nevile's Place must have caused his relatives. Camilla remembered with gratitude the care he had taken to make everything as painless as possible and she looked forward to meeting him again. It had helped, of course, that they had known him for years, and the late Mr Knight, accepting the inevitable with good grace, had done much to introduce Stephen to the estate and its workings. In the event, Mr Knight's premature death had surprised everyone, but the effects of his good sense had meant that the transition had been a smooth one.

She was sure Lady Ellwood would invite her cousin to join the house party, for he too shared the interest in amateur dramatics which their hostess enjoyed so much.

Ophelia slipped her novel back into her reticule and touched her mother on the hand. 'Mama! We are just turning into the avenue.'

'Waah?' Mrs Knight, caught out in her doze, woke with a start, her bonnet over one eyebrow. 'I was not asleep my dear, merely resting my eyes. Oh dear, what has become of this bonnet!'

The carriage wheels were crunching on the gravel as the coachman reined back the team by the front porch. The panelled door swung open and, with her usual lack of formality, Lady Ellwood swept out, almost flattening the butler, who was standing deferentially to one side. She was followed by her husband, both her sons, her daughters-in-law and what, to the Knights, seemed a veritable sea of small dogs and young children.

'Louisa! My dear!' Lady Ellwood waited impatiently for the footman to let down the steps, then enfolded her old friend of more than twenty years in a warm embrace. 'You look so well, dearest! How the Bath air has suited you—I swear you do not look a day older than when I saw you last!'

'emma, how wonderful to see you...' Overcome by emotion, Mrs Knight broke off, fumbling in her reticule for her handkerchief to wipe away her tears. 'It is such a joy…but to be back in Cambridgeshire, where I spent so many happy years…'

'There, there, dear, come inside and have a nice cup of tea,' Lady Ellwood soothed. 'You are tired from the journey. Camilla, Ophelia—my dears, how lovely you have grown!' She linked her arm through her old friend's and made vague shepherding movements with the other hand towards the door. 'Come along, all of you, inside.'

By the next day it seemed to Camilla and Ophelia as if the last three years in Bath had been a dream and they had never been away from the county of their birth. When they had lived at Nevile's Place the two households had been frequent visitors each to the other, and on the most informal terms. Both Lord Ellwood and Mr Knight had been supporters of the Whigs and had spent many an hour in earnest political discussion over their port. Their wives, knowing each other since they were young brides, had against all expectations become firm friends. Louisa Knight, always prone to an excess of sensibility, had found her confidence boosted by her friend's no-nonsense manner and energy. It had never occurred to Emma Ellwood, the daughter of the largest landowner in the area, that there might be any restriction on her doing exactly as she pleased. Aided and abetted by an indulgent older husband, she had soon become mistress of all she surveyed and famous locally for her unconventional house parties.

The present party found itself the next afternoon seated on rugs spread on the hillside overlooking the grounds, recovering from a picnic luncheon of some magnificence.

Lady Ellwood adjusted her parasol and sighed contentedly. 'Just look at this weather! And yet I declare this time last week it was positively cold. I am delighted, for I am quite determined to present our latest dramatic offering in the garden.'

'The garden, Mama?' Her elder son handed his latest offspring to its grandmama and regarded her quizzically.

'Yes, Charles, in your grandfather's grass amphitheatre.' She turned to the Knights to explain. 'You know, my father-in-law was very fond of chamber music and liked to entertain outside to the sound of a small orchestra in the summer? The lawn he created, sheltered by yews and with a raised turf platform at one end, it became quite overgrown—for my husband, as you know, cares little for music. But I have had it restored and I think it will answer perfectly.' Lord Ellwood, who had been sleeping gently under the shade of his hat, opened one eye and regarded his wife indulgently.

There was an immediate buzz of excitement, but Camilla's trained voice cut through it. 'It sounds wonderful, Lady Ellwood. Which piece do you have in mind?'

'Scenes from *The Tempest*, I thought. There are several which are quite unexceptional,' she added hastily, seeing the look of concern on her youngest daughter-in-law's face. 'And so suitable for an outdoor setting.'

Before she went to Bath Camilla would have been the foremost in planning the production, eagerly sharing ideas for casting and production. But now she sat back, leaving the discussion to her hostess, Charles, his wife and Ophelia. It had come as a shock how much she missed the stage, the frisson of excitement and nerves, the applause and approbation of the crowd. She longed to join in immediately with the discussion, but she was wary of exposing her professionalism and deep knowledge. Lady Ellwood knew her too well not to recognise the change in Camilla from the days when she had acted in one of the many charades and playlets that always took place at Fulbrook Hall.

Now she would have to put all her skill into acting the part of an amateur actress! Turning her shoulder on an animated discussion on casting, she smiled at Mrs Francis Ellwood, the somewhat staid wife of the younger Ellwood son. 'Have you taken part in one of Lady Ellwood's entertainments before?' she asked the dark-haired young woman.

'Indeed not,' she replied earnestly. 'Although I am very much looking forward to doing so. Thomas!' She broke off to call to a young child of about two who had escaped from his nursemaid and was toddling determinedly towards the fence separating them from a field of cows. The nurse ran after him and Mrs Ellwood, ignoring her son's wails of protest, turned back to Camilla. 'At first I was concerned about the propriety of play-acting, but, after all, if dear Lady Ellwood is happy to espouse it, there can be no objection. Do you attend the theatre often in Bath, Miss Knight? I believe there is a theatre of some renown in the city, is there not?'

Camilla found herself unexpectedly flustered. 'Er…no, I have not been in the audience often.' That was true enough.

Mrs Ellwood nodded seriously. 'Perhaps you devote more of your time to good works,' she suggested. 'Do you perhaps know my friend Miss Murgatroyd? She is very active in Bath charities, especially in that founded by Lady Isabella King some years ago. Perhaps you have heard of it?'

'I think not,' Camilla replied faintly. 'What is it called?'

'The Society for the Suppression of Common Vagrants and Impostors and the Relief of Occasional Distress and the Encouragement of the Industrious Poor,' Mrs Ellwood recited with justifiable pride.

Camilla firmly suppressed the desire to giggle, and equally the desire to tell Nicholas. How he would laugh! And then she remembered. She had severed all connections; she would never speak to Nicholas again.

'How very comprehensive,' she managed to say, before she was distracted by Charles Ellwood getting to his feet and waving his hat to attract a rider on the track below.

'Oh, look!' Mrs Knight exclaimed with pleasure, shading her eyes with her hand. 'It is Cousin Stephen! How well he looks,' she added, as the young man turned and cantered up the slope towards them. To her disappointment the Earl of Ashby had left Bath somewhat suddenly, dashing her hopes that perhaps there was something between him and her elder daughter. But, although not to be compared to an Earl, Stephen Knight would be a most eligible match for either of his cousins.

Mr Knight sprang down boyishly from his mount, tossing the reins to a footman who hurried forward. He bowed to Lady Ellwood, then, sweeping off his hat, saluted Mrs Knight on the cheek before shaking hands with his cousins and the others present.

Tall, blond and looking younger than his twenty-five years, Mr Knight was blessed with an open and pleasing personality, a conscientious approach towards his estate and tenants and a love of sport. He would never claim to be an intellectual, but his charming manners and willingness to join in and be pleased by whatever his hostess suggested made him a welcome visitor in all the surrounding houses. Those same hostesses—at least, those with unmarried daughters—agreed that it was about time that Mr Knight found himself a wife and settled to domesticity.

He took his place on the rugs surrounding Lady Ellwood, accepted a cold drink and was about to enquire after the Knights' journey when Charles Ellwood exclaimed, 'A fortuitous arrival, old chap, you are just in time to be cast in Mama's latest dramatic enterprise.'

Stephen sat up with enthusiasm. 'Another play, Lady Ellwood? Then count me in!'

Camilla had not realised that her cousin would be interested. 'Do you act, Cousin Stephen? I had no idea.'

'Oh, rather! Over the last couple of years Lady Ellwood has included me in all manner of entertainments.'

'And very good you are too, Mr Knight,' Mrs Charles Ellwood remarked, lifting the baby from her mother-in-law's arms and dabbing its chin with a napkin.

'Thank you, ma'am.' Stephen gave her a charming smile. 'I must confess I enjoy it so much that if the estates ever become mortgaged I will take to the stage as a professional!'

Mrs Knight looked down at her hands somewhat abruptly, Ophelia coughed as though a crumb had caught in her throat and Camilla waved her napkin in front of her face to disguise her mounting colour. 'So warm, is it not?'

'Indeed, somewhat too warm for the children now, I think.' Lady Ellwood got to her feet and brushed her skirts. 'Who will come in the carriages with me and who will walk down?'

Lord Ellwood swung up into the saddle of his cover hack and rode off with his sons to view a barn that needed reroofing. Lady Ellwood, the Mrs Ellwoods and Mrs Knight took the children in the two open carriages, leaving Stephen, Camilla and Ophelia to stroll down the hill back to Fulbrook Hall. Behind them the servants began to fold rugs and pack the hampers into the pony cart taking their time about it in the warm afternoon sun.

Mr Knight offered an arm to each lady, leaving

his horse on a loose rein to follow slowly behind. 'You all look extraordinarily well; the climate in Bath must be congenial,' he commented, but it was on Camilla's face that his warm gaze rested. 'I hope you intend to come over to Nevile's Place: I intend a few changes of which I hope your mother will approve. I would welcome your view first, however, for I would not wish to distress her by altering your old home.'

Camilla smiled affectionately at her cousin. 'You are too kind, Cousin; your sensibility and care for our feelings is much appreciated by all of us. I am sure Mama will be happy with any change that you make, for she will know you have only the best of intentions.'

Ophelia seemed very quiet. Camilla was puzzled, for her sister normally sparkled and flirted in the company of attractive young gentlemen. Surely she did not dislike Cousin Stephen now she saw him for the first time in almost three years? Camilla glanced across at her sister and saw that she was walking quietly, eyes downcast, one hand resting demurely in the crook of her cousin's arm. Perhaps she had a headache? It was unseasonably warm that afternoon.

'We are to perform scenes from *The Tempest*,'

Camilla remarked as Stephen conducted them carefully over the stile and down on to the hard-packed earth of the carriage drive. 'I expect Lord Ellwood will covet the part of Prospero.'

'Well, he is the only really *old* person in our party,' Ophelia said earnestly.

'Ophelia! Really!' Camilla chided. 'Cousin, I despair of my sister, she thinks anyone over the age of four-and-twenty is quite decrepit.'

Stephen turned his charming smile on his younger cousin. 'Then I must confess to being in my dotage, for I have just passed my twenty-fifth birthday.'

Ophelia raised wide blue eyes to his face and protested, 'Oh no, Cousin, I think that is a perfect age for a gentleman!'

Camilla cast her eyes upwards but managed to keep the smile off her face. So that was what was wrong with Ophelia! Well, this should be quite entertaining and would do Ophelia no harm, for Stephen was far too kind to either snub or take advantage of her. And, who knows, he might find he too was attracted…

Cousin Stephen was undoubtedly an attractive and eligible young man, and under other cir-cumstances she too might have harboured a *tendre* for him. But it was Nicholas who filled her thoughts, and at night when she fell asleep it was Nicholas's lips she felt on hers.

Abruptly Camilla asked, 'And what part would you like to play, Cousin? Ferdinand would be very appropriate, of course.'

'An attractive part indeed, if neither Charles nor Francis cared for it,' Mr Knight replied enthusiastically. 'Who would play Miranda? Yourself?'

A season ago at the Theatre Royal in Bath Camilla had played Miranda to great acclaim from both the press and the audience. But that was Mademoiselle Davide, not Camilla Knight, and she doubted whether she would be able to conceal her experience in the part from her close friends.

'Oh, no, I am too old. Ophelia is nearer the right age, or Mrs Francis Ellwood.'

They had reached the house as Stephen remarked, 'That is as may be, but I am sure Lady Ellwood has already decided on her casting and we will have little to say to it!'

Her cousin proved correct, for after dinner, to which Stephen was invited, Lady Ellwood waved aside the gentlemen's attempts to sit over their port and summoned the entire house party into the salon.

'Now then, we must cast our play,' she began briskly, once they had clustered round her as she sat in her wing-chair, the tea-tray disregarded at her side. 'Charles, pass me my tablets.'

Her elder son found the notebook and passed it to his mother. Lady Ellwood flipped over the pages and cleared her throat. 'Prospero: Lord Ellwood. Ferdinand: Mr Knight. Ophelia, you will be perfect as Ariel. Mary and Clara, you will be the Spirits: there should be more than two of you, perhaps the Williams girls will join us if their mama approves. Charles and Francis—you choose between Alonso and Sebastian.'

'And Miranda?' asked Stephen.

'Why, Camilla, of course.'

'Surely I am too old,' Camilla protested. 'Ophelia is nearer to the age of the character than I...'

'I do not think it would be *quite* appropriate, dear,' Lady Ellwood said carefully. 'You and I can look at the text and make one or two...amendments. For propriety's sake,' she added looking across at Mrs Knight. 'And of course, my dear, the part of Ariel must be carefully...er...amended to make it suitable for Ophelia.'

Mrs Knight nodded. 'And the costume too

must be most carefully considered! I will not permit Ophelia to flit about the stage in flimsy gauzes, and that is that!'

At the same time as Lady Ellwood was taking a blue pencil to the Bard of Avon's text—much to the relief of her old friend—Nicholas was stretching his legs in front of a blazing fire in Freddie's study. Lord Corsham had arrived home with his usual insouciant lack of concern for domestic detail and without sending ahead to warn his mama, the Dowager, of his expected date of arrival.

Finnan, the butler, had opened the door on his master without betraying the slightest sign of being discommoded by the arrival of not only his lordship but the Earl of Ashby to swell an already large house party.

'My lord.' He bowed to Freddie. 'My lord.' An equally dignified inclination of the head to Nicholas. 'My lady will be distressed to be from home, my lord, but not expecting you this evening has taken her guests to dine at Lady Robertson's.' He took hats and coats and summoned two footmen with a lift of one eyebrow. 'James, put a match to the fire in his lordship's study. William, ensure their lordships' valets have all the assistance they require. My lord, I will set dinner in the Blue Salon if that is acceptable to you.'

Freddie, never one to stand on ceremony, clapped the butler on the shoulder, causing him to wince more with anguish at the impropriety than at the impact of the blow. 'Just the job, Finnan, no need to rattle around in the dining-room. Mother well, is she?'

'Her ladyship enjoys her normal good health, my lord. I regret that Lady Cecilia has taken to her bed with a severe head cold and that two of your cousins have sore throats.'

'Confined to their beds as well, are they?' Freddie asked hopefully, waving Nicholas ahead of him into the study.

'No, my lord, they have bravely put their discomfort to one side in order to accompany your mother.'

'Oh, yes,' said Freddie vaguely, reaching for the decanter. 'Lady Robertson has three sons; I can see why they have forced themselves to go.'

Finnan, who had ambitions to serve in the most correct and formal household, stiffened his back and swept out.

'Poor old Finnan, I'm a great disappointment to him. He loved working for my father—a great stickler, everything done according to the book, and hell to pay if it wasn't. Brandy?'

Nicholas took the proffered glass and dropped into one of the fireside wing-chairs. He half raised it in a mock salute to his host, but then fell into a brown study, gazing into the flames which were just catching hold of the coals. However well he had suppressed the thought of Camilla on the long journey from Bath, it was at moments of relaxation like this that she filled his mind again.

He put his glass down on the table at his side, knocking his hand against the bowl of pot-pourri as he did so. A faint flower scent rose in the warming air, slightly dusty, but still redolent of the scent of honeysuckle and roses. Damn it! Why could he not forget her? Because she was different, he answered himself. She was beautiful, but then he had known plenty of beautiful women. She was well-bred and elegant, but then there were dozens of more eligible girls on the marriage mart. No, she had *quality*…that was the only word for it. And, whatever she thought of him there was that spark of thrilling sensual excitement that coursed between them every time they touched.

But he owed something to his name... Georgiana might favour the girl, but she did not know that Camilla had made him the butt of every middle-class matron's gossip in Bath. Let alone Camilla's other secret...

'Nick. Nick! Wake up, for heaven's sake, man!' Freddie had obviously been trying to attract his attention for some time, for he raised one booted foot and kicked his friend none too gently on the ankle.

'Ow! What the devil are you doing, Freddie?'

'Just trying to ask you if you want to go up and wash and change before dinner. Wish I had something to think about that produced the same smile on my face...'

'Shut up, Freddie. I was just thinking about my dinner.'

The combination of the best efforts of Freddie's French cook, his brandy and a day spent on the road combined to send Nicholas into a deep sleep, despite his gloomy conviction that he would spend all night thinking about Camilla Knight. His host gave strict instructions he was not to be disturbed, so it was ten o'clock before Nicholas found his way down to the breakfast-room. Freddie, always inclined to think that ten was the crack of dawn, had only just poured himself a cup of coffee, but the Dowager was leaving the room as Nicholas entered.

She paused as he opened the door for her. 'Dear Nicholas,' she patted him on the cheek. 'The Bath air has obviously suited you. And how is your sister?'

'Georgiana is very well, and sends you her best wishes, ma'am.'

'I am sorry to have missed you last night. If my son—' she sent Freddie a withering glance '—ever communicated with his poor mama, then all would have been ready for you and we would all have been at home.' She looked Nicholas up and down with the arrogant rudeness of her class and generation. 'You're as good-looking a dog as your father was—why aren't you married and setting up your nursery?'

Nicholas, normally more than capable of dealing with formidable gentlewomen, flushed slightly. 'I cannot find anyone willing to take me, ma'am,' he said with a slight smile.

'Nonsense. You cannot be trying hard enough.

Never mind, I have a houseful of eligible young women here…'

'Most of them with putrid sore throats,' Freddie muttered through a mouthful of beef. 'And those that haven't have squints.'

'Frederick!' snapped his irritated parent. 'Only Arabella has a squint, and her mama has every hope she will grow out of it.' She smiled again at Nicholas. 'Now, for goodness' sake, both of you, get out in the fresh air—I will see you at dinner.'

Nicholas pulled out a chair and raised an eyebrow at Freddie. 'How nice to see her ladyship in such good spirits.'

Freddie shot him a dark look. 'That's what you call it is it? She's already criticised my haircut, my neckcloth, my complexion—too many late nights, too much brandy, unspecified loose living—and the fact that she thinks my trousers are cut too tight. Oh, yes, and why aren't I married yet.'

Nicholas reached for the rolls and butter and the two men ate in companionable silence for five minutes. Freddie finished first, pushing his chair back and looking out at the bright sky with high white clouds chasing across the sun and casting shadows on the newly scythed grass. 'Looks as though the weather will hold: I've got to see a man about a horse—might as well do it today. Coming?'

Nicholas was only too happy to ride out with his friend, and was too preoccupied with his own thoughts to ask where they were going. It was enough to be out in the fresh air, the horse moving easily under him, the low, rolling countryside green and fertile around them.

Freddie, who was a good landlord, despite his air of caring for nothing but enjoying himself, stopped occasionally and spoke to small groups of estate workers they encountered. Nicholas, looking around as he waited for Freddie to finish talking to a man who was clearing a ditch, saw in what good heart the land was and felt a pang of homesickness for his own estates at Ashby in Buckinghamshire.

They gave the horses their heads after that stop and, watching the sun, Nicholas realised they were heading south-west of Newmarket. Eventually Freddie pulled up as they came over the top of a rise.

A substantial grey stone house lay comfortably in a swell of the hillside, terraced gardens running down to the stream below. 'Fulbrook Hall,' Freddie remarked. 'My godmama's place.' He pressed his horse into a canter again, jumped neatly over the gate into the parkland and led the way through an old Tudor gatehouse towards a sprawling stable block.

The head groom came out as they clattered through the arch into the yard. 'My lord! Good morning, gentlemen. Have you come to see the bay gelding, my lord? Lord Ellwood's gone over to the hunt kennels to see the new puppies, but he should be back in ten minutes or so. Would you care to go over to the house and I'll send a boy to tell him you're here?'

'No, it's all right, Griggs, we'll wait.'

'Did you say Ellwood?' Nicholas demanded abruptly, once the man had turned away, calling to the stable boy.

'Yes.' Freddie looked surprised at his friend's tone. 'Do you know them?'

'No,' said Nicholas slowly. 'No…I just thought I might know someone who is part of their house party this week.' Hell and damnation! Of all the houses, it had to be the one where the Knights were staying. He had known they were not far from Freddie's place—why the devil had he not had the sense to ask Freddie where they were going?

Ellwood was bound to ask them back to the house once he and Freddie had finished discussing the horse—how the blazes could he refuse to join them? Meeting Camilla seemed inevitable. If that were the case then he needed to clear his head and prepare for the encounter.

Freddie was heading with single-minded interest towards the horse-boxes. Nicholas put a hand on his arm. 'Look, old chap, those terraced gardens are just the sort of thing I was thinking of having done at Ashby. You wait for his lordship, I'll stroll over and have a look at them for half an hour.'

Freddie turned, a look of astonishment on his amiable face. '*Gardens?* Damn it, Nick…' But his friend was already striding through the archway. Lord Corsham pushed his hat back and scratched his head in puzzlement. 'Nick's behaving damned oddly. Must be in love…'

Chapter Nine

'This stage is quite superb,' Stephen said enthusiastically, taking Camilla's arm as they strolled
out through the yew arch on to a gently sloping
lawn, enclosed by high hedges and ending in a
low turf platform.

'It is lovely,' Camilla agreed, looking round at the
fresh greenery of the sprouting yew against the
close shaved turf. 'But do you think the audience
will be able to hear well?' She looked up at him, a
little frown of concern between her arched brows.

Stephen Knight looked down into his cousin's
beautiful face and came to the conclusion that he
must indeed be a man in love. Camilla glanced
away, unaware of his thoughts, measuring dis-
tances with practised, narrowed eyes.

'Cousin Stephen, could you go down the

lawn half-way, perhaps—I do not think the audience would extend back from the stage any more than that, do you?' She smiled at him, and he reflected that her air of decision, which in another woman might seem merely bossy, was charming.

He walked away, turned and saw she had climbed the three steps on to the turf platform. She raised a hand to shade her eyes and called, 'A little further back…there, that is perfect.' And she smiled, a smile of pure pleasure, and Stephen looked at the tall slender figure in the pale green muslin gown, jonquil ribbons fluttering from her blonde hair, knotted high for the morning.

Yes, he thought, it must be love. If he could look at all that loveliness and still want Ophelia, not her sister, then he could be sure of his own heart. Ophelia was not as perfect, not as intelligent, not as poised…yet it was Ophelia who made his heart beat faster, who could make his normally fluent tongue stumble over the most commonplace words. But she was very young, and her elder sister not yet betrothed—under such circumstances would Mrs Knight consent to an engagement?

Camilla lifted the pages of script in her hand

and took a moment to choose her piece. She felt almost happy this morning. The sun was shining, she was acting again, among friends. Almost she could forget Nicholas. She took a steadying breath and launched into Miranda's words on first seeing Ferdinand. *'I might call him a thing divine, for nothing natural I ever saw so noble.'*

'That was perfect,' Stephen called, strolling back towards the stage. 'I could hear every word. The only problem will be if we cannot all achieve the same projection of our voices as you can.'

'I am sure everyone will manage perfectly well with a little practice. Shall we try a scene now we are here?' Camilla asked as he joined her on the platform.

'I fear you will show me up dreadfully, dear Camilla. Everyone spoke of your talent, but I had no idea how beautiful your voice was. Why, if it were not such a shocking thing to say, one would think you almost a professional.'

It was indeed a shocking thing to say, and it explained why Camilla coloured and turned hastily away. 'Oh, I have had lots of practice. After all, we have been play-acting together for years,' she said modestly. 'Shall we try this scene?'

Stephen took his part and conned the pages. 'Here?' He cleared his throat and read, his voice strong and clear in the morning air.

> *'Wherefore weep you?'*
> *'At mine unworthiness, that dare not offer what I desire to give; and much less take what I shall die to want...'*

The words came back to her with perfect clarity. The pages of the script fell unheeded from her fingers and she was back on the stage at Bath playing Miranda, the heroine. Stephen, swept along with her reading of the verse, found himself gazing not into Camilla's eyes, but into Miranda's. The garden around him became Prospero's island and he stepped towards her, his face rapt with the magic of Shakespeare's love poetry as Miranda declared her love for the young prince Ferdinand of Naples.

'I am your wife if you will marry me.' She took his hands, her gaze intent upon his face.

> *'If not I'll die your maid. To be your fellow You may deny me, but I'll be your servant Whether you will or no.'*

Stephen, in thrall to the part, gathered her into his arms and a silence fell as she finished speaking.

Then the tranquillity was broken by the sound of one pair of hands slowly applauding. Stephen, expecting no one but another member of the house party, hardly moved, but in his arms Camilla froze. Her expression of shock slowly turned to dismay, and at that he did turn, to see a tall stranger standing regarding them sardonically from the nearest archway. No wonder Cousin Camilla was embarrassed—to anyone not aware of the house party's theatrical plans it would appear a most compromising and improper scene.

The man was wearing riding dress which Stephen, a man always careful of his own appearance, recognised as coming from the hands of a master tailor. 'Weston!' he exclaimed, his voice carrying clearly in the clear morning air.

'Schultz, actually,' Nicholas corrected drily, strolling towards them, hat and whip in hand.

Camilla stood staring at the two men, her head in a whirl. Why were they talking about *tailors*? And, more to the point, what was Nicholas doing here? Her heart jolted painfully as she watched him move confidently across the short cut lawn: the length of his stride emphasised by the leg-hugging riding-breeches, the polish on his high-topped boots, the sunshine glancing off his dark, burnished head. She fought down the impulse to throw herself into his arms, cover him with kisses, tell him how much he was filling her thoughts day and night.

His next words drove all thoughts of love out of her head. 'I do not think I have heard such feeling and projection since the last time I was in the Theatre Royal in Bath.'

Camilla felt the blood draining out of her cheeks. She stared at him, the realisation of what had just happened sinking home. He had seen her act as Mademoiselle Davide. In Bath she had chosen to ignore the slight references he had made, the hints he had dropped that he might have guessed at her secret. But now he had seen her—Camilla Knight—acting, as well as she had ever acted. And he was letting her know that he knew she was Mademoiselle Davide.

Ruin was staring her in the face, yet there he was, shaking hands with Stephen, introducing himself as though they had met at White's, acting as if this were a normal social occasion.

Would he betray her? Surely he was too much of a gentleman to do so deliberately, but then a slip of the tongue, a little too much wine over the gaming tables, a word in the wrong ear and the world of the Knight family would come crashing down. All hopes for Ophelia's come-out would be dashed, all hopes of the affection that she was sure was budding between Ophelia and her cousin Stephen would be at an end.

Nicholas looked up from where he was standing with Stephen and made a bow. 'Miss Knight.'

She bowed stiffly in return. 'My lord.'

Stephen, a sociable man, was delighted at the discovery that the two were acquainted. 'You know each other, then? But of course, from your reference to the theatre may I assume that you too have just come from Bath? A fine city with many diversions.'

Nicholas smiled thinly. 'Indeed, I found it most…diverting. The theatre, the Sydney Gardens, the rides…'

The colour had returned to Camilla's face with a rush. She knew she was blushing. To cover her confusion she turned away and strolled to the turf steps down to the lawn. But it only gave

Nicholas the opportunity to walk towards her and offer his hand to assist her descent.

She forced herself to meet his gaze and was startled by the chill of his blue eyes and the hard set of his mouth. It seemed that he was still angry with her, as angry as he had been as they parted company in the Sydney Gardens.

Low-voiced she asked, 'Have you received my letter?'

'I have received nothing from you,' he replied in clipped tones.

Mr Knight, seemingly oblivious to the atmosphere, enquired if his lordship would join them in the drawing-room for a glass of Canary. 'Not that this is my establishment,' he added hastily, 'but Lord Ellwood is out and about his estate and I am sure he would wish me to offer your lordship his hospitality.'

'Thank you, Mr Knight, but I am here with a friend. A small matter of a horse he wishes to discuss with Lord Ellwood—he is down at the stables now, awaiting his lordship's return.' His tone with Stephen was pleasant but guarded and his eyes on the young man were assessing. If it were not for the fact that he had made it all too clear that everything between them was over, she might almost have thought him jealous. But that could not be; it appeared that Nicholas Lovell did not forgive and was prepared to extend his dislike to her friends, Camilla reflected bitterly.

To her relief the scene was interrupted by the arrival of Freddie and Lord Ellwood, a gun-dog at their heels.

'There you are, Nick!' Freddie called. He turned to Lord Ellwood to make the introductions, then waited, smiling genially, as Lord Ellwood, in his turn, introduced his house guests.

Freddie bowed to Camilla, his eyes sparkling at the sight of such a beautiful young woman. 'Miss Knight, how do you do? And Mr Knight. Your brother, I presume?'

Camilla was probably the only one who heard Nicholas murmur, 'Hardly brotherly behaviour!' She ignored his reference to the scene he had interrupted and, obviously, misinterpreted. Her heart gave a little jump. Could he be jealous?

'Mr Knight is my cousin, Lord Corsham. Do you make a long stay in the country? The weather is so very pleasant, and the countryside so green: we are finding it such a refreshment after residing in Bath.'

Freddie fell in beside her as the entire group strolled back towards the house. He was not the most perceptive young man in the world, but there was something about Miss Knight that piqued him, piqued his memory. Surely he would have remembered such a gem if he had met her before, yet there was something about the timbre of her voice, her gracious carriage, the turn of her head on that long neck…

He pulled himself together and replied to her questions. 'Not sure how long I'm staying, Miss Knight, but my mother felt I'd been away from the estates too long so it's goodbye to the attractions of Bath and Town for a while. Still, Lovell's keeping me company, and Mama always enjoys Nick's company. Feels it's a challenge to get him married off, don't you know. Mind you, she says he's impossible to please. Still, she won't give up.'

Camilla, only too aware of Nicholas's rigid back ahead of them, could not resist dropping a barb to test whether Nicholas was listening. 'Oh hush, Lord Corsham,' she said lightly with a little laugh, 'Lord Lovell will overhear you, and I am sure he would not wish to be the subject of tittle-tattle.'

Nicholas's neck, between the line of his freshly trimmed hair and the collar of his coat, reddened. So he was listening, as aware of her as she was of him.

Lady Ellwood was very pleased to find her drawing-room full of unexpected guests, especially her godson, of whom she was inordinately fond. Freddie dropped a kiss on her cheek and, settling in a chair beside her with a glass of Canary, brought her up to date with all the news from his mama.

Lord Ellwood, Stephen and Nicholas seemed deep in conversation on the subject of gun-dogs, but Camilla was constantly aware of his cool gaze flicking over her from time to time. She felt very exposed: Mama and Ophelia had joined the two Mrs Ellwoods in a carriage drive, and never had she wanted their presence so much.

The morning was so warm that the long floor-to-ceiling windows had been opened fully. Camilla stood by one of them, grateful for the cooling breeze on her cheek, and tried to order her emotions. Standing across the room from her, watching her coldly, was the man she loved, the man in whose hands not only her reputation but that of her entire family rested. She wanted to throw herself into his arms and kiss him, yet she wanted to hit him for being so cold, so seemingly hostile. She was so afraid of what he might do with the knowledge of her secret, yet through the fear anger too was rising. He knew, he must have known almost from the beginning about her double life—just how did he intend to use that knowledge?

Abruptly she ducked under the raised sash and stepped down on to the flagged terrace. No one called after her, so she ran lightly down the steps and into the sunken rose garden where she could sit, hidden from the house. With a soft moan she put her head in her hands, cupping her hot cheeks in her palms. How could she desire Nicholas so much yet be so angry with him? How could she love him so, yet be so fearful of his motives? Surely being in love with someone shouldn't be this painful, this confusing?

'You cannot keep running away from me, Camilla.' He had followed her and was standing a few feet away, his arms crossed, his face as hard as his voice.

Camilla sprang to her feet. 'I am not running away,' she denied hotly. 'I just do not choose to be in your company.'

'Indeed? I would have thought you would be seeking me out, imploring me to keep your secret.' His eyes were blue chips of ice and she felt her own anger rising to meet his. At last he was being plain with her, at last he was admitting he knew she was Lysette Davide.

'I would have thought that unnecessary. I believed that your *honour* as a gentleman would have assured your silence. I have obviously misjudged you.' It was taking all her composure and her training to stop her voice from shaking with the anger that suffused her frame.

Nicholas smiled without warmth, without humour. 'Madam, I would do everything in my power, upon my *honour*, to protect the reputation of a *lady*.'

Camilla gasped as though he had thrown cold water over her. 'You…you…' She took two angry steps towards him, raising her hand, fingers curled.

'No, you don't, you hellcat.' He grasped her wrists, his fingers curling tightly around the thin bones and holding fast. 'If you had let me finish I would have added that your sister and your mother are both ladies whose reputations I would do much to protect.'

'And I, I suppose, can go to the Devil?' she asked wildly, her breath tight in her breast.

'Well, madam, you seem hell-bent on getting there without help from me. I hardly expected you to mope when we were apart, but I had not realised the speed with which you would be looking for the next likely mark. Mr Stephen Knight inherited the family estates, did he not? He has no title, of course, but I am sure that sort of financial security is attractive.'

Camilla stopped struggling; it hurt her wrists too much. Fighting for composure, she said icily, 'My friends are not of your business, but I believe I told you when we first met that I am not the sort of actress that could be bought.'

'Gifts of money—or anything else, come to that—hardly seem necessary in your case.' He stood looking down into her furious eyes. 'Every time you have been in my arms it seems all I need to do is this.' And he released one wrist, running the back of his fingers down her cheek-bone, down to the swell of her breast.

Camilla reacted, but fractionally, fatally, betrayingly too late. His touch mesmerised her, set the blood in her veins alight. But it was not that which held her still for that fatal second: it was his face, softened suddenly as those hate-fully cold eyes dropped from hers and his lips parted slightly as his fingers touched her skin.

Her freed hand came up, but unlike in Sydney Gardens he was ready for her. 'Oh, no, Camilla, you do not get a second chance.' Her wrist was back in that hard, imprisoning grasp and she was jerked against his chest, held tight as he found her mouth and kissed her.

He had kissed her before and each time it had been a kiss which had lived in her memory, coloured her dreams, sent her pulses racing. But this was a kiss meant to punish, to show his anger, to assert himself as master and not a man enslaved by a woman's charms.

Camilla tightened her lips into a thin line, fought with every muscle in her neck and back to resist him and kicked futilely with her thin slippers against his leather-booted shins. He responded by holding her even closer, crushing her breasts against his coat-front, seemingly seeking to draw every breath from her body.

Just when she felt sure she would swoon, he let go of her and she staggered back, grasping the arm of the bench to stay upright. Nicholas's eyes raked her coldly, taking in the crushed muslin and the disarrayed curls. 'You have my word I will say or do nothing which would harm your sister and mother. But you, madam, had better look to your behaviour. If you persist in throwing yourself at every man who crosses your path you will have no need of my assistance in betraying yourself. Or is your unfortunate cousin your insurance, your key to a *respectable* future?'

Nicholas spun on his heel and stalked back towards the house. There was the sound of voices on the terrace and then she heard Nicholas, his voice assured, calm, as though he had spent the last ten minutes discussing the weather, joining the conversation.

Camilla ran across the rose garden away from the voices, in through the open breakfast-room windows and up the stairs to the sanctuary of her room. Mercifully no one saw her.

She slammed the door behind her, turned the key in the lock and threw herself across the bed, pummelling a wild tattoo on the pillows with her clenched fists. 'I hate you, I hate you, I hate you!' she cried, her voice muffled against the bedding. Finally, out of breath, she rolled over on to her back and lay, gazing upwards, unseeing, the beautifully moulded plaster ceiling a mere blur.

Time passed, marked only by the chime of the little clock above the fireplace. Finally, as it struck the hour, she sat up, some semblance of calm restored. So this was real life, this was the reality she had been ignoring for so long, over-confident in the belief that her scandalous double life would never be discovered.

She had taken to the stage with all the courage of ignorance, a blind belief that she would always remain undetected. And as time had passed the belief had grown to the point where the nagging fear had dwindled into nothing and she had felt invincible in her deception.

Well, it had taken one man to shatter that illusion. One man to teach her that not only could she not keep her secret but she could not flirt with love. And now she had paid the price on both counts. The man she loved thought she was an immoral, deceitful hussy. The gossips of Bath were shredding her reputation and she had shocked herself to the core by the discovery of her own deeply sensual nature. Even now, hating Nicholas as she did, she knew that if he walked in, smiled at her, kissed her, caressed her, she would melt into his arms again.

For an independent, spirited, intelligent woman this was a humiliating discovery to make.

* * *

'There, that is the last of the invitations,' Lady Ellwood said with satisfaction, passing it to the younger Mrs Ellwood, who added it to a neat stack of gilt-edged cards.

Camilla laid aside the volume of Scott's *Waverley* without much regret and asked, 'How many is that?' The stack by her hostess's hand looked somewhat larger than she had imagined it would be.

'Forty, all told, but I doubt whether we will get more than thirty acceptances. The Hodgkinsons are away with his mother in Harrogate and I have invited the Canon, but he rarely accepts social invitations. Lady Browne may or may not…it will all depend on her bad leg.'

Camilla paused to steady her breathing and then enquired in a tone of studied nonchalance, 'Have you invited the Corshams?'

Lady Ellwood rose from her escritoire and crossed the drawing-room to tug the bell-pull. 'Tea, I think, my dears.' She settled in a rustling of puce draperies next to Camilla, picking up the novel as she did so. 'Ah! Sir Walter Scott. How are you finding this one? I have just finished

Guy Mannering, which I found somewhat slow in places.'

'I agree. To be honest, Lady Ellwood, I do not know why I persist with Scott; I am always disappointed. I will put this one aside and re-read *Emma*. But you were saying about the Corshams?' She wanted to add 'and their guests' but dared not.

'Indeed, so I was. Ah, there you are, Wilkins. Tea, if you please, and a plate of macaroons if Cook has any to hand.'

'Yes, my lady.' The footman bowed himself out and Camilla fought down the desire to scream.

'The Corshams?' she prompted again, wondering if it were her imagination or if Mrs Francis Ellwood was regarding her with interest.

No, she was not mistaken. 'Why, Miss Knight,' said Mrs Francis in a rallying tone. 'I declare you are very anxious to hear about the Corshams' party. Can it be that a certain young gentleman has the fortune to have attracted your sympathies?'

Camilla felt the blush spreading to her very hairline. 'Oh, indeed not! Why…why it is simply that it is such a very large house party from all accounts, and I know so few of them…'

Oh, what a mull she was making of this! If the other ladies had not been suspicious of Nicholas and herself before, they certainly were now, thanks to her embarrassed reaction.

Lady Ellwood regarded her with approving interest. 'Well, so that is how the land lies! Of course, I am very biased, but he is a wonderful catch: how he has remained single for so long defeats me.'

If the earth had opened up to swallow her Camilla would have been thankful. All she could do, while wondering wildly how Lady Ellwood came to know so much about Nicholas, was murmur, 'He is?'

'Of course!' Lady Ellwood looked surprised. 'The Corshams are a very old family, very distinguished. And of course the estates have always been so well managed. Added to that there is all the property in London too.'

'Oh!' Camilla felt quite dizzy with relief. 'Oh, you mistake me! I hardly know Lord Corsham— the merest acquaintance—although obviously the most amiable gentleman—there is not the slightest attachment between us, not on either side…'

I am protesting too much, she thought wildly. But fortunately further conversation was forestalled by the arrival of tea, and the necessity of giving Wilkins detailed instructions on the delivery of the invitations.

The weather continued warm and dry for the rest of the week, much to Lady Ellwood's relief. If it had been inclement they would have had to repair to the ballroom, but in its classical perfection it was hardly reminiscent of a scented isle, complete with spirits and shipwrecked sailors.

On the night of the performance the ladies were gathered to don their costumes and *maquillage* upstairs in Lady Ellwood's large dressing-room. The Misses Williams had enthusiastically agreed to make up the number of Spirits required, and their mama had been placated by the utter respectability of their garb. Camilla had reflected privately that no Spirit could have moved through the air in that quantity of fabric, but they made a pretty enough ensemble.

Mrs Knight was still clucking about Ophelia's costume, although after much work with the blue pencil the role of Ariel had been rendered suitably anodyne. 'Oh, the skirts of your tunic...' she wailed. 'Whatever you do, do not spin round and show your ankles!' She tweaked at her younger daughter's hems and enquired anxiously, 'Are you wearing both petticoats?'

'Yes, Mama,' Ophelia replied dutifully, edging her bare feet well out of sight under the chair. Her eyes were sparking and her colour high. Her mama put it down to excitement and stage nerves: what her feelings would have been if she had realised that Ophelia had every intention of luring her cousin Stephen into the conservatory that evening in the hope of provoking a declaration, heaven only knows.

Mrs Francis Ellwood, who was possessed of both a sharp eye and an equally sharp tongue, was watching Camilla. She was untwisting her hair from the rags in which she had knotted it all day, and arranging it carefully into the disarrayed locks suitable to a young woman stranded on a desert island.

'You are very quiet, Miss Knight,' Mrs Ellwood observed. 'Are you suffering from stage fright?'

'Oh, yes, indeed,' Camilla replied glibly. In fact she had no fear of either the audience or of the quality of this excellent amateur performance. No, it was the knowledge that Nicholas would be there, watching her. He would be able to compare her acting tonight with what he had seen in Bath. Then the thought struck her: there was another danger. Nicholas, after all, already knew the worst; this evening's performance would not change his opinion of her one whit. But Lord Corsham had also seen her act in Bath—what if he, seeing her tonight, put two and two together?

Then Lady Ellwood's betoqued head appeared around the door. 'Hurry, my dears, all is ready for us to begin!'

Swept along with the discipline of long practice, Camilla's mind cleared of all other thoughts and fears. Treading carefully in her bare feet, ignoring her mother's shriek as she realised that both her daughters were scandalously unshod and stockingless, she made her way downstairs and across the lawn.

The applause that greeted the final act was tumultuous. As she took her bows between Lord Ellwood, robed and bearded as Prospero, and Stephen, flushed with triumph as Ferdinand, she felt once again the familiar rush of excitement and achievement.

The principals stepped back to let the more

minor players take their bows, followed by a bashful group of footmen and bootboys who had been pressed into service as shipwrecked mariners.

Lord Ellwood was almost incoherent with admiration. 'My dear, you were magnificent. Equal, if not above, anything I have seen in Drury Lane. Why, one would have believed you were indeed in love with Ferdinand—all, of course, in the most refined taste, as one would expect of you.'

The applause swelled again and the three of them moved into the centre of the stage to receive the approbation of the invited guests. Camilla curtseyed low, and on either side the men raised her hands to their lips in gallant salutation.

Defiantly she raised her head and stared out over the improvised footlights into the blurred faces beyond. Virtually everyone had accepted the invitations, over forty people had attended, but it was Nicholas she sought, and Nicholas she found.

Their eyes met and locked, his dark and stony, hers bright with excitement and challenge. Suddenly seized by the desire to shock Nicholas out of his coldness, Camilla turned to Stephen, who was at her side, and threw her arms around him. Automatically her cousin picked up the cue, and they stood locked in the theatrical embrace which had marked their final kiss in the performance.

As Stephen released her Camilla sought Nicholas's eyes again defiantly, but he was no longer looking at her. His head was bent as he brushed a speck from the sleeve of his impeccable evening-coat. By contrast, beside him Freddie Corsham was clapping with gusto, his ingenuous face beaming, his voice ringing out, 'Bravo! Bravo!'

Dear Freddie, far too conventional, far too stolid ever to imagine that a woman like Miss Knight could have led a double life. No, there was nothing to fear from Lord Corsham.

Finally the applause died down and everyone trooped back to the Red Saloon for refreshments. Mrs Knight, scolding furiously, hurried her daughters upstairs and insisted on them putting on stockings and shoes before they could join the rest. 'What can you have been thinking about? Ophelia, as soon as you have tied your garters put on this fichu. Camilla, where is your shawl? You will catch your death…'

The Knights descended the staircase, modestly

shod, silk shawls draped over their elbows, and found themselves instantly the centre of attention. All the men clustered round and Ophelia, more than a little piqued, realised that all their attention was on her sister. Even Stephen, she observed with acute annoyance, had taken Camilla's hand and showed no sign of wanting to let it go.

Nicholas had not been the only one to observe that final embrace on stage with anger. Ophelia found herself quite cross with her elder sister: surely she could not be casting out lures for Stephen? She told herself that it was simply the thrill of the performance: still, it would not do to take risks with the man she was now convinced she loved. Unaware that Lord Lovell was observing the play of emotions on her pretty face, she let her brow furrow in thought.

Lady Ellwood had sent round the champagne and Camilla accepted a glass from Freddie, releasing her hand as she did so with a smiling glance at Stephen. Behind him she saw Nicholas, his face unfriendly as his glance took in both the clasped hands and the shared smile.

Stephen stepped back and was lost to her sight in the crowd which immediately surrounded him.

Feeling suddenly vulnerable, she turned to Freddie. 'Did you enjoy the performance, Lord Corsham?'

'I'll say I did! Dashed fine, and you, Miss Knight, were magnificent!'

'You are fond of the theatre, my lord?'

'Indeed, yes! Don't understand many of the plays, unless they're comedies, of course—too much philosophising. But I enjoy the acting and the atmosphere. And I have to say, Miss Knight, that you were equal to anything I have seen on the professional stage. Why, I would have to say you are as good in your talent as Mademoiselle Davide of the Theatre Royal in Bath.'

A very dry voice remarked, 'Really Freddie, what a very shocking thing to say to Miss Knight.'

Freddie blushed furiously and shot his friend a hunted look. 'I say, Miss Knight, I do apologise. Lovell, damn good thing you stopped me there. Oh damn…I mean, I apologise for my language, Miss Knight. Don't know what came over me! Not that I meant that you and she were in any way the same…I mean you are a lady…er…'

'Stop digging, Freddie,' Nicholas remarked, not unkindly. 'I think the hole is quite large enough already.'

'There is Godmama waving at me,' Freddie burbled frantically. 'Please excuse me, Miss Knight…'

There was a long silence. It was finally broken when Camilla said frostily, 'Poor Lord Corsham. You did not have to put him to the blush in that way. It was not kind.'

Nicholas shrugged. 'I thought it for the best. You should thank me: he is unlikely to speculate again on any similarities between yourself and Mademoiselle Davide.'

Camilla, knowing he was right, but in no mood to forgive him, watched silently as he turned to take two more glasses of champagne from a passing footman. Erect and immaculate in the formal evening wear, Nicholas was by far the most striking man in the room, but in contrast to the laughing faces all around, his was set and cold, his eyes glittering.

She glanced round, hoping no one had noticed the tense exchange between them, and realised she had lost sight of her sister. Instinctively she cast round for their cousin. Nicholas, observing her scrutiny enquired, 'Who are you looking for?'

Startled by his abrupt question, Camilla replied without thinking, 'Stephen.'

Still conning the room, she did not notice Nicholas's lips tighten. Then she saw the backs of Stephen and Ophelia disappearing into the conservatory. Ah, good. If their cousin did not declare himself tonight, he was not the man she thought he was. A small smile touched her lips as Nicholas turned back and handed her a glass.

'Something amuses you.' It was a statement, not a question.

'Why should it not?' she replied coolly. 'Everyone is enjoying themselves—except, apparently, you, my lord.'

'Indeed, you seem to have had quite a little triumph.'

'And you grudge me that? How ungracious you are, my lord.' The glass she raised to her lips was not quite steady.

'You are very unconciliatory for someone so much in my power,' Nicholas remarked tightly.

'In your power?' Camilla's brows arched haughtily. 'Why, indeed, I might be, but I have no fear that you would say anything to cause Mama and Ophelia distress. If you betray me, you betray them.'

'You are pleased to be confident in me, Miss Knight.'

'I have every confidence that you would do nothing to diminish your own good opinion of yourself, my lord,' she fired back. 'Excuse me, there are other people I wish to speak to. Friends of mine.'

Weaving her way through the crowd, exchanging nods and pleasantries and receiving compliments as she went, Camilla finally found herself alone on the terrace. She held up her hot face to the cool rays of the moon. An owl hooted from across the park but otherwise she was alone, and the noise from the room behind was cut off abruptly as the heavy curtain swung back across the window.

So that was that then. There could be no going back from that chilly parting. Not wanting to be disturbed, Camilla trod slowly down the mossy steps and into the shadows of the topiary which dotted the lawns. As she did so the noise from the reception room swelled again and instinctively she turned, drawing back against a yew peacock.

A shaft of moonlight suddenly pierced the light, high cloud and illuminated the man standing on the terrace as surely as a theatre limelight. Nicholas, a champagne flute in his hand, stood for a long moment scanning the garden. Then he said out loud suddenly, viciously, 'Oh, to hell with it. To hell with it all,' and threw the glass into the darkness.

There was a sharp tinkle as it hit the slender trunk of a young tree and then he was gone.

Chapter Ten

At ten o'clock the next morning Camilla sat at the breakfast table tearing pieces off a bread roll and sipping at her now cold tea. Her preoccupation was fortunately going unnoticed amongst her companions, who were variously suffering the effects of too much excitement, too much champagne and too little sleep.

Only Ophelia was bright and breezy, her voice loud and animated, causing her mama to say repressively, 'Do try for a little moderation in your volume, my dear, we are all feeling rather fatigued this morning.'

No one but Camilla appeared to notice how Ophelia's eyes sparkled and what an uncommonly pretty gown she had put on that morning. Camilla could hazard a shrewd guess as to why her sister had threaded pink ribbons through her hair to match the rose quartz necklace encircling her neck and why she was almost bubbling with expectation and excitement.

Her suspicions were confirmed when there was the sound of hoofbeats on the drive, followed shortly by the bang of the knocker on the front door.

Lord Ellwood clutched his aching forehead and grumbled, 'Who on earth is calling at this hour?'

His elder daughter-in-law got to her feet and peered carefully around the draperies at the long window. 'I do believe it is Mr Stephen Knight's horse—that handsome new bay he was riding the other day.'

No sooner had she spoken than the sound of Stephen Knight's voice was heard in the hall and the butler appeared. 'Mr Knight has called requesting the favour of a word with Mrs Knight, my lady. I have shown him into the Blue Salon, madam, while I enquire if Mrs Knight is at home to visitors.'

A look of puzzlement crossed Mrs Knight's face. 'Mr Knight? For me? I cannot conceive what that might be about. Perhaps a problem with one of our old servants... Would you excuse me for a moment, Emma dear?'

Camilla shot Ophelia a very hard stare, but her sister looked back at her with wide, innocent blue eyes. 'More tea, Camilla?'

Aware that Mrs Francis Ellwood was watching the by-play with her usual beady regard, Camellia merely said, 'Thank you, Ophelia,' and passed her cup.

A silence fell, during which no one was so ill-bred as to speculate on the reasons for Mr Knight's early visit. After ten minutes or so the door to the breakfast room opened again on the butler. 'Miss Ophelia, Mrs Knight requests your presence in the Blue Salon.'

Ophelia laid her napkin down with great care, stood up, smoothing the skirts of her pretty muslin gown, and followed the black-clad figure with a demure smile of apology to her hostess.

This time Mrs Francis Ellwood could hardly contain herself until the door shut once more. 'Well!' she exclaimed, putting down her chocolate cup with emphasis. 'We can all guess what that is about!'

'Can we?' Camilla asked, calmly and repressively.

Mrs Francis was not to be snubbed. 'Oh, you

think your mama might not agree to Mr Knight's proposing to your sister as you yourself are not betrothed? After all it is unusual for the younger sister to be turned off first.' Her black eyes were snapping with excitement and a not unpleasurable sense of the elder Miss Knight's discomfiture. After all, as she would observe later to her sister-in-law, Mrs Charles, 'A charming and talented enough young woman, but she does put herself forward for an unmarried girl. Her sister's success will perhaps put her nose out of joint.'

Lady Ellwood, sensitive to the undercurrents around her breakfast table, chided her daughter-in-law gently. 'Yes, we really should not speculate on such a delicate matter. Lord Ellwood, will you be dining at home this evening? I must tell Cook how many covers are required.'

At that point Mrs Knight almost burst into the breakfast-room, her face glowing with excitement, her hands clasped tightly to her bosom. 'Camilla dearest, Emma, dear friends... such joy! Dear Mr Knight—Stephen—has asked for little Ophelia's hand! Such a surprise, such a happiness!'

Lord Ellwood, ever practical, remarked, 'An

excellent match, and brings the estate back into the family to boot! You are to be congratulated, madam.'

Mrs Knight, much struck by this thought, sank down in her chair, her handkerchief clasped in her hand. 'Oh, yes, how happy her poor dear lamented papa would have been to see this day!' And promptly burst into tears.

What with mopping up her mama's tears, receiving congratulations from the assembled guests and then, somewhat belatedly, repairing to the Blue Salon to chaperon the newly engaged couple, Camilla did not have much leisure at first to continue brooding on her own troubles.

Her sister and cousin, although receiving her good wishes politely, made no secret of their desire to be alone. Mindful of her mama's wishes, Camilla could not allow that, but she did retire behind a large potted palm and gave them what privacy propriety would allow.

The lovers withdrew to the bay window and, heads close together, exchanged murmured conversation. Camilla sat back and tried to discipline her mind to making lists of items for her sister's trousseau. Then she realised the others had fallen silent, and in parting the fronds saw that Stephen had bent his head to kiss Ophelia gently on the lips.

It was such a chaste, touching and innocent caress that Camilla felt a lump rising to her throat. She had not the heart to intervene and drew back into her corner. But all hope of occupying her mind with wedding lists had been shattered by the sight of that salute. Unknowingly her fingers strayed to her lips, as though feeling again that last angry, punishing kiss that Nicholas had pressed on them in the rose garden.

He would never kiss her now with that gentle adoration that Stephen was showing her sister. Perhaps once there had been a glimmer of hope for them, but now all that was left was the anger and mistrust and that undeniable sensual attraction that sparked between them whenever they touched.

Finally her mama reappeared and Stephen reluctantly took his leave, agreeing plans for the ladies to spend the next day at Nevile's Place, where Mrs Knight could indulge in an orgy of list-making and Ophelia could reacquaint herself with what would be her new home.

Amid the excited bustle of the house, Camilla slipped away into a corner and tried to concentrate on being happy for her sister and not on thinking about a pair of hard blue eyes finding hers across the garden as the play came to an end.

The owner of those same blue eyes was at that moment standing beside Lord Corsham on the banks of his trout lake, which his friend regarded with deep displeasure. 'Damn me if it's not those poachers,' Freddie was saying. 'I keep giving orders for it to be restocked, but every time I go fishing I never catch a darned thing.'

Nicholas stooped to pick up a stick and stirred the mud at the lake edge with it. Freddie, glowering moodily at the water, skimmed a stone across the glittering surface as if hoping to provoke a rise of fish. They stood together silently, Freddie's mind entirely on fishing, Nicholas's on something quite different.

He stirred the muddy water unseeingly, his mind's eye full of Camilla: her slender form caught up in Stephen Knight's embrace on stage, her passion as she declared the lines of the play, the defiance as she deliberately sought his eyes across that crowded garden.

God! He wanted her: wanted to kiss her, undress her, make love to her… He should never have kissed her like that in the rose garden. It was not her he had been angry with, it was himself—and he had taken that anger out on her. Why had he let himself get involved with a woman like that? A woman in her position? She was everything he had hoped of finding in a wife—and she was totally ineligible. Gripping the stick, he hurled it with all his strength at the opposite reed bed, sending a heron flapping upwards in panic and showering Freddie with muddy water.

'I say! Dammit, this is a new shooting jacket, Nick!' He glanced up as more droplets fell. 'Oh, hell, now it's raining! And if we go back to the house we'll be driven out of every room by giggling girls. What was my mother thinking about asking them all to stay?'

'Let's run away, Freddie,' Nick suggested abruptly, hunching his shoulders against the sudden shower. 'Now—today.'

Freddie drew him under a sheltering willow. 'Good idea, but where? London's dead, too early for Brighton, no hunting, too early for shooting anything decent...'

Nicholas frowned. Where indeed? Anywhere without memories of Camilla Knight would do.

At that moment, like a messenger from the gods in answer to their question, a rather damp footman rounded the coppice.

'Letter for you, my lord,' he called as he drew near, adding rather darkly, 'Mr Finnan said I was to bring it out, said you wouldn't be far from the house.' He glanced down at his mud-spattered stockings and pulled his jacket tighter around his shoulders.

'Thank you, Jenkins. Cut along back now. No point in you getting any wetter. Come on, Nick, we're half-way between the house and the village—let's go down to the Corsham Arms and have a brandy by the fire.'

Ten minutes later the two of them were sitting comfortably, legs thrust out towards a crackling fire, the soles of their boots steaming gently and bumpers of the landlord's best brandy at their elbows.

'And not a woman in sight,' said Freddie gratefully, slitting the seal on his letter. 'Oh! It's from George—says Bath's pretty dull now that Mademoiselle Davide's no longer there and we've gone. Says he hasn't forgotten that wager and time's running out...' He conned the rest of the page and added, 'Here we are, the answer to our prayer! George says, had we heard about a big mill near Buckingham in three days' time?'

'A prize-fight?' Nicholas raised an interested eyebrow. 'Who's involved?'

'Alfred Dyson, the Slough Bull, and the challenger is some character called Patrick Shaughnessy. Never heard of him, but George writes that he's trained with Thomas Cribb and the smart money's going on him.'

'Capital! Write back to George and invite him and Hendricks to meet us at the Black Horse in Buckingham. The mill won't be far out of town—probably at Rickett's Farm—that's where they usually hold them. Then we can all go on to Ashby afterwards and I'll promise you a week without any giggling girls! We can play cards and drink claret if nothing else.'

'Damn good idea,' Freddie agreed. 'Tell you what, I'll get my groom to hack Thunderer over along with my curricle and team and you can try him out—see what you've missed, not winning that bet over Mademoiselle Davide.' He shot Nicholas a mischievous glance. 'Don't glare at me, Nick, I've noticed you studiously ignoring my invitations to try him out while you've been here. Not like you to be a bad loser.'

'I've not lost yet; I've got until the end of the month.' Nicholas retorted, draining his glass and getting to his feet. 'Come on, it's stopped raining. Perhaps I'll throw a leg over him this afternoon.'

'Well, I suppose it is asking for a lot, expecting you to seduce a woman when you don't know where she is,' Freddie said fairly to his friend's retreating back, then wondered why the back of Nick's neck suddenly flushed red.

It was past luncheon, and still raining heavily, when the same postboy who had delivered George's letter reached the Ellwoods' estate. The butler, tutting under his breath at the damp state of the letters, brought them to his lordship on a silver salver.

'Bills, bills, one for you my dear—what handwriting your nephew has to be sure!—one for you, Charles, another bill and a letter for you, Mrs Knight. Somewhat rain-spattered, I regret to say.'

Mrs Knight slit the seal, unfolded the single sheet within and squinted at the heavily crossed and recrossed lines. 'Camilla dear, can you read it? It is from Miss March—our old nanny, you know,' she explained to Lady Ellwood. 'I cannot make out a word. She *will* write too close together—a habit I was always fearful she would pass on to you girls.'

Camilla rose and took the letter, smoothing down the page and scanning it in the light from the window. 'If only we could persuade her to use a second sheet, but her habits of economy die hard and she will always cross the page to save the postage. Oh dear, someone has died…ah, her brother-in-law.'

'That was hardly unexpected, my dear,' Mrs Knight intervened.

'Yes, but her sister collapsed and was quite ill, and then poor Margaret had to nurse her and the strain in turn made her…oh I cannot read this; it must be *ill*. And now there is trouble with the will and the property and can you ask Mr Brooke to look at it because of course she won't—surely that cannot be "consume"?—oh no, it is *presume* to approach him herself.'

'What a moment to get involved with this!' Mrs Knight exclaimed in exasperation. 'Of course she cannot be expected to know of Ophelia's happiness, but even so, why she does not simply send a note to Mr Brooke herself I cannot imagine. She knows him well enough.'

'Now, Mama, do not be harsh. You know what trouble poor Marchy has always had with her sister and her nerves. And of course they are in Cheltenham, so she cannot speak to him in person.'

Mrs Knight flapped her hands irritably. 'Well, can you write to Mr Brooke, my dear, and explain? I am sure he will sort it all out in a moment. Such a capable young man,' she added to Lady Ellwood. 'Just like his dear father.'

'Very well, Mama, and I will write to Marchy as well and tell her not to worry. She sounds quite worn down, poor woman.'

Writing to Mr Brooke proved more difficult than Camilla had anticipated. She felt she needed to explain the background to Miss March's current dilemmas, but at the same time she did not feel authorised to go into too much detail about the affairs of her old nurse's sister. Two drafts of Lady Ellwood's expensive hot-pressed paper were consigned to the waste-paper basket. One version had been too wordy, the other too abrupt. Really, it would be so much easier simply to speak to Mr Brooke direct.

Camilla put down her quill and wandered over

to the window. The glass was streaked with rain and a wet peacock wandered by, his soaked tail trailing on the gravel. He looked as miserable as she felt.

Oh dear, this would get her nowhere! She felt drained by the anticlimax at the end of the play, drained by trying to be happy for Ophelia when her own heart was in pieces. The house felt like a prison. All people spoke about was weddings and lists and trousseaux;
 and not being able to share fully in her sister's happiness made her feel so grudging, so guilty...

Then as she sat at the desk and dipped her quill once more in the standish the idea struck Camilla. It was so simple! She would go to Cheltenham, collect Miss March, reassure her sister that they would consult with Mr Brooke and then return home to Bath! By doing so she could leave Mama and Ophelia happily engaged in wedding plans. She would leave Nicholas far behind and in looking after Miss March and helping her with her affairs she would have something to occupy her unruly thoughts.

Dropping the pen back on its stand, Camilla sprang to her feet and ran lightly to the Blue Salon, where the ladies were sitting.

'Mama, it occurs to me that if I were to return to Bath at once and speak to Mr Brooke myself it would be much easier than trying to arrange this all by letter—and quicker too. I do not like to think of poor Miss March worried by this after all the strain she has endured these past few months. And,' she added shrewdly, 'if I return and require a chaperon, then Marchy will *have* to leave her sister. I could go to Bath by way of Cheltenham; it would not be so very far out of my way. After all, the unfortunate woman will never gather up her nerves if Marchy is always there beside her.'

Mrs Knight's furrowed brow spoke of her doubts at the wisdom or propriety of this scheme, but her elder daughter added hastily, 'And I could set in train the orders for Ophelia's trousseau. Linen and so forth. There is much that will not need a particular decision by Ophelia…and I can ensure that Miss Forbes will be free to devote herself to Ophelia's gowns.'

It worked, as Camilla had known it would. Her mother's face brightened. 'What a good scheme, my dear. And if you could have a word with Madame Le Brun about hats…she is after all, the best in Bath.'

Lady Ellwood nodded encouragingly. 'We will, of course, place both the chaise and servants at your disposal for tomorrow, Camilla, if you are determined to go.'

'Tomorrow? I had thought to set off at once.' Her mind made up, this delay seemed intolerable.

'No, no, not to be thought of,' said Lord Ellwood, who had come into the room and overheard the plans. 'That heavy rainstorm last night has brought a tree down over the millstream. The road is flooded and although they are digging drainage channels to carry the water off on to the fields it is best to leave it to tomorrow and make an early start then.'

But Camilla, fired as she was by the desire to return home—and the desire not to think about Nicholas again—remained restless. After luncheon she donned stout walking shoes and her pelisse and set off across the park, determined to see the state of the mill and the river for herself.

Despite the storm of the previous night, the day had now become warm, and she quickly took off her bonnet, swinging it by the ribbons as she squelched across the grass of the park towards the mill which she could see beyond a distant stand of trees. Everything gleamed wet and green in the watery sunshine and the smell of burgeoning growth filled her nostrils with the restless scents of spring.

Finally, panting somewhat with the effort of walking across the heavy ground, Camilla arrived close to the riverbank. The area around the old mill was thronged with men and horse teams and she craned to see what they were doing. But the bank was too high and at her feet a small ditch, its bottom silted with wet mud and weeds, barred her way.

Clear water was running off the fields into the ditch, making it far too wet to ford. Camilla decided to follow its course, certain that somewhere she would be able to cross, and sure enough after a few minutes she came upon a crossing place where an old plank had been laid from bank to bank. The track to the mill lay beyond.

Picking up her skirts, Camilla set foot cautiously on the wood. It dipped, but seemed firm enough, so she edged out towards the middle of the eight-foot span. Half-way across she began to wonder at the wisdom of what she was doing. The plank was bowing and she cast an anxious eye at the distance which yet remained.

Gingerly, she stepped forward, testing the strength of her bridge. The clear spring air was suddenly full of the sound of powerful hoofbeats and instinctively Camilla looked up to see who the rider was. As she did so, she and the plank wobbled, her precarious foothold gave way, and she teetered wildly, arms spread out for balance.

She caught a glimpse of a great black horse, of a familiar figure astride it, and heard Nicholas's voice call her name. It completely destroyed both her concentration and equilibrium. The next moment Camilla was standing up to her knees in cold water. She gasped in shock and dismayed discomfort as her shoes filled with mud, seeping through her stockings and between her toes.

Seconds later she was being dragged, none too gently, on to dry land. Nicholas was grasping her arms above the elbow, his fingers hard even through the thick pelisse. And, despite the fact that she was now out of the ditch, he showed no inclination to release the hold.

Camilla, although she would have denied it vehemently, had cherished a very detailed fantasy about the circumstances under which she and Nicholas would have their next encounter. She would be exquisitely gowned and groomed and on the arm of some impossibly handsome and unimpeachably aristocratic gentleman who had just laid his heart and his fortune at her feet. She would be able to dismiss with a cold glance the presumptuous greetings of Lord Lovell, who would, by this time, have realised how mistaken he had been in her.

And instead she was wearing a very ordinary gown, a positively dowdy pelisse, her hair was in rats'-tails from the damp wind and her skirts were mired to the knees. She could have screamed with fury and humiliation.

'Unhand me, my lord!'

'Certainly, Miss Knight.' Nicholas let go of her as abruptly as he had seized her, causing Camilla to slide once more down the slippery grass slope.

'Oh! Help!' She flailed wildly for balance, caught his gloved hand and was hauled towards him, this time on to the hard surface of the track. Her cheeks flushing hotly, Camilla realised she had nowhere to go. She could hardly flounce off over that treacherous plank—even if one could flounce with one's boots full of ditchwater. And pushing past Nicholas towards the mill would only expose her to the interested gaze of a dozen yokels.

Defiantly she raised her eyes to meet his, as if daring him to comment on her predicament. At her sides her fingers clenched tight until the seams of her kid gloves creaked. And Nicholas—Nicholas merely stood there, his horse's reins looped over negligent fingers, his clothing, despite his rescue of her, immaculate, his blue eyes dancing and at the corners of his mouth just the faintest twitch of amusement.

'Don't you dare laugh at me!' she stormed, stamping her foot. It was a mistake. There was an unpleasant squelching noise and mud oozed out of the lace holes of her boots. Nicholas, quite unforgivably, laughed out loud.

All the anger drained out of her, leaving her feeling cold, miserable and verging on the edge of tears. Camilla squinted furiously in an effort not to cry. She knew the end of her nose was going pink; all the better to match her cheeks, she thought in despair. Her skirts dragged coldly at her legs and she felt her stockings dragging too, dankly. 'Oh, just go away!' She averted her eyes quickly, determined that he should not see her tears.

'Oh, Camilla, don't cry!' His arms came round

her, warm and comforting, and despite herself she melted into them.

'No, I'm all muddy,' she protested feebly, making no effort to free herself from the strength of him.

'I know, and very pathetic you look too,' Nicholas said, his voice warm.

'But someone will see us.' Her voice was muffled against his riding-coat.

Nicholas took a step back and held her at arms' length, looking into her face. His own had lost its amusement. 'Whatever is the matter, Camilla? Worried that word might get back to Cousin Stephen and make him think twice about making you an offer?'

'Stephen?' Her cousin was the last thing on her mind. Camilla struggled to follow his train of thought. 'But Stephen has made an offer.'

'And it has been accepted?' Nicholas demanded abruptly.

'It has, my lord. And why should that be any of your business?' Ignoring her wet skirts and disarrayed hair, Camilla drew herself up and regarded him with some *hauteur*. 'Or is it your opinion that Mr Stephen Knight is too re-spectable to marry into our family?'

'Doubtless he feels that after his very public display of affection at the very end of the play he has little choice but to make you an offer.'

'Make *me* an offer?' Camilla regarded Nicholas as though he had run mad. 'My lord, you have quite mistaken the case. Stephen is engaged to marry Ophelia.'

For a long moment she could not read his face, then he said softly, 'Oh, poor Camilla.' His gloved finger traced her cheekbone. 'No wonder you want to cry. Is that what sent you out for a walk on this damp afternoon?'

Camilla was so furious that she was out of his grip and across the plank bridge before she was even aware of moving. Safe on the other side she stood, anger shaking her slender form, and stormed at him. 'You, sir, are presumptuous, impertinent and, and…jealous! How dare you speak of my cousin in those terms? I am delighted that he and Ophelia have found happiness together and I never want to see you again so long as I live!'

Nicholas swung up on to Thunderer's back, checking the horse's immediate inclination to canter off and his own to put the animal at the ditch, ride after Camilla and scoop her up on to the saddle in front of him. He watched the muddy figure stumble away across the wet, tussocky meadow, then pulled the horse's head around and rode off. He thought of her words all the way back to Freddie's. Jealous? Him? What a ludicrous notion. Why, dammit, he could have any woman he wanted—including the sanctimonious Miss Knight. But the pure and respectable Miss Knight had a double life, however reluctant she was to admit it. How dared she lecture him?

More and more furious, he dug his heels into Thunderer's black flanks and gave the stallion its head. He almost flattened Freddie as he came clattering into the yard, powerful emotion still coursing through his veins. Tossing the reins to the groom, who led away the sweating animal, he dragged off his tight gloves.

'You certainly put him through his paces, Nick,' Freddie remarked, sauntering over the cobbles to perch on the mounting block. 'Damn good animal, isn't he? Shame you'll never get to own him. I know it's not the end of the month, but surely you'll concede you've lost the wager?'

His friend's eyes when he looked at him were glittering strangely and Freddie had the uncanny feeling that it wasn't him that Nick was looking at. 'I wouldn't be too sure about that, my friend. I can take Thunderer off you any time I wish.'

Chapter Eleven

Camilla closed her book of tablets with a snap and threaded the pencil through its ribbon loops before tucking it into the reticule which sat on the carriage seat beside her. The sound of the horses' hooves changed as the chaise turned into the yard of the inn and she picked up her bonnet and replaced it on her head, tying the grosgrain ribbon in a bow.

'Oh! We're here, miss!' Mathilda the maid said with a squeak of excitement. 'Ooh, it does look *big* Miss. And aren't there a lot of people about?'

Camilla reflected wryly that virtually every-thing they had encountered along their route that day had seemed big to the little chambermaid. Mathilda had never set foot beyond the village before and was quivering with the excitement and the responsibility of being a *real* ladies' maid

Camilla, who had set herself resolutely to construct the most comprehensive list of personal and domestic linen that her sister could possibly require when married, had been constantly distracted from her task by cries of wonder and amazement from Mathilda. But that too had been a welcome distraction from thoughts of Nicholas and her own appallingly unladylike behaviour yesterday. The man seemed to bring out the very worst in her, which was a very lowering reflection.

The postillion had jumped down to open the carriage door for her, and as she stepped on to the cobbles Camilla realised that for once Mathilda had not exaggerated. The yard was thronged with people of every class and station and with vehicles ranging from modest gigs to at least one elegant equipage with a coat of arms emblazoned on its gleaming black door.

Camilla lifted her skirts carefully to negotiate a puddle and found herself the object of an unashamedly admiring member of the dandy set, his quizzing glass trained upon her ankles. She shot him a frigid glance, then, turning her head, realised that the interest was shared by a very down-at-heel ruffian, a terrier under his arm, who was lounging against the mounting block.

'Come, Mathilda, don't dawdle,' she said sharply, leading the way towards the inn door. Lord Ellwood had recommended this hostelry most particularly: what on earth was afoot to transform it so?

The landlord was just inside, wiping his hands on his vast white apron and looking harassed. Around him there was a throng of potboys carrying out tankards of ale to those waiting outside, a valet demanding assistance in getting his master's trunk taken upstairs, and a small child wailing because its kitten, taking fright, had dived under the oak settle.

The man saw Camilla and his expression changed from harassment to dismay. 'Oh, I beg your pardon, ma'am, but as you can see we're terrible busy today. There's no private parlour left, I'm sorry to say, but if you would care to step through to the back room with your maid, my wife will attend you there.'

Camilla raised her eyebrows and began to draw off her gloves. A servant came in with her valise and waited at her side. 'I am Miss Knight. You should have a room for me, bespoken by Lord Ellwood's messenger this morning.'

The landlord looked even more flustered. 'Oh

dear, ma'am. We did get the message, and there is one room for you, ma'am, because the gentleman who had ordered it was taken ill on the way here, but I don't know if you'll be wanting it, things being as they are.'

At that moment a somewhat boisterous group of young bucks swaggered in calling for ale and clapping one another on the shoulders as they shared a jest. The landlord hastily opened a door and ushered Camilla out of the passage. 'You see how it is, ma'am, no place for a lady.'

'Lord Ellwood assured me that the Black Horse was the most respectable hostelry in Buckingham. Are you telling me that this is not the case?'

'Well, ordinarily, ma'am,' he said with some pride, 'I wouldn't hesitate to make that claim myself. I say we keep the most comfortable house, the finest food and the best-kept ale for fifty miles around! But you see, it's the prize-fight over at Rickett's Farm tomorrow, and the town is packed out. It's a big fight, you see—the Slough Bull against a new Irish challenger.' He licked his lips eagerly. 'There's a lot of money riding on it, ma'am, and that's brought them all in from miles around.'

'So I see. I have no interest in such matters,'

Camilla replied with some asperity, but inwardly her heart was sinking. So much for setting out alone: at the first hurdle everything was going horribly wrong and for some reason she did not feel able to rise to the challenge with her usual confidence. 'Well, is there another inn you can recommend, somewhere quieter?'

The man shook his grizzled head. 'Not this side of Chipping Norton, ma'am. As I said, this is a big fight, they're coming from all over and putting up where they can.'

'*Chipping Norton!* Why, that must be all of twenty miles away! I have driven from Cambridge today and have no desire to drive any further than I have to.'

'It's nearer thirty mile, ma'am, to the Prince's Arms, which is the nearest I could recommend to a lady with any confidence under the circumstances,' the man said apologetically. 'Look, now, you sit down—you won't be disturbed here—and I'll get my wife to wait upon you. You can have a look at the bedchamber, ma'am, and see what you think. But you'll have to eat in your room. There's no private parlour to be had, and you'll not want to be seen in the public rooms.'

The landlord left to summon his wife. Camilla gazed around the little parlour, her spirits lowering by the minute. So much for independence, for activity to chase thoughts of Nicholas from her mind and make her feel in control of her life once more! Raucous laughter swelled from the public bar beyond and she clutched her reticule, her fingers tight on its handle. With long experience in the Green Room she had thought herself more than able to cope with any awkward situation: now, more than anything, she wanted the reassuring presence of a man, of Lord Ellwood, of Stephen, of Nicholas...

The door opened and Mathilda came in looking scared, her little face pinched with worry. 'I don't like it here, Miss Knight. It's full of undesirables, it is. Can we not find another lodging?'

With someone to look after, Camilla rallied her spirits. 'Now, Mathilda, don't look so afraid. The landlord's wife is coming to attend us and show us to our room. We will be confined to it until tomorrow morning, I am afraid, but we will be comfortable, I am sure. We must make the best of it,' she added briskly, and was rewarded by seeing the maidservant brighten at this show of confidence.

Mrs Whitwell, the landlord's wife, proved to be a cheerful little bird of a woman, very sensible of the delicacy of Camilla's position. 'Now, you just come along with me, ma'am, and we'll soon have you comfortable. A nice little room, if a little out of the way. Not that that's any bad thing today,' she added.

Loud voices echoed down the passage demanding, 'More ale, and hurry up about it!'

The Black Horse was a substantial, rambling establishment which appeared to have been added to almost by whim over the centuries. It fronted the main street of Buckingham, growing backwards and sideways to eat up the gaps between the other houses beside it and to surround the great stableyard.

Camilla's head spun as they went up and down short flights of steps, crossed landings and finally arrived at a large panelled door. Mrs Whitwell peered round it and then ushered Camilla and Mathilda through and into a parlour with other doors leading off.

'I'm afraid the parlour won't be available to you, ma'am,' she apologised. 'And all the rooms off have been taken by a party of gentlemen,' she added warningly. 'But down here—' she disappeared down a narrow passage '—here's your chamber, ma'am. It's quiet—well, as quiet as anywhere will be in Buckingham tonight—and no one's any reason to come down here. There's a truckle bed for your maid, and a table and chairs over here by the window.' She bustled across and tugged back the curtains to let in more of the late evening light. 'Now, I'll bring you a nice cup of tea, and then when you want your dinner—or anything else—just you pull the bell over there, ma'am. I'll attend you myself, never fear.' She bobbed a curtsey and bustled out.

Camilla paced round the room slowly, watching her maid unpack her overnight valise. Mathilda, her spirits restored, went about her new duties with a pride and care that brought a small smile to Camilla's lips. The girl was rising to this challenge, and was probably even now constructing a dramatic retelling of that afternoon's events for the servants' hall.

They drank their tea when it arrived and Mrs Whitwell lit the fire. Seated by the window, Camilla gazed down into the alleyway below which was all the view the room afforded. The view of the crowns of a large number of hats, both smart and disreputable, was entertaining for a short while only, and Camilla was soon re-gretting being so forgetful as to fail to pack something to read. Sitting brooding, trying not to think about that last mortifying encounter with Nicholas, she was brought back to the present by a sharp pang of hunger.

Looking over her shoulder, Camilla realised that not only was the light in the room quite dim, but that Mathilda had curled up on the truckle bed and, her hand beneath her cheek, was fast asleep. The clock on the mantel shelf struck seven rather tinnily and Camilla tugged the bellpull. At least dinner would provide a welcome diversion and occupation, and she could retire to bed afterwards. Doubtless those attending the prizefight would set off at the crack of dawn, so she would find the inn more con-genial in the morning.

The clock struck the quarter and she realised that no one had answered her summons. Impatiently she tugged at the cord again and was rewarded by the entire length falling at her feet, leaving a frayed end beyond reach above her head.

Camilla gave a sharp, exasperated sigh. Now what was she going to do? She thought briefly of rousing Mathilda, but the girl looked so young and so tired that she hadn't the heart to send her off into the noisy bustle of the inn. She turned the key and opened the door, listening. But there was no sound of movement or voices from the private parlour beyond, so she stepped out, closing the door behind her, and walked along the short stretch of corridor and into the room. The doors were all safely shut and the passage beyond empty.

Emboldened, Camilla walked across, and had nearly reached the far passage when she heard the sound of booted feet striding towards her and then taking the short flight of stairs two at a time. Her heart thudded, and she looked around wildly for somewhere to hide. A second later the man she least—and most—wanted to see in the world strode in to the parlour, his face alive and animated.

They stared for a long moment at each other and then almost as one they took a step forward and stopped. Camilla felt as though she was being torn in two: one part of her just wanted to throw herself into Nicholas's arms, but another part could recall only too clearly their angry exchanges over the past few days and Nicholas's mocking, bitter words on the riverbank. She stood watching him like a wary animal, ready to turn and run at the first sign of aggression.

'Camilla, my dear…'

His voice sounded so tender! Was he then so happy to see her? had he followed her? 'How did you know I was here?' she managed to say.

'I did not know. I had no idea you had even left Cambridgeshire. I left because I could not bear it there any longer. The thought of a bachelor party at my home following this prize-fight seemed an ideal distraction from what was ailing me.' His smile was rueful.

'I could not bear it either,' Camilla whispered. 'And, it seems wicked to say so, but the sight of Ophelia's happiness stung like a burn. I had to be busy and my old nurse needs me, so I left.'

Nicholas opened his arms and she walked into them instinctively, desiring only to be in his embrace.

'Camilla, darling, I cannot believe you are really here,' he whispered into the soft mass of her hair. 'Camilla, look at me…'

She raised her eyes to his and saw him smiling down into her face. Her heart almost stopped in her breast as he lifted one finger to trace the full, sensual curve of her lower lip. 'Nicholas…I…'

'Shh.' He bent and swept her up in his arms, and in one stride had shouldered open a door. He set her down inside the room as he heeled the door closed behind him. Glancing round, Camilla realised she was in his bedchamber. His many-caped driving-coat had been thrown carelessly over a chair, but his valet had obviously already unpacked his valise and evening clothes lay out ready on the bed. Her heart gave a little thud of happiness mixed with fear at the realisation of what she was doing and where she was.

Camilla knew she ought to go now, this moment. If anyone saw her here she would be utterly compromised. But somehow she just did not care, because Nicholas had turned from the door and she was in his arms again. He was kissing her gently at first, then, as she responded, with increasing passion, his tongue exploring, demanding, sending wild thrilling urges coursing through her.

All the anger that had been between them had miraculously disappeared, without a word being said. The anger had become passion and Camilla realised hazily that that was what it had been all the time.

But thought was not easy, and sensible,

prudent thought impossible. Nicholas's lips were moving down the column of her throat, kissing, nibbling, teasing the soft flesh there, the pulse throbbing against his lips. Camilla entwined her fingers in his hair, compelling his head down to the swell of her breasts. He pushed impatiently at the lace of her fichu until his lips rested hot on her skin.

With a groan he raised his head and, looking deep into her eyes, pushed her gently back on to the bed, quite heedless of the shirt, neckcloth and immaculate tailcoat which were crushed beneath their weight as he joined her there.

Camilla realized that somehow she had lost both her kid slippers and that Nicholas's fingers were trailing shockingly up her foot, her ankle, the curve of her calf to her knotted garter.

'Nicholas…darling…stop, we should not…' It was a terrible effort to say it, she felt as though she was fighting all her instincts, the clamouring desire of her body, and above all, the waves of happiness that they were together, that the anger had gone, that he needed to be with her.

'Camilla, hush.' He paused, his fingertips caressing the bare flesh of her thigh. 'Do not be afraid. I love you, I want to be with you, but I only want what you are willing to give me. You must know I want to be with you…always. Finding you here is like a miracle; I thought I had lost you for ever.' His lips dropped once more to her breast, teasing, licking the aroused tip.

Camilla stiffened at the shock, at the pleasure he was giving her, then his words struck home. This man she loved had just told her that he loved her too, that he wanted to be with her, always. He wanted her to be his wife, she realised deliriously, as his fingers moved once more to stroke the silky softness of her inner thigh.

Nicholas shifted his weight above her and for the first time she felt his arousal. The heat of him burned through the fine lawn of her gown and his breathing was ragged, catching in his throat. She gazed up into his face, saw his eyes intent with passion. She put up her hands and cradled his hot face tenderly. 'Nicholas…' She let her fingers stroke across his cheekbones, her heart brimming over with love for him.

She knew she should not be doing this, should not be here with him, but he loved her as she loved him, and they would be married. Driven by mutual passion, they were only anticipating the inevitable—and that could not be wrong, could it?

'Camilla…my darling, I love you, I want you, but only if you want me too. You know what I am asking, don't you?'

His fingers were doing things which made it difficult to think, to breathe, to do anything but arch gasping into his embrace. In answer to his question all she could do was seek his mouth blindly, clinging to him as he took her into realms of pleasure she had never known could exist.

Suddenly, shockingly, a chorus of male voices filled the air, shattering their hidden sensual world. Boots clattered on the parlour floor, chairs scraped, and the sound of valises being dropped on the boards reverberated through the unlocked door.

Nicholas swung off the bed and in one movement turned the key in the lock, standing listening intently with his back against the door panels. Camilla scrambled up against the pillows, instinctively gathering the disordered lace of her bodice together in one hand. 'What…?'

'Shh!' Nicholas whispered urgently. 'It is the others—my friends. They must not find you here.'

'Others? Which others?' she whispered back,

dismayed, her heart thudding in her chest, her whole body aching with interrupted passion.

'Freddie Corsham, George Marlow and William Hendricks,' Nicholas murmured, crossing the room and tugging his neckcloth back into some semblance of order. He tucked his shirt-tails back into his breeches and shrugged into his jacket. Stooping to the mirror, he raked his fingers swiftly through his disordered hair where Camilla's searching fingers had locked in it. 'Are you here alone?'

'Yes, I have only my maid. I was on my way to Cheltenham,' she whispered. It seemed somewhat late in the day to be discussing whether she was chaperoned! 'Why…what are they doing here?' she whispered frantically. All it needed was for Mathilda to be awakened by the men's voices and come looking for her for all to be quite lost.

'They are here for the prize-fight and to meet me,' he murmured. 'Give me ten minutes and I'll get them downstairs.' He looked at her white face and crossed to kiss her reassuringly on the lips. 'Don't worry, my love. It will be all right. Trust me.'

'I trust you, Nicholas,' she whispered back against his lips, her eyes huge in her face.

'Stand behind the screen while I open the door,' he urged. 'Remember, give me ten minutes.'

Camilla stood behind the screen which surrounded the washstand and heard the door open and close. Nicholas's voice, raised in greeting came back clearly through the panels, as did the responses of his three friends. Camilla hastily retied her garters, pinned her fichu back into place and did what she could with her tousled coiffure.

Emerging from behind the screen, she saw her left slipper by the bed. She lifted the coverlet and peered underneath, but there was no sign of the other shoe. Puzzled, she cast around the room, but still could not find it. She would have to risk lighting one candle, for the room, lit only by the firelight and the reflected light from the yard, was very dim now. Groping on the mantel she found some spills which caught quickly from the smouldering fire. But even with the candle in her hand she could see no sign of her other kid slipper.

She was starting to panic when she heard Nicholas say rousingly, 'Come on, stop sitting around here in this fug. Let us go down to the saloon bar and see how the betting is going. I have sovereigns burning a hole in my pocket even if you do not.'

To her relief she could hear the sound of chairs being pushed back and of the men rising to leave. Then a voice she recognised as Lord Corsham's rang out. 'Here! What's this? Upon my oath, there's a pretty little slipper if ever I saw one! And where's the lady, eh? Nick, you dog, you've not been here an hour! That is good going even for you!'

This sally was greeted with laughter, a few spicy comments which brought the blush to Camilla's cheeks, and speculation about who the hidden beauty could be. A voice she had never heard before said, 'Come on, Nick, don't be greedy. Introduce us to the lady!'

Terror lent speed to her feet and she virtually ran across to the door and twisted the key in the lock. The click sounded awfully loud and was obviously audible to the men outside. A cheer went up, and the second voice said banteringly, 'A shy one, eh? Well, Nick, we aren't going to move from this room until we meet your ladybird. Come on, Hendricks, ring for dinner and a couple of bottles of claret: who knows how long Nick's modest companion will take to emerge?'

Nicholas's mind raced. If the hidden woman had been a member of the muslin company then he would have no reason to hide her; they were all men of the world. But by refusing to reveal his companion he was as good as admitting it was a lady of quality with a reputation to lose. If he told them this was the case they would behave like gentlemen and leave while she came out, but Freddie at least might put two and two together— he certainly would if he saw Camilla next morning about the inn. And how had she arrived at the inn? In Lord Ellwood's carriage? If that were the case, his coat-of-arms would be on the doors. Damn it! Was there no way out of this coil?

'Nick? Just who have you got in there?' George Marlow asked slyly, putting his feet up on the table with the unmistakable air of one who was going nowhere.

Inside the room Camilla had pulled herself together and was casting around for escape. She crossed to the window, but looking out realised it gave out on to the main inn yard, still thronged with coaches and ostlers. No escape that way, even if she could have climbed down the ivy which clustered around the casement.

She brought up her hands to her lips in a gesture of despair and then saw her fingertips were sooty from the taper she had lit at the fire. It seemed at that moment as though the plan arrived in her mind complete, without the need for further thought. She could not leave this room as Camilla Knight, but she could act her way out of it!

Frantically she threw open the clothes press doors, rummaging recklessly amongst the carefully folded garments. There, gleaming in the subdued light, was the answer to her prayers.

The dressing-gown was an extravaganza of oriental silk which would have pleased even the exotic tastes of the Prince Regent. Dragons writhed across it, breathing fire in slashes of colour. She pulled it out and held it up against her: it was long, it must be full-length on Nicholas—against her it pooled on the boards. Camilla pulled off her dress, heedless of the ripping sounds she created. She swathed the dressing-gown around her body, arranging the folds and securing it with the cord which had caught back the bed curtain. She had another use for the sash, long, wide as a cummerbund and lavishly fringed.

With a practised hand she wrapped it round her head, totally enveloping her blonde hair in its folds and with the help of a tiepin creating a perfect turban. She lit a second candle and blew out the first. As she'd hoped, the wick was charred enough to provide enough black to darken her brows and lashes dramatically. She cast round for further cosmetic aid and smelt, before she saw it, the pot of geraniums which rested on the window ledge, still warm from the evening sun. Two petals crushed against her lips reddened them outrageously and she was transformed from a demure young lady into an exotic creature.

Out in the parlour Nicholas's mind was racing desperately. Appeals to his companions' better natures, bribery and outright threats had all failed. Pleading had merely made them more obdurate, and the arrival of the claret set the seal on their determination to enjoy themselves.

George waved the waiter away and poured the wine himself, pushing the glasses across the table to his seated companions in turn. 'Sit down, Nick, and relax: we are not going anywhere, so you may as well resign yourself to showing us your hidden beauty.'

'Over my dead body,' Nicholas responded grimly, taking the proffered glass and drinking deep. As he spoke the unmistakable sound of the key turning in the lock froze them all. Four pairs of eyes turned to the door of Nicholas's chamber. Three pairs were alight with mischievous curiosity, the fourth with appalled resignation. Well, they were all old friends of his: however much they might tease him they were gentlemen too. He knew he could rely on their discretion—but he was only too aware of what an ordeal this was going to be for Camilla.

The door swung open on to complete silence, broken only by the sound of four wine glasses being set down on the table and a hoarse whisper from George. 'By all that's holy—it's…it can't be…it's Mademoiselle Davide!'

'Nick! You lucky devil!' Sir William gulped, swinging his boots down off the table with a thud.

The apparition swayed languidly into the room. '*Oh, non monsieur*. I can assure you luck has nothing to do with it.' Mademoiselle Davide reached Nicholas's side, smiled up into his rigid face, then, with a sensual possessiveness which made Freddie moan faintly, ran her fingers down his cheekbone, along his jawline and let her hand rest lightly on his lapel.

He bent, appearing to nuzzle her ear furthest from the onlookers and whispered, 'You little witch. I've been dying a thousand deaths out here!'

All Camilla's nerves, her fears, had vanished. The parlour was the stage and she had a part to play, the most vital of her life. There was her reputation, her family's name to protect, but most of all there was Nicholas's good name. If she failed in this his friends would know that the woman he was intending to marry had made her living as an actress. And that would put her—and him—beyond the pale of polite society.

She turned, her hand still resting on Nicholas's shoulder, and shared a welcoming smile amongst the three men. 'Are you not going to introduce me to your friends, *chéri*? They look fun—and you.' She turned and pouted crimson lips at Nicholas. 'You I have not yet forgiven for shutting me away in that boring room instead of letting me share your company.'

Hendricks darted forward, his cheeks flushed. 'Mademoiselle, please take this chair. Let me offer you a glass of wine—George, ring for another glass!'

For once in his life George Marlow did as he was bid by his old schoolfellow, jerking the bellpull with such force that the waiter appeared at a run. 'Dammit, where have you been! Another glass for the lady, and more candles. And where's our dinner? Hang on, hang on,' he called to the lad's fast retreating back. 'Set a cover for the lady, and make sure there's something fit for her to eat!'

'Yes, sir—right away, sir!' the boy gasped, hurrying out. Cor! That was a prime article and no mistake—and you saw a few in this job! He could hardly wait to get down to the kitchen and tell them all about it. If Cook sent up something really special, there might be a good tip in it as well.

Camilla glanced from under her lashes at Freddie, the only man who had met her as Miss Knight and the only man who knew that Miss Knight was a good amateur actress. But there was no look of recognition on his face, nothing but admiration and envy that Nick had secured such a prize. Nonetheless, it would be best to keep him at a distance, especially as George Marlow had sent for more candles.

She patted the chair next to her and fluttered her sooty lashes at William Hendricks. 'Please,

sit by me, sir. And you must introduce yourselves, as Nicholas seems determined not to do
so.' She indicated the other chair and turned her
attention to George. 'And you, sir, you have the
advantage of me, for you know my name. Can
it be that you have done me the honour of
coming to see me act?'

They sat hurriedly, both flushed, and George
began the introductions. 'Sir William Hendricks
upon your right, ma'am. Lord Corsham—'
Freddie bowed '—by the fireplace. And I am
George Marlow, your most humble and devoted
servant.' He bent over her hand. 'We are all firm
devotees of your art, and all of us devastated by
the suddenness of your retirement.'

'Yes, indeed, mademoiselle,' William almost
gabbled, reduced to schoolboy gaucheness by
the nearness of his goddess. 'Could we not beg
you to reconsider? Is there nothing we could do
to persuade you to return to the stage?'

Camilla reflected wryly that it was a good
thing that none of them realised that they were
indeed seeing Mademoiselle Davide's final performance! She lifted a hand and waved vaguely
in Nicholas's direction. He came across and
caught it in his, giving it a warning pressure

which she completely ignored. The terror had gone, as stage fright always had, to be replaced by exhilaration, by the power she had over these four men.

'Nicholas, you are a very naughty boy not to introduce me to your friends before. I am quite cross with you. They are all so very charming!'

Nicholas circled the table to sit opposite her, shooting her a glance that suggested quite clearly that she was in danger of over-egging this particular pudding. Camilla, her eyes dancing wickedly, blew him a kiss and turned to George. 'Now, you will tell me all about this prize-fighting, because I do not know anything about it, except that it sounds very exciting, and Nicholas will not explain. I expect you understand it much better than he does...'

George coughed pompously and shot his cuffs. 'Well, it isn't really a subject for a lady, but I must admit it is by way of being a passion of mine and I am generally acknowledged to be somewhat of an expert on form.' Encouraged by her wide-eyed admiration, he continued. 'Now, the challenger is an unknown Irishman called Patrick Shaughnessy, who has been training with Thomas Cribb...'

Camilla clapped her hands. 'Oh, I have heard of him. He is very famous, is he not?'

'Clever girl. He was the champion heavyweight of all England.' George patted her hand. 'Now, the defender is known as the Slough Bull, and he has been undefeated for his last ten fights.'

'But which one is going to win? Will it be this *toreau*?'

'Ah ha!' George tapped the side of his nose knowingly. 'That is where the bets are going.'

Camilla put her hand on his sleeve and gazed at him admiringly. 'But you know better, do you not, *Georges*?'

George flushed and admitted that he flattered himself that indeed he had a better grasp of form than most gentlemen.

Two waiters appeared at that moment, and this prevented George from being soundly abused by his friends, who were becoming restive in the face of this shameless self-promotion.

Nicholas, joining in the general banter while the waiters unloaded their trays heaped with food, wine and more candles, reflected that Camilla was magnificent and that he had never been so scared in his life. Like riding a tiger, it was exhilarating while you were in motion, but the thought of what would happen if—when—you fell off was terrifying.

How Camilla thought she was going to bring this theatrical dinner party to an end he could not imagine. But suddenly he stopped worrying and allowed himself to be swept along with the animated talk and the pleasure of watching her perform.

The clock struck one. The plates had long been swept aside, more claret had been sent for and consumed, and the conversation had flowed freely from prize-fighting to the stage, to the latest French fashions—about which Freddie was surprisingly knowledgeable—and finally to the precarious health of the King.

'No, I have never acted before the Prince Regent, and now I never will. It would have been a great honour, of course. Oh, but *messieurs*, regard the clock. I must retire. I need my beauty sleep and *sans doute* you gentlemen will all be up at some ungodly hour making a great deal of noise.'

'Never say you need beauty sleep, mademoiselle—how could one improve upon perfection?'

'You are too gallant, Sir William,' Camilla responded gracefully as she got to her feet. 'No, no, there is no need to open that door for me. I shall go to my own chamber and leave you all to your brandy and your betting. Goodnight, gentlemen.'

Nicholas followed her down the corridor to her chamber. Once they were safely round the corner he took her in his arms and kissed her. 'My God, you were magnificent! I have never been so terrified in my life—or so excited.'

His breathing was ragged as he kissed her hard. Camilla, all the exhilaration ebbing from her body, suddenly felt very tired, but very happy. Gently she pushed Nicholas away. 'No, darling, go back to your friends. When will I see you again?'

Nicholas looked down into her face and smiled. 'Just as soon as you get back to Bath. I will be waiting. You know my sister's direction. You have only to send for me.'

Camilla watched his tall, elegant figure disappear back towards the parlour. She leaned her aching shoulders against the wall, suddenly overcome by how much she loved him. She was tired, so tired, but also restless, as she had often been after a particularly draining performance. She could not go out, and if she went to her room her fidgeting would doubtless wake her maid. Instead, on silent bare feet, she began to pace up and down the empty passageway.

She reached the bend just before the parlour and stopped, safely out of sight. The men had fallen silent as she had left them, but now as Nicholas reappeared he was greeted by a chorus of admiration.

'She is more beautiful close up than she is on stage,' Sir William sighed moonily.

'You lucky dog, Nick,' George growled, draining his brandy.

'Luck has nothing to do with it,' Nicholas retorted. Camilla flushed at the note of triumph in his voice, then told herself that of course he too had a part to play in this charade.

'No, indeed it hasn't!' Freddie suddenly exclaimed. 'You know what this means, don't you? Nick's won the bet—he's won Thunderer!'

'He's run out of time,' George stated dogmatically.

'No, he hasn't,' Freddie said gloomily. 'We

gave him to the end of this month, and it's the first of June tomorrow.'

'Sorry, old chap,' Hendricks agreed. 'I don't think there can be any doubt that Nick has succeeded in making the Unobtainable Mademoiselle Davide his mistress, just as we agreed that night in the theatre. Thunderer is his.'

George got up unsteadily, scraping his chair back, and raised his glass to Nick. 'Here's to you, Nick, and well earned, I say. A stallion for a stallion, what?'

The men's laughter rang mockingly in Camilla's ears as she ran back to her chamber.

Chapter Twelve

Mrs Babbage was perhaps the most lachrymose individual Camilla had ever had the misfortune to meet. She knew she should feel nothing but compassion towards Miss March's widowed sister, but she was finding it very hard indeed to deal with a woman whose only response to every question, every decision, was to dissolve into tears and wail, 'If only dearest Mr Babbage was here!'

Camilla refrained, with difficulty, from pointing out to the widow that if Mr Babbage was there the situation would not have arisen, and, further, from mentioning that the unfortunate gentleman had suffered a long and difficult illness, and that no charitable person could wish him to be other than at peace with his Maker.

Yet, whatever the provocation, she could not

regret her decision to come to Cheltenham, for poor little Miss March was worn to a thread, as Camilla could see from the moment she set eyes on her old nurse.

'Marchy darling,' she had cried as she tumbled down the steps of the carriage into the outflung arms of her oldest friend and ally. They had both burst into tears: Miss March because she was tired, drained and once more in the company of her dearest 'Lilla, Camilla because she was so shocked by the sight of Miss March, suddenly old and helpless.

She had sat numbly in the carriage all the way from Buckingham, forcing herself to make responses to Mathilda's eager questions, simply counting the minutes until she could fall into her old nurse's arms and have it all made better. But the miles passing by on the turnpike milestones had brought her not someone who would pat her and soothe her and tell her it was all going to be well, as she had told a young Camilla so many times in the past. Instead she found herself needing to support an old lady at the end of her tether, whose innocent mind could never have comprehended the scandalous toils her charge had entangled herself in.

Miss March, who had never set foot in a theatre in her life, had not quite understood what it was that Camilla was about night after night as she changed in her cottage and then slipped away with a kiss, leaving her to her night-time indulgence of a cup of chocolate. It seemed that darling 'Lilla was involved with a group of like-minded friends who enjoyed dramatics, and as this was a *slightly* daring thing to do it was better if she returned via Miss March's. After all, the old nurse had reasoned, if Mrs Knight was complaisant about it, then it must be perfectly all right, although it was a pity that dear 'Lilla seemed so tired every evening.

So, exhausted, humiliated and with her life in tatters around her feet, Camilla had dismissed Mathilda to unpack, drunk a strong cup of tea, pushed her handkerchief firmly back into her reticule and set herself to discover how she could disentangle Miss March from Cheltenham before her health finally gave way.

If Mrs Babbage had been a torturer in full possession of Camilla's scandalous secrets she could not have inflicted more pain as she held forth to her enlarged audience. 'Dearest Mr Babbage, such a tower of strength for fifty years!

I will not hide from you, Miss Knight, that I fell for him the moment I saw him! Oh, you do not yet know the felicity of falling in love with a fine gentleman, of receiving a declaration from his lips, of yielding your life and fortune into his hands, but you will, you will. And I pray you will never know the horror of seeing him snatched from you, leaving you all alone, alone…' And here she trailed off into tears again.

'Indeed I do not,' replied Camilla with such emphasis that Miss March looked startled and hurried to put right what she saw as her sister's tactlessness.

'You will do so, my dear Miss Knight, never fear! Somewhere there is the right gentleman for you. You have only to wait and he will come to you, rest assured.'

Neither lady was surprised when Camilla snatched her handkerchief from her reticule, burst into tears and fled from the room.

'Such sensibility, such a sympathetic understanding of your feelings,' cried Miss March.

'Indeed,' her sister sniffed. 'Dear child! So unlike so many young people of today!'

The Babbage house, although modest and neat, was well-appointed and the late Mr

Babbage had allowed himself the indulgence of a small conservatory at the rear. Here Camilla took refuge and at last found the privacy and peace for a good cry. Last night she had been unable to sleep, lying awake and taut listening to Mathilda's snuffles and snores as the night became darker and the inn finally fell quiet.

Curled up in a tight ball of misery Camilla had crushed her handkerchief against her teeth to stifle her sobs and had lain silent while her thoughts whirled in a nightmare, mocking dance.

How *could* she have been so mistaken in Nicholas? How *could* she have believed him to love her when all he had wanted was her seduction? And for what? In order to win a horse! He must have known right from the beginning that she lived a double life. He must have sought her out cynically, intending her ruin simply for a bet. She had known of his reputation as a rake, but stupidly, innocently, she had also believed that he would treat her as a gentleman should a lady. She could only conclude that in his eyes, by following a career on the stage, she had forfeited that status and that protection. She had believed him when he said he loved her—perhaps he did, after his fashion, in perhaps the only way a rake could understand love. Doubtless he would have offered her a *carte blanche*: at least she had been spared the ordeal of discovering his intentions in his presence.

Her whirling thoughts had become no calmer as the inn had begun to come alive again. In the deep darkness before the dawn she'd heard the ostlers walking across the yard, the noise as stable half-doors swung open and horses whickered for their feed. From downstairs had come the rattle of grates being riddled and the clang of the pump-handle as chilled kitchen boys pumped the first buckets of water of the day.

All those people, awake and happy in their way. All knowing their role in life and what their expectations and dreams were. And in her chamber, gradually filling with light as the day dawned, Camilla had remained in a wretched huddle, swathed in the heavy silk of Nicholas's robe.

She'd stirred, and a waft of the sandalwood cologne he had sometimes used drifted up, warmed by her body. It had brought her to a recollection of how she must look, what she was wearing. Mathilda must not see her like this! She could not explain to the girl why she should preserve silence about such an odd occurrence, and the risk that she might innocently blurt something out was too great.

Cautiously Camilla had slipped out of bed and shed the robe, folding it as small as possible and tucking it into a calico bag she had brought to place linen in for laundering. The sash had swiftly followed, and the tiepin she'd tucked into her jewellery roll. That had just left the curtain cord, which she'd dropped on the floor by the window. Mathilda, sleeping the sleep of the very young, had slumbered on as Camilla wiped the soot from her brows and lashes with cold water from the washstand and scrubbed the geranium stain from her lips. The sting of the towel on her soft flesh had been a penance, and she'd scrubbed harder, trying to drive the memory of Nicholas's betraying mouth teasing those same lips.

The enormity of his betrayal flooded back to her now, as she sat in the respectable little glasshouse, unheedingly shredding the leaves of the fern which grew in a pot by her side. Nicholas had been so clever, so cynical, playing her like a fish on a line: alternately respectful and teasing, admiring and then apparently uninterested. He had kissed her, exploiting her innocence, her susceptibility to him.

And then how shocked and angry he had appeared to be after he 'discovered' her secret. And she had thought herself a good actress! Why, he was worth ten of her when it came to dissembling and deceit.

Not that she could accuse him of doing anything to damage Ophelia and Mama: no, he would not do that. They were *ladies*, and his code forbade him to do anything to hurt them. But she, Camilla, was another matter. She had forfeited his regard by her actions and so he could use her to his own ends as he chose. But to count her virtue as of less worth than the possession of a horse...

Suddenly angry, she sprang to her feet and began to pace up and down the short alleyway between the benches. What hypocrites men were! It was not just Nicholas: why, those three friends of his were the same—such fun to be with, so open, courteous and pleasant to her— but they would cut Mademoiselle Davide dead in the street if they met her when they were in company with their mothers or their sisters. Before they knew who she was they had bayed like hounds on the scent to discover her, for she had simply been Nicholas's 'bit of muslin' in their eyes.

Then her own innate honesty brought her to a standstill. No, she could not blame it all on Nicholas. What was he to make of a 'lady' who quivered at a touch from him, who returned kiss with kiss, who after a chance meeting in a strange inn was ready to surrender her virtue to him? Camilla closed her eyes in shame at the memory of how she must have looked, tumbled and half-clad on his bed.

She covered her eyes with her palms for a long moment until her breathing calmed a little and made herself think. Men had tried to kiss her before and some had almost succeeded. She had met many handsome, rich and eligible men in her time, had flirted and been flirted with, received admiring glances and even passionate poems. Yet not once had her heart been stirred, not once had her flesh quivered with response under a touch or a caress. Her dreams had been blameless, her imagination untouched by every man she had met.

Until she had met Nicholas. Yes, she could acquit herself of being an abandoned, over-

sensual woman who would have responded like
that to any passable man. She had been attracted
to Nicholas from the first moment, had fallen in
love with him long before she had allowed
herself to acknowledge it with anything except
her betraying body.

Camilla stared unseeingly through the glass to
the small garden beyond. She loved Nicholas,
loved him despite his betrayal. She knew she
would never feel like this about any other man
so long as she lived. Was the world full of foolish
girls who had jeopardised their virtue for a rake
and then spent the rest of their existence regret-
ting it? She supposed she could not be the only
one. Occasionally you heard the whispers.

'Lady Y has been a long time in the country—
quite eight months, is it not…?'

'Young Miss B is looking very pale. Has not
her engagement to Lord X been announced
yet…? Strange, is it not, that she fainted at the
dance last night…?'

She should be grateful to Nicholas's boisterous friends. They had saved her from the
ultimate folly as effectively as any three fierce
chaperons could have done. How would she be
feeling now, counting the days until she could be

sure she was not carrying his child? How would she feel if those comforting signs did not come and her body told her that she was? Appalled, Camilla realised that she would be glad, not sorry to find that was the case. There was nothing for her now except the empty shell of her old life without even the stimulus of the stage: the thought of a little house in the country, a new identity as a young widow with her child was curiously attractive.

Carefully she smoothed down her gown, took a deep breath and made her way back to the front parlour. 'Shall I ring for tea? I am sure we would all feel better for some.'

What was Nicholas doing now, what was he thinking? Did he feel any qualms about his actions?

Nicholas was indeed feeling qualms, but not about Camilla. After a long and highly satisfactory day at the fight, where all four had reaped the benefit of George's advice and won handsomely on the Irish challenger, he was driving his curricle homewards with a deep furrow between his brows.

To his friends' surprise he had refused to ride

Thunderer back to his estate but had left him to his groom to lead, choosing to drive off alone as soon as the last bout had finished. 'I will head back to Ashby now: you collect my winnings, Freddie; here are the slips. I will see you all in time for dinner, but I must have a word with my head keeper this afternoon if we are to have any sort of sport while we are there. It will only be pigeons, I expect.'

If Camilla had known the tenor of Nicholas's thoughts as he drove the fifteen miles back to his estates she would have been deeply wounded, seeing it as just another example of the hypocrisy of male 'honour'.

But Nicholas, his conscience quite clear as far as she was concerned, was acutely aware that he had just won Thunderer under false pretences and could see no way of getting out of it. The bet had been to seduce Mademoiselle Davide within two months, and not only did Mademoiselle Davide not exist, he had not seduced her either. Another five minutes in that bedroom... The match bays snorted and sidled as his hands tightened unconsciously on the reins, pulling his full attention back to the road.

Nicholas negotiated a tight bend, steadied the

pair as he saw the mail coach ahead, then with a flick of the whip gave them their head and was round and away with a clear straight road ahead of him.

Three days at Ashby, then back to Bath and to Camilla: his mouth curved into a smile and Camilla would have recognised with a thudding heart the sensual droop of his eyelids. Meanwhile he supposed he *could* admit to Freddie that he had not actually seduced Mademoiselle Davide. Nicholas winced at the thought of Freddie's expression, let alone his likely comments. Or he could fabricate an opportunity to wager Thunderer again and lose him back to Freddie. A few really poor hands of whist ought to do it; Freddie was a good enough player to make that plausible if he thought Nick was off his game.

Camilla, meanwhile, by dint of agonising patience and persistence, had managed to establish which problems with Mr Babbage's will were causing such an upset. 'Yes, I see what you mean. How very worrying,' she agreed, after half an hour peering at the crabbed script. 'What a pity Mr Babbage did not see fit to place the making of his will in the hands of his solicitor but instead wrote it himself. I have no idea what the legal position might be, of course…'

Both older ladies nodded and clucked in agreement. After all, what mere female could understand these male mysteries. Men were so *clever* at business…

'*But*,' Camilla persisted, 'I think I understand the problem well enough to be able to explain to Mr Brooke, and I am sure he will be willing to act for you. After all, I am sure Mr Babbage cannot have intended to leave the house to the Home for Widows and Orphans and only fifty pounds to you, Mrs Babbage. He appears to have got the two things muddled up.'

'And Mr Brooke is so wise,' Miss March explained to her sister, for the fourth time. 'And yet still quite young. Most handsome and well set up, you know,' she added with a sideways glance at Camilla, who was trying to make a copy of the will to take to the lawyer and fortunately did not hear her.

'Indeed!' Mrs Babbage, finding a subject of interest at last, looked at Camilla with sudden attention. 'A younger son?'

'Oh, no…'

Camilla's hopes of bearing Miss March and the copied documents back to Bath the next day were foiled by both ladies, full of concern for her health. 'You look so tired, 'Lilla dear,' Miss March explained, slipping into using her nursery name the moment they were alone. 'Such dark shadows under your eyes. I am so grateful to you for coming all this distance out of your way for me; I do so hope you have not caught a chill.'

Camilla, casting round for excuses to escape the cloying atmosphere of Cheltenham, finally told Miss March about Ophelia's engagement. 'But please do not tell anyone, even dear Mrs Babbage. As she is not yet out, Mama does not wish it to be widely known.'

Miss March, happily assured that she had an explanation for Camilla's tiredness—excitement and late nights helping her dear mama make plans—stopped fussing and allowed Camilla to convince her that she had done her duty and that her sister would be the better for a few days by herself. 'And then that nice Mr Brooke will come and visit her, and perhaps once that worry with the will is straightened out she can go and stay for a month or two with dearest Cousin Emily…'

'And I do not know how I can go on in Bath if

you do not come with me, Marchy, for I will need a chaperon, and there is so much I am charged with doing for Mama and Ophelia,' added Camilla mendaciously. 'We will have the Green Bedchamber made up for you, if you do not dislike that idea, and there will be no need for you to chaperon me to any sort of party you might not wish to attend while in mourning, for I am sure one of Mama's friends will be more than willing to do that.'

Miss March hurried away to supervise the packing of her best black silk, just the thing for a chaperon to wear. Whatever the sacrifice she would be at dear 'Lilla's side, even if it meant attending a ball at the Assembly Rooms!

Camilla was heartily glad to be home once more, but even the inescapable tasks that were waiting for her did nothing to soothe her mind or her aching heart. Cook, finding her absent-minded over the week's menus, was not to know that Miss Camilla had found a little cameo brooch in her jewellery box, or if she had, she could never have guessed it had been given to a certain Mademoiselle Davide in the Green Room of the Theatre Royal.

And Miss March, finding herself having to

repeat for the second time her request for dear 'Lilla to pass her the blue embroidery silk, could not know that Camilla was looking bleakly into her heart at her image of Nicholas. Try as she might, she could not adjust her picture of him as strong and honest, wickedly funny, tender, sensual and exciting, and replace it with that of a heartless seducer, a man blinded by the conventions of the day to her love and to what she could bring him.

Mr Brooke, calling to peruse Camilla's copy of the Babbage will, thought her much changed, and of all her friends guessed most nearly at the cause. So, she had flown too near the sun and had her wings singed, he thought pityingly. Well-bred as Camilla was, it would be an ambitious step to aspire to marry an earl. Damn the man for leading her on! Mr Brooke was a patient man and, although not one given to deep passions, had been more cast down than Camilla realised when she had refused his first proposal. Perhaps if he were to wait a month or two, he mused, he could hazard his fortune again.

'This, I make no bones about telling you, Camilla, is a confused mess!' He poked with his quill pen at the sheets of paper covered in

Camilla's flowing hand. 'However, there is some virtue in its very weakness. No judge, should it come to it, is going to believe that this was Mr Babbage's true intention. Leave it with me, for it is perfectly possible for a will to be amended after death provided all parties are willing. It will not look good for a charity devoted to widows to be seen to profit at the expense of just such an unfortunate person. I am sure, if Mrs Babbage is prepared to offer them a small additional sum, we can reach a satisfactory conclusion. I will leave for Cheltenham tomorrow and speak to her myself.'

He rose and unexpectedly took her hand in his, raising it to his lips. 'You are tired, my dear Camilla. Please look after yourself, for your friends do not care to see you so cast down.' The look he gave her was a speaking one, but she was hardly aware of it. 'I have acquired a new carriage: would you permit me to take you out in it soon? The fresh air and diversion will do you good.'

Camilla stood for a while after he had shown himself out, having reached agreement on the day for their drive. She raised the hand he had kissed to her cheek, unconsciously grateful for the comfort. Arthur was a good, caring friend. She looked out over the rooftops at the waters of the river below and remembered Nicholas staring out of this same window. It seemed very long ago. So much had happened between them since then.

After several minutes she gave a little start and walked determinedly into her bedchamber. Pulling out a stool, she reached up for a hatbox which she had pushed well to the back of the clothes press and lifted it down.

Inside were the folded dressing-gown and sash and Nicholas's tiepin. The heavy folds of silk felt alive and sensual under her hands and seemed to resist her efforts to fold them neatly and be trapped within the layers of brown paper she was parcelling them in. The scent of sandalwood rose rich and exotic to her nostrils, and she had to fight the urge to bury her face in the richness and drink in the scent of Nicholas for one last time.

Carefully she wrapped the tiepin in tissue paper and slipped it into the parcel, then she knotted the string and lit a candle. The hot red wax dripped onto the knot, sealing it with a dreadful finality.

She sat at her writing desk, pulled a sheet of paper towards her and began to write without hesitation or correction.

Miss Knight presents her compliments to the Earl of Ashby and takes the liberty of returning to him some items which have come into her possession during the course of a recent journey and which she believes belong to his lordship.

Miss Knight begs that the Earl will not trouble to acknowledge this trifling service and regrets that it is unlikely that she will be at home should his lordship call.

Miss Knight would like to take the opportunity to congratulate his lordship upon the acquisition of a very fine new horse and observes with interest what gratification his lordship's skill in games of chance gives his lordship's closest friends. Miss Knight will endeavour to learn from this example of the relative values placed upon friendship and the winning of a wager.

Camilla folded and sealed the envelope and rang for the footman. 'Please deliver this parcel and this letter to the residence of the Countess of Forres to await the arrival of the Earl of Ashby. There is no need to wait for a reply.'

The parcel and letter sat for two days upon the dresser in Nicholas's usual room in his sister's house. When he finally arrived from Ashby he was late for dinner and Georgiana, for once tolerant of informality, urged him to delay merely to wash. 'I will forgive you your riding-boots this once, Lovell,' she declared. 'You and I will be eating alone this evening. Henry has a bad head cold and has retired to bed so I have been forced to cancel this evening's visit to the theatre. Hurry down and tell me all the gossip from the country, for I swear not a thing of interest has occurred in Bath these two weeks past.'

The parcel was unnoticed in the shadows as Nicholas made himself respectable and ran downstairs again to join his sister. It suited him well enough to dine quietly at home that evening, for he was too late to visit the Paragon and Camilla. The delay added piquancy to his desire to see her and he was smiling as he entered the dining-room, wondering what she would be wearing next morning and whether she had managed to get all of the soot out of her eyebrows.

'You are looking very pleased with yourself, Lovell,' Georgiana observed tartly. 'Now tell me, how is my dear Lady Corsham? Not managed to marry off that scrapegrace son of hers yet, I see.'

Nicholas grinned. 'Poor Freddie, he was very much in his mama's bad books, I am afraid. Still, he has escaped once again, despite her best efforts. Lady Corsham is very well and begs to be remembered to you. So does Lady Ellwood. We attended a fine entertainment at their house one evening—amateur dramatics of a very high order. Lady Ellwood staged the whole thing outside on a grass stage: very effective, if unconventional.'

'Indeed? Pass me the gooseberry sauce, my dear. Really, I do feel this bird is a trifle tough. How is the salmon? And who was at Lady Ellwood's entertainment that I would know?'

Nicholas recalled a list of names, prompting a flow of reminiscence and faintly scandalous stories from his sister. 'And Mrs Knight with her daughters. One of them has become contracted to her cousin, who inherited the family estates, so there is much rejoicing as you may imagine.'

Georgiana looked up sharply. 'The Knights? The Knights from the Paragon? And which daughter has become betrothed?'

'The younger, Miss Ophelia.'

'Indeed!' Georgiana toyed with her meat, finally pushing the plate away. 'Benton, you may tell Cook that this goose is tough.'

'Yes, my lady.' The butler removed her plate and left the room.

'And how does the elder Miss Knight take to her sister's engagement? I do not think that many would have wagered on her having her nose put out of joint by that child becoming betrothed before her.'

Nicholas shrugged and helped himself to burgundy. 'This is a fine bottle; remind me to ask Henry where he got it from. The Knight engagement is not yet announced, you understand. Miss Knight seems happy for her sister's good fortune, that is all I can discern.'

'Humph. When do they plan to return to Bath?'

'I cannot say when Mrs Knight and Miss Ophelia will come home, but I believe Miss Knight may have already returned.'

It was Georgiana's turn to smile. 'Unusual to have left her mother and sister and travelled alone. Shall I call upon her?'

Nicholas returned the look blandly. 'Just as you wish, sister dear. I am sure she would welcome your company. For myself, I shall call tomorrow morning.'

It was not until Nicholas was shrugging on his dressing-gown the next morning, after a belated and prolonged breakfast and was waiting for his valet to whisk his shaving soap into a rich foam, that he noticed the parcel on the dresser.

'What is that?'

'A parcel delivered a few days ago, my lord. There is a letter with it I understand.'

Nicholas picked up the letter and sat in the chair, raising his chin to allow the valet to swathe him in a large towel. The man began to strop the razor as Nicholas broke the seal and opened the pages. His oath and the abruptness with which he sat up caused the startled man to leap backwards.

As he said afterwards to the butler, 'I'm still shaking now, Mr Benton. How I didn't take off his lordship's ear I'll never know, and my hands were all of a tremble. It's a miracle I didn't cut him shaving.'

'Years of experience,' the butler said graciously. 'Whatever it was, it's sent his lordship off with a rare scowl on his face, that's for sure.'

Chapter Thirteen

Nicholas's long legs and furious temper took him towards the long hill up to the Paragon without him even noticing the early morning scene around him. The smart set were out in their carriages or on foot, nodding and greeting each other as they went in and out of the many fashionable shops.

The pavements were newly swept and gleaming with wetness where shopkeepers had swilled them down. It was all lost on Nicholas as he wove his way through the crowds on the pavements, stopping occasionally to let a lady past, or nodding in acknowledgement of a 'good morning' called by a passing acquaintance.

He was walking around the Circus, heading towards Bennett Street, when there was a splintering crash as the owner of a sporting gig misjudged the angel at the corner and hit the kerb with one wheel. Chaos ensued; the horse got its legs over the traces, a sedan chair, cornering at the trot, collided with the rear, its Irish bearers filling the air with Hibernian oaths. All the traffic in the Circus ground to a halt, and Nicholas, unwilling to force his way through the throng of onlookers, found himself standing at the edge of the pavement.

Over the hubbub a feminine voice, carrying with the clarity of a performer, reached his ears. 'Oh, that poor bearer, I do hope he is not hurt!' It was Camilla, seated beside the driver of a very dashing tilbury.

Her attention was all on the accident, but Nicholas stepped back slightly behind a large matron wearing a toque and carrying a parasol. Through its silken fringe he could observe Camilla and her companion. Damn it! It was that sober-sided solicitor Brooke! Not, after all, quite such a puritan if he was prepared to splash out on such a sporting equipage.

Nicholas had thought how Camilla would look when he next saw her, but he was not prepared for just how very lovely she did look, perched up beside Arthur Brooke. Her slender form was sheathed in a fine wool walking-dress of spring green, with daffodil-yellow ribbons in her chip straw bonnet and yellow kid gloves on her hands, one of which carried a ridiculously small parasol, tilted rakishly over her shoulder.

She looked absolutely stunning, and was attracting the admiring attention of many of the gentlemen who had stopped to take in the scene. This attention had not been lost on Arthur Brooke, who could not but feel a certain smugness: not only was he driving the very latest sporting vehicle, but the lady beside him was a beauty of the very first water.

Neither he nor Nicholas could know what it had cost Camilla to rally her spirits and make the effort. But she was determined not to pine, and dear Arthur deserved that she made every effort to enjoy the treat he was offering her.

The blockage was cleared, the traffic moved on and Nicholas was left looking after the tilbury as it bowled once more towards the Paragon. 'Hell and damnation!' he swore, not quite enough under his breath to escape an outraged stare from the dowager behind whom he had been sheltering.

His expression by the time he reached the Knights' residence was still thunderous, a fact reflected on the footman's face as he answered the heavy knocking on the front door.

'I am sorry, my lord, but Miss Knight is not receiving today.'

'She will receive me.' Nicholas took a firm step over the threshold, thrust his hat, gloves and cane into the startled man's hands and opened the door into the salon. 'I will wait in here.'

He had a long wait. Finally, after the clock on the mantel had struck both the three-quarters and the hour, the footman returned. 'Miss Knight asks me to say she is not at home, my lord.' He held his breath for a long moment, wondering what he should do if Lord Lovell marched off to look for Miss Knight. It would no doubt be his duty to try and stop him, but he didn't fancy his chances...

'Indeed. Then please find me pen and ink.'

Relieved that the alarming visitor was showing signs of departing, the man hurried to obey. Nicholas took up the pen, scratched one line, signed it with a single initial and dusted it with sand. 'There. Take this to Miss Knight immediately, if you please.'

Camilla, sitting over her account books with Miss March mending linen beside her, heard the footman return and saw with relief he was carrying a note. 'Has his lordship gone?'

'No, Miss Knight. He said to give you this.'

Camilla unfolded the note and spread it out on top of her accounts.

Come to me, or I will not leave this house until I have searched every room.

The bold arrogance of a single 'N' filled the rest of the sheet.

'Are you quite well, dear?' Miss March enquired. 'You have gone positively white.'

'Thank you, Marchy, I am quite well. There is a gentleman here to see me, and I am afraid that if I do not allow him to speak to me he is going to take up residence in the salon. Would you be so kind as to accompany me?'

Miss March exclaimed at the early hour, speculated as to what he might want and who it was, worried that it might be a message from Mrs Knight with bad news, and generally managed to prevent Camilla achieving a single coherent or helpful thought before they reached the salon.

Camilla let the footman open the door and dismissed him with a smile. 'Thank you, James. His lordship will not be staying long enough for us to require refreshments.'

Nicholas stood as she entered, his eyebrows raised somewhat at the sight of Miss March.

'Miss March, may I introduce the Earl of Ashby? My lord, Miss March—my companion.'

Nicholas threw Miss March into a tizzy by bowing over her hand with exquisite grace. He lifted her little paw in its lace mitten in his and led her to the door before she had a chance to protest. 'Miss March, I have long desired to meet you, and I trust I will have the opportunity before long of making your better acquaintance. However, I am afraid that I have a matter of the utmost discretion to discuss with Miss Knight and I simply cannot have another person present. I am sure you will understand.'

She was almost out of the door before she realised what was happening. 'But my lord! I must chaperon Miss Knight!'

'I promise I will not seduce her this morning,' Nicholas replied, with such sincerity that she was reassured and was half-way back to the parlour with the salon door firmly closed on her before what he had said penetrated her brain.

'How dare you say such a thing?' Camilla knew she was white. Her hands were shaking so much she had to clasp them tightly together.

'Surely you do not expect me to seduce you here; it would be most inappropriate.' He strolled across and stood very close to her. 'Will you not sit down and tell me the meaning of that letter you wrote me?'

For a moment Camilla found she had no power to move or speak. Whether it was anger or misery that froze her she had no idea. Finally she managed to sit down, still clasping her trembling hands tightly together and said, 'You should be more careful where you discuss your successful wagers, my lord. I overheard your friends in the inn congratulating you. Surely you cannot be surprised if I resent my virtue being the subject of a public bet?'

There was a long silence before Nicholas spoke. 'Miss Knight's virtue has never been in question, nor discussed,' Nicholas said quietly.

'You are playing with words, my lord,' she said sharply, looking up at him. There was nothing to read in his face except a mild regret at her anger. 'I am both Mademoiselle Davide and Camilla Knight. You have always known that. I realise it now. You have played with me, toyed with my affections, manipulated the way I felt about you—and all because you made a bet with your friends over a horse and an actress! Are you not ashamed of yourself?'

'I did not know who you were when I made that bet.'

'But you soon did, did you not? It would have been very easy to have walked away, Nicholas— I made it easy for you by vanishing as Mademoiselle Davide. No one would have thought anything of it if you had failed to find one actress who chose to retire completely. Your friends would have had no reason to mock your much vaunted virility and success with women, would they? Nick the stallion? Nick with the devil's own luck with women? Even he cannot be expected to seduce a woman who isn't there. But, no, you had to seek me out and play with me like a cat with a mouse.'

He walked away and stood with his back towards her, looking out of the long window. 'You seemed to welcome my company.'

Camilla bit her lip until the pain steadied her. 'You mean I appeared to welcome your embraces.' She managed to say it without blushing crimson, even when Nicholas turned to regard her steadily.

'Yes, those too.'

'It did not occur to you that I had fallen in love with you?'

He met the challenge in her eyes, returning her stare. 'Not at first. I did not know, you see, what experience you might have had in your other life.'

'You must think me a very good actress if you could not tell I was a virgin!'

'I do think you are a good actress. You proved it at Lady Ellwood's house.'

Camilla got to her feet with a jerk and took one angry pace towards him. 'And you decided to take the opportunity I so foolishly gave you to win your bet! You could have warned me you were expecting your friends the moment you saw me in that inn. At best I could have left the place, there and then. At worst I would have spent the night unseen in my room. But, oh no, it was too good a chance, was it not? You made love to me. You told me you loved me…'

Her voice cracked, but she steadied it with an effort, throwing up a hand to still the step he made towards her. 'I was such a fool I thought you meant to marry me. I suppose I am not the only woman who has made a fool of herself over a man. But I did believe, my lord, that you were a gentleman, that you would not split hairs to the point of protecting my mother and my sister but not caring what happened to me.'

Nicholas's face was dark, his mouth tight. He seemed to remain where he was by a great effort of will. 'You seem determined to think the worst of me.'

'I do,' she spat back. 'And do not think I do not think badly of myself as well! Are you telling me that that horse is not in your stables now?'

'Yes, I am. It is in Freddie's.'

'How come?' Camilla raised a skeptical eyebrow.

'Because I could not accept it: I had not won the wager, so I lost to Freddie at cards that night—with Thunderer as my stake.'

Camilla sat down again, staring at him. 'Let me understand this aright. You gave the horse back. Not because it was an ungentlemanly thing to have done to have wagered my virtue on it or because you had betrayed me. You gave it back because you *failed* to seduce me and therefore you had won it under false pretences?'

'You really do not understand, Camilla. Now

listen to me…' Nicholas raked his hand through his hair as if wrestling his words into an order which would convince her of what he was trying to say.

'I understand only too well, my lord!' Camilla was in no mood to be mollified.

'No, you do not.' He took two long strides towards her, then stopped at the look on her face. 'I had to make things right with that damned horse and Freddie, then I had to come and see you…'

'For what purpose? Do not try and pretend I have stung your *honour* to the point of feeling you need to buy me off! Well, my lord? What have you come to offer me?' Camilla sat back in the seat and regarded Nicholas with cold disdain, but her breathing was far from steady

'I came to offer you an apology, although quite frankly, Camilla, just at the moment all I feel inclined to do is box your ears!' He looked as though he might carry out the threat and Camilla sat upright with a grim determination not to give him the satisfaction of seeing her flinch. 'I also came in order to ask you to marry me,' he finished.

'To marry you!' She was on her feet again, face to face with him, eyes sparkling with fury.

'You ask me to marry you after what happened in Buckingham!'

'That seems a very good reason,' he retorted hotly. 'After all, I damned near took you…' He pulled himself up and added, 'I mean, I compromised you.'

'*Took me*! How dare you use such indelicate language to my face? And to marry you for *that*! It is the worst reason I can think of! Let us be quite clear about this: why did you not ask me to marry you before? In the inn you told me you loved me.'

'Lovells do not marry actresses. You may have kept your scandalous secret from all but your family but that is hardly the point: you have behaved in a way totally unfitting for the Countess of Ashby.' Nicholas had his temper on a tight rein again. It was obvious that he considered this to be an adequate explanation.

Two spots of colour burned high on Camilla's cheekbones.

'Oh, I see. Lovells do not marry actresses. Well, that is plain enough, my lord. How irritating I must be, confusing your rigid code of honour! Sometimes I am an actress, but I am always a lady. And now, because you made a botch of seducing the actress and your precious

honour will not let you risk the lady being compromised, you have gritted your teeth and
decided to make the best of it!' Camilla side-
stepped neatly, away from the anger which
burned in Nicholas's blue eyes. 'Well, my lord
Earl, you may take your very gracious offer and
remove yourself from this house! I never want
to see you again!'

She swept over to the door, wrenched it open,
and finally lost her composure. 'Oh, go away,
I hate you!'

Faced with an interested audience of the
footman, Miss March and Cook holding a
rolling-pin, Nicholas produced an impeccable
bow, snatched up his hat and cane and stalked
through the front door.

Under Camilla's smouldering gaze the
footman scurried to close the door, then
removed himself swiftly through the green
baize door.

Miss March, clutching Cook's arm, looked at
her charge in astonishment, but words were
beyond her. Camilla turned to the cook and addressed her loftily. 'Mrs Powes, I do not believe
I have seen this week's menus as yet. Will you
be so good as to bring them to the salon imme-

diately? Oh, and I think Miss March will be better for a cup of camomile tea.'

She gathered her skirts and swept off to the salon, followed by Miss March in a state of great disarray and emitting faint clucks of disapproval. 'Dearest 'Lilla…that man…'

If Nicholas had thought about it at all he would have assumed that his sister would be out making morning calls, but Lady Forres, far more interested than she had let him guess in the progress of his relationship with Camilla, was hovering in the drawing room with the door ajar.

She heard his key in the lock and put down her tambour frame with a look of alert interest in her eyes. Now, how had her incorrigible brother gone on with the lovely Miss Knight? Then the sound of his cane and hat hitting the hall stand made her wince and she slowed in her eager advance to the door. The butler's voice as he arrived in the hall was faintly reproachful.

'I must apologise, my lord, for not being here to open the door to you. May I take your gloves, my lord? Is that your hat on the floor, my lord, doubtless your valet will be able to do something with it. Her ladyship is in the…'

'I have no need to disturb her ladyship at the moment, thank you, Benton. Please have my valet attend me in my chamber immediately: I will be leaving this morning.' The words were clipped and Georgiana came to a complete halt, her lower lip caught between her teeth.

So, his suit had not prospered. What on earth had happened to put him in such a temper? And how had he managed to fail with Miss Knight? Georgiana, having seen them together, was convinced that Miss Knight had a distinct partiality for her brother. What was the girl thinking of? He was the Earl of Ashby, after all!

Emerging into the hall, she followed the sound of his footsteps up the sweeping stairs and along the landing, pushing open his bed-chamber door without ceremony. Her brother was sitting at his writing-table staring at a blank sheet of paper, the pen in his hand. Without turning his head he said curtly, 'Stevens, pack my things at once. We leave as soon as maybe.'

'Lovell, why are you in such a pet?' Georgiana demanded, sweeping into the room and sitting firmly on the end of the bed.

'I am not in a *pet* as you put it, my dear sister.

I am just writing you a note: I find I have to return to Ashby urgently.'

'Nonsense. You have received no message from Buckinghamshire.' The door opened and the valet appeared, looking startled at the sight of the Countess perched unconventionally on the bed. 'You may go, Stevens. His lordship no longer requires you.'

The man effaced himself quickly and hurried off. Mr Benton's expression when he had given him his lordship's summons and the dented hat had spoken volumes: perhaps the butler could throw some light on his lordship's black mood.

'Georgiana, I would be obliged if you did not countermand my orders to my own servants.' Nicholas tossed down the quill and got to his feet.

'Sit down, Lovell, and stop pacing; you are making me feel tired. Now, what have you done to upset that lovely Miss Knight?'

Nicholas regarded his sister blankly, then his face relaxed and he laughed. 'I see you are taking your usual measured view of life, Georgiana dear! I beg you, never allow your ignorance of the facts to stand in the way of your opinions.'

The Countess flapped her hand at him irritably.

'Never mind all that! Now, I assume she has refused you?'

'And what makes you think I have made Miss Knight an offer?'

'You have been in love with her for weeks…'

'Have I?' her brother asked faintly.

'Of course, although no doubt your frivolous friends might not notice. And she, of course, is head over heels in love with you.'

'Is she?'

'Stop sounding like a parrot, Lovell. Despite the fact that Miss Knight is an elegant, well-mannered and refined young woman, her true feelings cannot be hidden from an experienced woman of the world such as myself…'

'In that case,' Nicholas responded wryly, 'you may tell me why she has refused me, and why she is out and about with her damned man of business—who, if I'm not very much mistaken, aspires to be rather more than that to her.'

'Presumably because you have done something to upset her,' Georgiana declared. 'Really, Lovell, you men are so clumsy in matters of the heart.'

'If she loves me,' Nicholas asked, the wry smile still twisting his lips, 'would she not forgive me, whatever I have done?'

'It depends what she has to forgive you for.' Georgiana eyed him closely. 'And only you know what it is—and just how unforgivable you have been. Nick,' she said suddenly, seizing his hand and pulling him down to sit beside her, 'what has gone wrong?'

Nicholas stared down at his sister's heavily beringed hand clasping his and knew he could not begin to tell her of Camilla's double life. 'Nothing I can tell you about: it is not all my secret to tell. You are right. I have given Miss Knight quite unforgivable provocation.'

'Then,' Georgiana said gently, 'you may have to face the fact that for once in your life there is something which being the Earl of Ashby cannot secure you.'

Chapter Fourteen

Next morning Mr Brooke called at the house in the Paragon at the respectable hour of half past eleven and found Miss Knight, clad in a gown of soft sea-green, sitting alone in the salon with a book of poetry in her hand.

Camilla laid the volume aside as he came in and smiled with pleasure at the sight of her old and trusted friend. It was so good to see Arthur Brooke; she had always regarded him as a friend as well as her man of business, and now she wished they were on such terms that she could confide in him as a brother.

After they had exchanged greetings and he was sitting beside her on the sofa he enquired, 'A new volume? Would you recommend it?' He picked it up and scrutinised the spine.

'I really cannot say,' Camilla confessed. 'I intended to cut the pages, but as you can see I have been sitting here quite idle all morning.'

She spoke lightly, as though mocking her own indolence, but Mr Brooke could sense a falseness in her tone. Her skin was pale, there were slight shadows under her eyes as though she had not slept, yet her hair and grooming were, as always, impeccable. It was as though something—or someone—had sapped her spirits. Yet when he had left her yesterday she had been quite her old self.

'I have come to let you know what progress I have made with Mr Babbage's will,' he began, conscious that he was engaging only part of her attention. 'I believe you were quite correct in assuming he had simply confused his intentions when he began to write them down. I have consulted a colleague with much experience in this area of law and he says…'

Camilla listened dutifully, but the words washed over her and afterwards she could not have repeated what Mr Brooke had imparted.

'…no need for a judge to be involved at all,' he concluded. She looked at him blankly, so he added, 'Good news, do you not agree?'

'Oh, yes…thank you so much for all your trouble.'

Arthur Brooke cast round the room looking for inspiration. He could not think of a pretext to keep the conversation going but he did not want to get up and leave Camilla when she was so obviously out of spirits. Her eyes were cast down, the long lashes fanning her pale cheeks and he felt a sudden desire to take her in his arms, protect her from life's hazards.

'That is a pretty cameo,' he finally remarked for lack of something else to say—or do. 'Is it new? I do not think I have seen you wearing it before.'

'I…it was a present, given to me by…someone who was a friend but is no longer so. That made me reluctant to wear it, but I am trying to overcome such foolishness. It is a pretty thing, is it not?' Her tone was studiedly neutral, but knowing her as he did Arthur sensed deep pain, even betrayal, behind those few words. Betrayal? Was he becoming melodramatic? he chided himself. The atmosphere in the room was beginning to affect him with a sense that some catastrophe had taken place and Camilla was hiding it from him.

She gazed down at the cameo that Nicholas had given her that night in the Green Room and touched it with one fingertip. Mr Brooke could not see the expression in her downcast eyes, but he saw the soft curve of her lip tremble and he found he could be sensible no longer.

'Miss Knight…Camilla. I realise this is sudden, and that I should speak to your mama first, but you cannot be insensible of the regard in which I hold you and the strength of my feelings for you. Will you not be my wife, my dear Camilla?'

Camilla, finding her hands seized in his, looked up in astonishment. 'Mr Brooke—Arthur—this is indeed sudden. When you asked me this question before, did we not agree that we would be better remaining friends?'

'Yes, but my feelings for you have undergone a change. I find myself quite…enamoured of you.' His honest brown eyes looked earnestly into her face as if seeking her answer there. 'I cannot offer you luxury or a title, but I can promise you every comfort, a good home, my devoted protection.'

Camilla met his gaze for a long moment. She could accept him—and the marriage would be everything he said. He would be a good, affectionate husband and in time she would learn to be content, but the minute she thought it she rejected it as dishonest. She did not love Arthur, and what was more she loved Nicholas. She could not betray Arthur in that way by giving him second best, despite the fact she had been betrayed herself.

Gently Camilla disentangled her hands from his. 'Arthur, my dear, you are a very good friend to me and I know you would make a wonderful husband.' She saw hope dawning in his face and hurried on before he could misunderstand her. 'I hold you in high regard, Arthur, but I do not love you and I do not believe I ever can, not as a wife should. And,' she added with an attempt at lightness, 'I would make a very bad wife for a lawyer, you must admit!'

'You love someone else, do you not?' he asked soberly.

Camilla looked him straight in the face and said simply, 'Yes.'

'I think I can guess to whom you refer.' Camilla held up her hand as if to stop him saying the name. 'But you will not marry him either?'

'No. I will never marry, I think.'

'Then what will you do with your life, Camilla?' He was looking at her with concern and affection.

'What I always intended,' Camilla replied with a little shrug. 'Be a companion to Mama, a support to Ophelia. She is to marry our cousin Stephen Knight, so perhaps I will have an aunt's duties in the fullness of time.'

The small silence stretched on, then Arthur enquired gently, 'And that will be enough for you?'

'It will have to be,' Camilla said with sudden determination. 'I have no intention of moping, in fact I have moped quite enough already. We will say no more about it. Let me call Miss March in and you can explain to her what you have achieved for her sister.'

'No!' To her consternation Arthur Brooke fell to his knees beside her. 'No, Camilla! I cannot permit you to sacrifice yourself in this way because some personable rake with charm and a title has toyed with your heart and then cast you aside.'

Camilla put out one hand and touched his shoulder. 'Please, Arthur, do not say any more.' This was hurting so much.

'I will say more! Your nobility of character, your generosity of spirit that would set aside your own hurts to support your mother and sister without thought for self, only serves to endear you even more to me. Please, please reconsider, Camilla. I only want to make you happy. You like me a little, do you not? We are friends, are we not? We can build love on that foundation—so many people go into marriage with far less, yet become happy!'

Camilla felt under siege, not only from Arthur Brooke's passionate declaration but also from her weaker self. How easy it would be to say yes. Arthur would always be a good husband, and he would make a good father too; she sensed that. Perhaps marriage to him would be the only chance she ever had to have a family of her own.

Overwhelmed by affection for him, and a deep sense of regret that she was going to have to disappoint him, Camilla took his earnest face in both her hands and leaned forwards to kiss him gently on the cheek. As her lips brushed his face she murmured, 'No, Arthur, I am sorry. You are my dearest friend; let us at least keep that.'

Arthur Brooke was too human not to turn his lips to meet hers. If this was going to be the only opportunity he ever had to hold her in his arms, then he was going to seize it. As his lips touched hers the door swung open and Nicholas strode in, his progress unimpeded by the protesting footman in his wake.

For a moment the four people in the room froze. It was Nicholas who spoke first, his words cutting across the silence.

'I will thank you, sir, to unhand Miss Knight!' Damn it! He had come to tell her he loved her, tell her he knew he had been an arrogant fool, to humble himself and lay his heart at her feet only to discover this! That bloody little solicitor, with his stiff disapproval and his dusty ways kissing her on the hearthrug!

There was a sharp click as the door shut behind the footman, for once showing admirable discretion and effacing himself.

Mr Brooke, his face flushed with anger and embarrassment, jumped to his feet, revealing himself as far from the little clerk that Nicholas had mentally labelled him. As tall as his lordship, in his dark, impeccably cut suiting he looked every bit as formidable in his anger as the Earl.

Camilla too jumped to her feet, 'My lord, Arthur…please…' They both completely disregarded her.

'How dare you burst in upon Miss Knight's private apartments in this way, my lord?' Arthur Brooke's hands were clenched at his sides, his eyes locked with Nicholas's.

'It is a good thing for Miss Knight that I did. In the absence of her chaperon, who knows what liberties you would have taken next, sir!' To Camilla's frightened gaze Nicholas was looking extremely dangerous. His sword hand was flexing automatically, although naturally he wore no weapon; his face was set and hard, his eyes cold and glittering.

Hastily she stepped forward, placing herself between the two men, and said as steadily as she could to Nicholas, 'Your behaviour and your accusations are unwarranted, my lord. Mr Brooke has only the most honourable of intentions.' Nicholas's eyes narrowed at this palpable hit, but she swept on. 'Whom I choose to receive in my own house, with or without a chaperon, is my business and mine alone!'

'It strikes me, Miss Knight, that you should be thanking me for preserving your reputation, not roundly abusing me. What would your mama have said if she could have seen that pretty little tableau just now?'

'*You* speak to me of my reputation?' she stormed at him, completely forgetting the presence of Arthur Brooke. 'When has my reputation ever been of the slightest concern of yours? My mother would have no qualms about my receiving an *honourable* declaration, nor would she appreciate your interference in this family's affairs. You, my lord, are neither my father, my brother nor my husband, and as such have no influence or rights over me!'

Her breasts were rising and falling in the close-fitting gown with the strength of her emotions, her cheeks were flushed rose and her eyes sparked fire at him. Nicholas thought he had never seen her look more beautiful nor more desirable. 'For heaven's sake, Camilla, stop this nonsense. Dismiss this clerk. You know you are meant for me.'

Before she realised what he was about Nicholas had taken her by the shoulders, pulled her towards him and fastened his mouth on hers in a hard, urgent kiss.

The embrace lasted only seconds before Camilla found herself being lifted bodily out of the way and Arthur Brooke standing in her place, almost toe to toe with Nicholas. He drew back his clenched fist and, before she could cry out, drove it with punishing force straight at Nicholas's chin. He saw it coming, but the two men were far too close for him to avoid it connecting.

The blow sent Nicholas back a pace, then he recovered and threw an answering punch which sent the lawyer sprawling on the sofa. Camilla cast herself on Arthur's chest as the only way she could think of stopping Nicholas following up with another blow. 'Stop it—stop it both of you!'

Arthur shook his head as if to clear it, then put Camilla firmly on to the sofa beside him before getting to his feet. 'My lord, you will meet me for this.' Camilla was shocked by the cold menace in his voice: this was not the Arthur Brooke she knew.

'With pleasure,' Nicholas responded, equally coldly. He was massaging his bruised knuckles but his eyes were fixed on his opponent. 'Name your seconds, sir. Lord Forres will stand my friend.'

A fire of fury swept through Camilla from head to toe. How dared they brawl over her like this? She stood up and spoke sharply to both men. 'Stop this. Stop it now! Both of you can take yourselves out of this house and agree your stupid duel somewhere else. I have had about as much of your male honour as I can take; it leads to nothing but grief and heartache. Now *go*!'

The two men, both still obviously in the grip of icy rage, bowed to her and left, punctiliously giving way to each other at the door.

They parted on the doorstep with a stiff bow, Arthur Brooke striding off up the hill, Nicholas, who had no wish to keep him company, going down towards the town. Mr Brooke reached Walcot church and turned blindly into the churchyard. He needed somewhere to sit and think, and the bench beside the aisle wall seemed as good a place as anywhere.

How the devil had he got himself into this coil? It was quite obvious that Nicholas was the man Camilla loved, and it seemed equally obvious that he was in love with her. He was certainly exhibiting violent possessiveness towards her. Killing or wounding the man she loved was hardly going to win over Camilla, he reflected, before common sense got the better of him and he had to admit to himself that if anyone was going to be hurt it was going to be him. The Earl, as the challenged party, had the choice of weapons, but whatever he decided upon he was going to be more than a match for his opponent. The best he could hope for was that the Earl would choose pistols. For himself, he would delope rather than risk hitting the man.

With a sigh Arthur Brooke got to his feet and set off to find a discreet friend to act as second for him, and to check that his will was up to date.

Four hours later, at the Forres house in the Crescent, Nicholas was hardly having a more enjoyable time than his erstwhile opponent.

'You bloody idiot, Lovell!' his unsympathetic brother-in-law yelled. 'Georgiana is going to go mad when she hears of this.'

'We must make sure she doesn't,' Nicholas said firmly, jamming his bruised knuckles still further into his pockets. He had finally tracked down Lord Forres in his study, moodily contemplating a pile of bills, and had done nothing to improve his temper by informing him that he was to stand as his second in a duel with a respectable Bath solicitor.

Both men fell silent and were still contemplating the situation when there was a knock on the front door. A few moments later Benson came in with a card on a silver salver.

'A Mr Murray to see you, my lord.' Henry scooped up the card and scanned it swiftly.

'Ask him to wait in the front salon, Benson. Is her ladyship at home?'

'No, my lord, she asked me to say that she will not be in until after dinner. She is dining with Lady Richardson.'

Henry waited until the door closed behind the butler. 'Well, that's a small mercy at any rate. I wouldn't care to try and keep this from Georgiana with the house full of this other chap's seconds.'

Nicholas got to his feet. 'Is that who he is?' He flipped over the card and read,

"In the matter concerning Mr B."

'Well, how conciliatory do you want me to be?' Henry asked. 'Are you going to apologise?'

'Damn it, no! He was kissing her.'

Henry's eyebrows rose. 'So? You are not engaged to the lady. Was she in distress?'

Nicholas grimaced and raked his hand through his already unruly hair. 'No, she was kissing him back.'

'Then why did you hit him?' he asked with irritating reasonableness.

'Because I was going to ask her to marry me,' Nicholas said through gritted teeth.

'Sounds to me as though you should be apologising all round, old boy. Damn if I wouldn't have hit you myself in his shoes. Still, if you are determined to fight, what weapons do you want? I suppose it doesn't really matter. You can kill a provincial solicitor with either sword or pistol, I imagine.'

'Pistols. It will make it easier to delope.'

'Humph.' Henry got to his feet. 'Well, just hope your man hasn't a good eye, because while you are busily aiming over his head he could be winging you.'

The early-morning mist was still shrouding Claverton Down the next day as Nicholas and Lord Forres climbed out of their carriage and looked around. 'Six o'clock on the nose,' Henry remarked, consulting his pocket watch. 'There's the surgeon's gig. And here comes your man. He's not a shirker, that's for sure.'

Mr Brooke, looking unusually pale in his dark clothing, descended from his carriage accompanied by his second, Mr Murray, and waited while the two seconds came forward to discuss the field.

After a few minutes Lord Forres came back

and indicated a flat area. 'That'll do. Now, I've brought my pistols. Which do you want?'

Nicholas took one at random and waited while Henry took the other over to Mr Brooke. In silence the two men obeyed the seconds' directions to turn and pace away from each other.

Waiting, the pistol held at his side, for Lord Forres to raise the white handkerchief, Nicholas looked at Arthur Brooke and wondered just how good a shot he was. He would not want to kill this man and find himself having to flee the country, but an inexperienced shot might well aim to wound and make too good a job of it. Would he ever see Camilla again?

Henry raised the white cloth and both duellists took aim. A vision of Camilla's face swam before Nicholas's eyes as he heard Henry call, 'In your own time!'

The still morning air was rent by two almost simultaneous cracks. Through the swirl of smoke from his own pistol, Nicholas could see from the angle of Arthur Brooke's arm that he too had deloped and fired well over his opponent's head.

Nicholas's heart was still beating loud in his ears as he walked slowly over to where Brooke was standing, one hand on the side of the carriage, a rueful grin on his very pale face.

'Mr Brooke, are you satisfied?'

'I am, my lord.' He cleared his throat. 'Not an experience I should wish to repeat, I must admit.'

Nicholas touched his shoulder. 'Nor I, sir, nor I. Come, there is a tavern down the hill; will you join me? There is a matter I would discuss with you.'

At the same time as the two duellists were talking over a glass of brandy in the Claverton Arms, Camilla was pacing her chamber. She had slept very little and now felt slightly sick as she contemplated the day before her. What was going on? She knew nothing—had never wanted to know anything—about the etiquette of duelling. How long would it take for the seconds to make the arrangements? A day or two, surely. Did she still have time to stop this madness? How could she? What could she say or do to change their minds once they set on a course of honour?

After a desultory breakfast, where she crumbled more bread than she ate, Camilla spent the morning pacing the drawing-room, driving Miss March to distraction by refusing to tell her what was the cause of her agitation. 'Oh dear, well if you will not tell me what is amiss, my dear, I will go and sort that old linen cupboard, for I declare I cannot sit here a moment longer,' she stated, as near to irritation as she ever got with her dear 'Lilla.

Fortunately for Camilla, a note arrived shortly afterwards in Mr Brooke's hand. For a long moment she stared at it. Was it to say he had killed Nicholas? Or had he written it before the two men had met, in case he was killed himself…?

It was pointless tormenting herself. Taking a deep breath, Camilla slit the seal and unfolded the stiff sheet.

My dear Miss Knight, I write to put your mind at rest. Both his lordship and I are unharmed, having met this morning and both fired into the air. Honour having been satisfied, I am now leaving for Cheltenham, but hope to call on you as speedily as I can upon my return. Believe me, I am, and will remain, your good friend and servant Arthur Brooke.

Camilla's legs gave way and she dropped into the chair, the letter crumpled in her hand. So that was that. They were both safe, thank the Lord. It was plain from Arthur's note that he had accepted that she could never be his wife, but that he would remain her friend. That was good: she would have hated to hurt him and she was going to need his friendship now that she must give up all hope of Nicholas. But he would remain in her heart and her dreams and that must be enough. The future of spinsterhood that she had outlined to Arthur Brooke was all that remained to her.

Two days later, as Camilla and Miss March were sitting down to afternoon tea, Samuel came in with a letter on a salver. 'For you, Miss Knight.'

The handwriting was familiar, and it was with a slight frown that Camilla slit the seal. What could Mr Porter of the Theatre Royal be writing to her about now? Their connection was at an end, as he knew only too well!

Mr Porter presents his compliments to Mademoiselle Davide and requests the favour of an interview with her upon a matter of some urgency.

Mr Porter finds himself in possession of

the sole rights to a remarkable new play which he has no hesitation in saying would be the theatrical sensation of the decade.

The playwright has created the leading female role for Mademoiselle Davide and Mr Porter considers that no other thespian could undertake the role with such success as he anticipates she could bring to it.

Camilla, with mounting excitement, scanned the rest of the letter. It did indeed sound a fascinating role. She turned to the second page.

Mr Porter requests a reply from Mademoiselle Davide this very day. He apologises for this unmannerly haste, but time is of the essence if this manuscript is to be secured. Mr Porter will be in his office between four and six this afternoon, and can assure Mademoiselle Davide of complete discretion if she condescends to call upon him there.

Her immediate instinct was to throw the paper in the fire, but something stopped her. She spent half an hour debating with herself, then, suddenly decisive, she ran to her dressing-room.

As she tucked the last tendril of blonde hair under the dark wig and fastened the long cloak around her shoulders, Camilla felt the old excitement stirring. This was madness; she had sworn to renounce the theatre. But now what had she got to lose? Her life was empty, Nicholas was gone, and at least she could fill the emptiness with the hypnotic world of make-believe.

With her hood pulled well up to hide her hair and face, she asked the footman to call a sedan chair and soon found herself outside the Theatre Royal stage door. Inside it was dark in the unwindowed corridors, the air heavy with the smell of dust, limelight and greasepaint. It was so familiar, so welcoming, she felt her blood stir in excitement.

But the silence was so odd and unsettling. She had never known the theatre without the bustle of stagehands, the banging of the scene-makers' hammers, the raised voices of rehearsals on stage.

The door at the foot of the stairs to Mr Porter's office was ajar and she began to climb. As she gained the landing, her heels sounding loud in the silence, a thought struck her. How had Mr Porter known where to send the letter and to whom to address it? She had never told him or anyone else at the theatre who she really was.

Camilla hesitated, suddenly very unsure of the wisdom of being there. But before she could turn and go the door in front of her opened inwards. Well, she could not go back now and never know who had discovered the key to her identity. Taking a deep breath, she stepped inside the theatre manager's office.

Of Mr Porter there was no sign, but the office was not empty.

'Hello, Camilla.' Nicholas stood up from the edge of the desk where he had been sitting. 'You came very promptly.'

'You! What are you doing here? And where is Mr Porter?'

Nicholas shrugged. 'Mr Porter is where I have paid him to be—in the local coffee-house, I suppose. Forget Mr Porter. Come to me, Camilla darling.'

Camilla, feeling as though she was in some sort of dream, walked forwards into his open arms and clung to him. 'Oh, Nicholas, what is this about?' But, in truth, for the moment she did not care why he had summoned her. She just wanted to be here, in his arms, her face pressed against his chest, drinking in the subtle smell of him.

She felt his hands on her head, then he had

tugged off the wig and tossed it aside. 'It is about getting rid of this,' he murmured into her tumbled hair. 'It is about saying goodbye to Mademoiselle Davide, Camilla, my love.'

Camilla thrilled to his touch, to his endearments, but she still felt dizzily uncertain of what he intended. That searing scene in the Sydney Gardens when he had so angrily informed her that he had no intention of making her an offer of *any* kind still haunted her. 'Nicholas, what do you want from me?'

'I want you to be my wife, Camilla. I love you. I want to spend the rest of my life with you.'

Camilla pushed herself away from his chest and looked up into his face, lit with the light from the dusty window. 'But you told me that Lovells do not marry actresses. You are the Earl of Ashby!'

'And you are no longer an actress. But even if you were, I do not care. I love you. No one knows your secret, but that is neither here nor there—if the whole of polite society discovered that you were Mademoiselle Davide tomorrow I would not heed them. After all, I *am* the Earl of Ashby, and I do not give a damn what society thinks of me.'

Nicholas pulled her close again. 'Oh, I was so angry when we overheard those two old witches gossiping about us in the Sydney Gardens! Not angry with you—not particularly angry with them; they were only acting true to type—but so angry and ashamed at myself. I knew I should either have gone away, hugged my family pride to myself and forgotten all about you, or I should have told you that I knew your secret and that I did not care. Told you that I loved you and wanted to marry you…'

'Why then were you so cold, so angry with me?' she asked softly against his shirt-front.

'I do not think I have ever put myself quite so thoroughly in the wrong! I can only blame my damnable pride for what I said and how I said it. The other day when I found you with Arthur Brooke I was coming to tell you that. Coming to apologise for my arrogance, for hurting you so much. When I saw him kissing you I thought I had lost everything, every chance of happiness I could ever hope for.'

He buried his face in her sweet-smelling hair and said huskily, 'The morning of the duel, as I stood there waiting, all I could see was your face—all I could think of was that I might never see you again. Afterwards I spoke to Arthur Brooke, told him something of what a fool I had been. It was he who convinced me that I could still win you back, that he knew you loved me. He only proposed because he thought we would never marry.' A tinge of laughter touched his voice as he murmured, 'You made me so jealous, you know: your cousin Stephen, Arthur Brooke… I suffered torments imagining you with them. If nothing else, that pain should have told me all I needed to know about my feelings for you.'

Camilla clung to him. 'Nicholas, I was so frightened I was going to lose you. I love you so very much. I had made the decision that if I could not have you then I would have no one.'

Nicholas tipped up her face to his and she thought she had never seen his eyes look so tender.

'Camilla, tell me you will marry me. I want you to be my wife more than anything I have ever wanted in my life.'

'Oh, yes, Nicholas, I would very much like to marry you. Very much indeed.'

His kiss seemed to last for a lifetime. Finally, still holding her gently against him, Nicholas lifted his mouth from hers and smiled down into her happy face. Seeing him, seeing his look of love, she could not doubt he meant everything he said.

'Nicholas, why did you come back to me that day?'

'Because of something my infuriating sister Georgiana said. She told me that in you I had found the one thing that my rank, my fortune, my place in society could not secure for me. And at that moment I realised I cared nothing for any of them, that they were meaningless if I could not have you, Camilla.'

He kissed her again and she kissed him back with an intensity that convinced him that his love believed him, forgave him, and was his for ever.

* * * * *